CONFESSIONS

MADALYN MORGAN

Copyright © Madalyn Morgan, 2019, 2023

The moral right of the author has been asserted.

To request permissions, contact the publisher at rights@stormpublishing.co

Ebook ISBN: 978-1-80508-237-8
Paperback ISBN: 978-1-80508-239-2

Previously published as *There Is No Going Home*

Cover design: Debbie Clement
Cover images: Arcangel, Shutterstock

Published by Storm Publishing.
For further information, visit:
www.stormpublishing.co

ALSO BY MADALYN MORGAN

Foxden Acres

Destiny

Betrayal

Redemption

Legacy

Reckoning

Secrets

Confessions is dedicated to my late parents,
Ena and Jack Smith

LONDON 1958

PROLOGUE

Ena dived to the floor, pulled off an earring and threw it behind the jewellery counter.

'May I help you, madam?'

From being on all fours, Ena rocked back on her heels. She poked her head above the glass display cabinet and scanned the room. The woman she had successfully avoided was striding across the ground floor of Selfridges department store towards the door leading to Oxford Street.

'I dropped my earring,' Ena said, looking up at the sharp features of the middle-aged shop assistant standing over her.

'Is this it?' The woman bent down and picked up a white plastic earring between her forefinger and thumb. Holding it at arm's length, as if she feared she would catch something from it, she dropped the bauble into the palm of Ena's outstretched hand.

'Thank you.' Getting to her feet Ena glanced over the assistant's right shoulder to where seconds before she had seen the woman. She had gone. Ena lifted the earring up to her ear. Her hair was in the way so she dropped it into her pocket. 'Costume jewellery,' Ena tutted and wrinkled her nose. 'But I wouldn't want to lose it, it has sentimental value.' In an attempt to make light of the situation, she gave the woman a quirky smile. 'I shall be more careful in future.'

The assistant didn't respond. Her lips remained a thin red line, her eyes emotionless. 'Customers are not allowed on this side of the counter. If you don't mind...' Like a policeman directing traffic, the snooty shop assistant waved Ena to the front of the counter.

'Sorry.' Ena sidestepped the woman and headed briskly for the exit.

She emerged out of the cool store into the warm still air of late summer, put her hands up to shade her eyes from the bright sunshine and froze. She spun round and pretended to give the window display serious attention. The woman she had avoided in the store was standing a few feet away from her talking to a middle-aged man. Ena strained to see what the man looked like in the reflection of the shop window. Taller than the woman by several inches, he wore a lightweight suit in a brown herring-bone weave. An attaché case hung from his right hand and a camel-coloured overcoat was draped over his arm. He had not bought his clothes off the peg at Burtons, Ena thought. His suit and coat were bespoke. They had been tailored for him in Savile Row, she would put money on it.

Trying to get a look at the man's face beneath his brown trilby, Ena edged along the window to where a display of ladies' swimsuits and two-piece bathing costumes were being replaced by autumn jackets and raincoats. As she moved, the man moved. He leaned forward until his face was almost touching the woman's face and said something that made her laugh. She pointed to Selfridges' door, then she kissed her fingers and transferred the kiss to his lips. The man smiled, shrugged, and looked north in the direction of Oxford Circus. Ena could see even less of him now. The woman's reflection wasn't as clear from this angle either. Not that it needed to be. Her posture, the way she walked, laughed, and the forthright way in which she had spoken to the man, were all too familiar. She looked different. But then she was fourteen years older, as was Ena, there was no mystery there. That the woman was standing behind her was the mystery. Feigning interest in the curling battlements of a cardboard sandcastle as it was being dismantled, Ena was able to observe the woman more closely.

Elegant in a powder blue costume, the skirt hugging her slender figure came to just below her knees. The short box jacket was the height of fashion. The collar and cuffs were piped with navy blue silk and to complete the ensemble the woman carried a navy-blue handbag, wore matching high heeled court shoes, and sported a white wide-brimmed hat on perfectly coiffed blonde hair. 'Bleached,' Ena said, under her breath. She had been a brunette when Ena knew her. She smiled. Brown hair or blonde, Ena would know her anywhere.

Keeping an eye on the couple, Ena sauntered past a display of dresses and coats to the corner of the building. Within reach of the side entrance, she turned and quickly slipped through the door. Unseen she walked to the front of the shop and stood behind two young female window-dressers dismembering mannequins. The interior of the shop was as dark as the outside was light. Ena could see the couple clearly without them seeing her.

There was no doubt about it. The woman Ena was told had taken her own life in the winter of 1946 was alive and standing yards away from her, separated only by a glass window.

ONE

The man was the first to leave. He took the woman's hand and pulled her to him. As he bent down to kiss her, the woman lifted her head and her lips brushed his. He kissed her the way someone who had lived on the Continent would do, briefly on both cheeks. Ena watched the man walk to the corner of Orchard Street. He waited for only a second before a silver Rover pulled up and the driver, wearing a peaked hat and a dark uniform stepped smartly out of the driver's side of the car. He walked swiftly round the back of the vehicle, opened the rear passenger door and the man lowered himself into the car without looking back. A second later the driver was behind the steering wheel and the sleek silver Rover was gliding effortlessly along Oxford Street in the morning traffic.

As soon as the Rover was out of sight the woman hailed a cab. Ena watched as she gracefully opened the door and got in. 'Damn!' Ena hissed. From inside the store she wasn't able to hear the address the woman had given the driver.

'Damn!' she said again, and turned with such force she collided with a boy carrying several boxes. Balanced precariously on top of the square tower was a round hatbox. The boy took a step backwards to avoid Ena, stumbled, and the hatbox began to slide.

Ena made a grab for it, missed, but seized the rest of the boxes. She managed to steady them, but not before the hatbox had fallen to the floor.

'Nooo!' the boy cried, as the hatbox rolled away from him along the ground.

Ena pulled the remaining boxes towards her, but the boy pulled them back. 'Go after the hat,' she shouted. 'I'll look after these for you.'

A look of indecision flashed across the boy's face. He was clearly unsure about leaving one customer's purchases with another.

'Go on! Quickly!' Ena ordered. 'Get the hat!'

A look of gratitude replaced the look of doubt in the boy's eyes. He relinquished his grip on the boxes and chased after the escaping hatbox, stopping momentarily when it careered past the feet of the snooty shop assistant with the pinched face that Ena had crossed swords with earlier at the jewellery counter.

Ena made no attempt to take the boxes to the assistant. She held them at arm's length and waited for the woman to come to her. Hoping to distract her long enough for the boy to retrieve the run-away hatbox, Ena smiled. It was not reciprocated. The look on the woman's face as she stormed towards her was one of fury, which told Ena the boy would later get the rough end of her tongue.

'Sorry again,' Ena said. Feigning embarrassment, she lowered her voice. 'I wasn't having any luck getting a taxi, so I decided to go up to the cafeteria for a cup of tea. I came into the dark store out of the bright sunshine and didn't see the young man until it was too late.' The woman's face was puce and her eyes sparkled with rage from beneath heavy eyelids. She whipped the proffered boxes out of Ena's hands. 'I'm entirely to blame that the hat... I hope the young man won't be in trouble for something that wasn't his fault.'

The woman's nostrils flared. Ena half expected to see fire come out of them. She looked along the floor to where she had last seen the hatbox. It wasn't there. It was heading for the size nines of an elderly man coming out of Gentlemen's Outfitting.

Ena winced as the man brought his foot down on the round container. The box stopped rolling, the lid came off, and a large brimmed hat, similar to the one the woman in the taxi was wearing but in cherry red, escaped.

In one hurried movement, the boy swept up the hat and put it back in the box. Replacing the lid, he nodded his thanks to the man and walked shakily back to the store's entrance where he waited for his superior to join him. Shamefaced the boy focused on the ground and followed the miserable female assistant out of the store to the waiting taxi. She placed the boxes carefully on the back seat and, after a few words with the woman, closed the cab door.

As the taxi pulled away the woman assistant marched back to the store – the boy trailed behind her – and Ena made her exit through the side door.

Ena ran to the road waving her hands in the air. She had every intention of jumping into the next available taxi and telling the driver to follow the cab the woman was in. Instead she watched the cab turn into Tottenham Court Road. A second later it was out of sight.

When a taxi stopped a few feet away from her, Ena waited for the elderly woman to pay her fare. By the time she had sorted through her change to give the cabbie the right money, Ena was in two minds about taking a cab. After all, Madame Romanovski, at 7 Dean's Crescent, Holland Park would no doubt be at home tomorrow or the next day. Ena smiled to herself. It had only taken her a second to read and commit to memory the name and address on the Selfridge's boxes.

'Where to, miss?' the cabbie called.

'I've changed my mind. I'm going to walk.'

Muttering, 'Bloody women,' followed by, 'can never make up their minds,' the taxi roared off causing a bus and the car behind it to brake sharply. The driver of the car gave several blasts on his horn, the bus driver thrust his arm out of the window and made a fist, and the taxi driver retaliated by sticking up two fingers. The sound of screeching brakes and horns blasting, caused other drivers to slow down. Some pulled into the kerb, stopped and got out of their vehicles to see what the kerfuffle was about.

Responsible for bringing the traffic on Oxford Street to a standstill, Ena turned her back on the scene and started walking towards Oxford Circus. A woman stopped her and asked if she knew what was going on. Looking over her shoulder at the near accident she had almost caused, Ena shook her head. 'No idea,' she said, and walked on.

She slowed her pace as she neared Oxford Circus underground station. Next to the railings on the far side of the steps leading down to the tube trains was a telephone box. She ran to it and pulled open the heavy glass-panelled door. As it closed behind her she picked up the receiver and inserted three pennies into the coin box.

'What number would you like, caller?' the operator asked.

'Mayfair one-five-five,' Ena replied.

Almost at once the clipped voice of MI5's switchboard operator said, 'Leconfield House, which extension would you like?'

Ena pressed button A.

'Five,' she said, breathless with excitement – and with her fingers crossed that Henry was in the office.

A moment later her husband came on the line. 'Green, here.'

'Henry, it's Ena.'

'Hello, darling.'

'Frieda is alive.'

'What?'

'Frieda Voight. She's alive and she's living in London.'

TWO

It was November 15, 1940, the day after the Coventry Blitz that her working relationship with Freda King developed into a friendship. Mr Silcott, the owner of the factory where she had worked since the beginning of the war, was needed in Coventry. Extensive damage had been done to the main factory, and he asked her to accompany Freda to Bletchley Park. She had never heard of Bletchley Park. Until that day she only knew that the work she did was destined for a place called Station-X. She remembered even now – eighteen years later – how excited she had been to be going to such an important place. If she had known what was to come, she would not have been so eager.

A feeling of nausea swept over her as she brought to mind the day Mr Silcott had been beaten up and left for dead in the gents toilet on Rugby station. It was the same day that she had been drugged and her work had been stolen. She could still hear the voice of the man who had almost killed her. He had initiated the conversation by asking her if she was all right, as she looked pale. She told him she suffered from travel sickness and sucked pear drops when she travelled. Out of politeness, she had offered him one. He took the packet, looked at its contents, and commented on the different colours before taking a sweet and handing the packet back to her. Putting a pear drop in her mouth was the last thing she remembered until she was woken by the ticket collector at Euston.

When she eventually arrived at Bletchley Park she was interrogated by military intelligence. Although the head of Bletchley, Commander Dalton, didn't accuse her outright of sabotage, she knew that she and everyone she worked with would be under suspicion.

At the time it had been unthinkable that anyone at Silcott's Engineering could have been involved in sabotage. Mr Silcott would have been fighting for his country if the government hadn't told him he was needed to provide vital equipment for the war effort. Besides which, he wasn't on the train. And it couldn't have been Freda because she was at Beaumanor Hall, the other Station-X facility that Silcott's did work for. She was sure it was someone from Bletchley Park who had stolen and later sabotaged her work.

That was the last time she took work to Bletchley on her own. If there wasn't enough petrol to drive down in the car, Freda went with her on the train. It was on one of those occasions that Freda was attacked. She had been walking along the corridor from the toilet when she heard Freda scream. She burst into the compartment to see a man with his hands around Freda's neck. He turned when he saw her, lunged and tripped. At the same time she had swung the case of work towards the man and the corner met with his chin. He staggered backwards, fell, and hit his head on the brass ashtray attached to the window ledge. She could see him now, his eyes rolling back in their sockets. Then he let out a rasping breath, closed his eyes, and slumped sideways.

Freda had felt the man's wrist for a pulse and said there wasn't one. Overwhelmed by the reality that she had killed a man and overcome with grief, she thought she would faint.

Freda had told her that by killing her attacker she had saved her life. It didn't make her feel better.

When she arrived at Bletchley she told Commander Dalton who immediately telephoned MI5. The director of Five said he would send two men to meet the train and deal with the body. Later the commander had told her that there was nobody – dead or alive – in that compartment or any other compartment on that train.

For two years Freda had watched her become more and more consumed with guilt. Freda sometimes brought up the *accidental* killing of the man on the train, always assuring her that it was their secret.

She had thought of Freda as a loyal friend, until the day she had found her out to be an unscrupulous liar with secrets of her own. By chance, she had found a key taped to the back of Freda's desk. On closer inspection, she realised it was a duplicate of the one that opened the safe where blueprints and classified documents from Bletchley Park were kept. She also found petrol coupons from the accounts department at Bletchley, which would have allowed them to take work down in the car. Freda had intercepted the coupons. The date on the envelope was three days before Mr Silcott had been beaten up on Rugby station: the day that she had been drugged and her work had been stolen.

No wonder Commander Dalton had looked at her with disbelief when she told him they had to travel to Bletchley that day by train because they hadn't received the petrol coupons.

What had prompted her to telephone the commander on the day she found the duplicate key to the safe and the missing petrol coupons was finding three one-way tickets to Ireland on the Lady of Liverpool ferry in the names of Frieda King – not Freda but Frieda spelt with an i – Walter King, Freda's brother, and H. Villiers, their uncle. With the tickets was a letter from Walter. It began, "Darling, I cannot wait until we are home. I will be on the Liverpool train, as arranged." It ended with, "Wear the red beret I bought you in Paris, it reminds me of the times we spent together when we were young."

Her next visit to Bletchley Park had been to receive instructions on how to play her part in getting Freda King – her brother and her uncle – arrested for treason.

The time soon came for her to put what she had learned into practice. She had felt nervous walking along the station platform and had to take several deep breaths. Feeling calmer she had boarded the train to Liverpool wearing a red beret and clothes identical to those she had seen Freda wear. When the train left the station she felt more relaxed. Except for the empty seat next to her, she knew at least four of the seats in the compartment were occupied by military security and MI5 personnel.

Remembering the events that followed sent waves of fear searing through her. The train had pulled out of Northampton before she was joined by Freda's brother Walter. She recognised him immediately as the man Freda told her she had killed two years before. He recognised her at the same time and took a knife from his pocket. With the blade at her throat, King forced her off the train at Rugby.

At the exit barrier, King ordered her to produce the train tickets. She opened her handbag, but instead of taking the tickets from it, she took out a gun that Commander Dalton had given her.

The last she saw of Walter King, who she now knows as Walter Voight, he was lying face down on the northbound platform of Rugby station. Later she learned that Freda, whose real name was Frieda Voight, had been arrested in Liverpool trying to board a ferry to Ireland. H. Villiers, if he ever existed, has never been found.

THREE

Ena left the underground at Green Park and walked the short distance to Leconfield House where her husband Henry worked. Crossing the road at the junction at South Audley and Curzon Street, the windowless ground floor headquarters of the Security Service and MI5 – the United Kingdom's domestic counter-intelligence and security agency – came into view.

Leconfield House was a smart building; a palace compared to the nondescript bomb-damaged dwelling where Ena spent her days scrutinising cold cases. Number 8 Mercer Street, a stone's throw from Covent Garden and Leicester Square, equal distance from Long Acre and Cambridge Circus, was surrounded by cafés and shops. She had wanted to work with Henry at MI5 after the war, but couples – engaged or married – were not allowed to work for the agency. Relationships of a romantic nature between operatives were seen as invitations for spies to kidnap one or other of the couple and blackmail them into giving away the country's secrets. It was happening, Henry let slip one night, though Ena hadn't heard anything. She didn't know anyone who had, except Henry, who seemed to know everything that went on at MI5 but shared nothing with her.

Ena loved her job. Attached to the Home Office, the cold case department was also top secret. She was not based anywhere as prestigious as Mayfair, but Covent Garden was what they called, up and coming. She liked working out of Mercer Street, there was always something going on. She liked the men she worked with too.

Sid, the older of her two colleagues, was in his mid-forties. During the war, Sid had been a code breaker first at Beaumanor, and then at Bletchley Park. He had also spent a short time at Scotland Yard. His Home Office file said Consultant. What kind of consultant Ena didn't know. She had never asked him and he had never said. Sid was a clever man. He was also a bit of a fusspot, which as far as Ena was concerned made him thorough.

Artie Mallory was a good looking man in his early thirties. He was tall with dark wavy hair and wore fashionable clothes – blazers and slacks and open neck shirts. In contrast, Sid wore dark suits, white shirts – was never seen without a tie – and you could see your reflection in his shoes they were so highly polished.

Artie was as relaxed about his work as Sid was serious. Sid would work until he had dotted all the i's and crossed all the t's. Artie, on the other hand, was always ready to leave and go to the Salisbury pub on St Martin's Lane, or a club in Soho. Artie was a chatterbox and often gossiped, Sid was economical with his words and, unless he and Ena were on their own, only spoke when he had something to say. To her knowledge neither men had ever been married.

You could set your watch by Sid. He was always on time. Artie occasionally tipped up half an hour late with a hangover. But, like Ying and Yang in Chinese philosophy, the two men complemented each other, worked well together, and, more importantly, they got results.

Ena sighed. Henry didn't see her job as important. She

dealt with cold cases and he dealt with current cases, many of which were "red" hot. Henry occasionally went overseas, which thankfully she didn't have to do. Ena was happy working in the Mercer Street office. The work she did was fascinating, even though the hours were long and she often got home at night exhausted.

She entered the plain marble foyer at Leconfield House and approached the reception desk. 'I've come to see Henry Green. All right if I go through?'

'Mr Green has just left,' the receptionist said.

'He said he'd wait for me.' Ena looked up at the clock on the wall. 'I'm late. You wouldn't know where he's gone, would you? It's important that I speak to him.'

'I'm afraid not, Mrs Green. He's usually back within forty-five minutes. If you'd like to wait.' The receptionist pointed to a row of chairs by the window.

'I'll try The Boar's Head. I've met him there before.' Leaving the MI5 building Ena walked along Curzon Street for fifty-or-so yards until she came to the pub.

She was peering through the window when Henry, putting his arms around her, said, 'Are you looking for me?'

'Yes, I am.' Ena turned to greet him. 'You won't believe me when I tell you how it happened.' Henry's brow furrowed. 'How I saw Frieda. Buy me lunch and I'll tell you everything. It's been an age since I had breakfast, I'm starving.'

Taking her by the hand, Henry led Ena across the road to the café opposite. It was bustling with office workers, but no sooner had they entered than a table became free. They ordered two steak and kidney pies with mashed potatoes and peas, and two cups of coffee. Ena was bursting to tell Henry about seeing Frieda and began her tale while they waited for their food.

'I first saw her in Ladies Fashions. I needed some shoes so I popped in on the way to the office.'

Henry gave her a look of disbelief. 'Okay, perhaps Selfridges isn't exactly on the way to Mercer Street, but it isn't far out of my way.' Henry laughed. 'Anyway, listen.'

At that moment the waitress brought their food. Ena waited until she left, before continuing with her story. 'My heart nearly stopped when I saw her. She looks taller. I expect it's because she's thinner than she was when we worked together. Oh, and she's a blonde.'

'Doesn't sound much like the Frieda we knew.'

'The blonde hair is out of a bottle,' Ena said, 'you can tell it isn't natural. It was Frieda all right. I know I haven't seen her for ages, but you don't forget someone who tried to have you killed, do you?'

Henry looked at Ena's food. 'Eat your lunch or it'll be cold.'

'All right! But this is important, Henry. You don't seem to realise just how important.' Ena sliced through the crust on her pie, stabbed a chunk of meat with her fork and nudged some mashed potato up against it. 'It's good.' After a couple of mouthfuls she put down her cutlery and, deep in thought, said, 'I wonder who the man with her was.'

Henry shook his head.

'He looked foreign. He could have been a Russian spy or an Eastern European gangster. She's from Berlin and he looked Germanic. He's probably on Five's wanted list.'

'Shush,' Henry said, looking around the room. 'We'll talk about *Frieda*, later.'

Ena raised her eyebrows and slowly shook her head. 'You don't believe I saw her, do you?'

Now it was Henry's turn to put down his knife and fork. He wiped his mouth with a paper napkin and looked into Ena's face. 'I believe *you* believe you saw her, Ena, but Freda King– Frieda Voight, is dead. You know she is. We went to her funeral.'

They ate the rest of their meal in silence. Henry finished his pie and mash, Ena pushed hers around her plate. The waitress cleared their dirty dishes, replacing them with two steaming cups of coffee. Ena took a sip, put the cup back in its saucer and, sitting side-on to Henry, stared out of the window.

'It couldn't have been her, Ena. You do know that, don't you?'

Ena didn't answer.

'It has been twelve years since you last saw her.'

'Fourteen, actually!' Ena snapped. 'And I admit she looked different. Her face was narrower and her lips were fuller. But it's fashionable to have pouting movie starlet red lips.' An involuntary smile crossed Ena's face. 'We worked together for four years and in all that time I never once saw her without make-up. She always wore too much lipstick, and she was always the height of fashion.' Ena looked into the mid-distance to remind herself of the woman who had befriended her and then tried to kill her during the war. 'One thing that hadn't changed was the way Frieda held herself. I would know that haughty posture anywhere.'

Henry spoke volumes by his silence.

'Do you think I could ever forget the person who had me believe for two years that I had killed a man?'

Henry put his hands up in a gesture of surrender. 'Okay! Supposing the woman you saw was Frieda Voight?'

Ena shot him a look of incredulity. 'It was!'

'Then whose funeral did we go to in forty-six?'

'I don't know, but it wasn't Frieda Voight's funeral because she isn't dead!'

'Okay. So, you think the woman you saw in Selfridges was Frieda Voight.' Ena opened her mouth to correct her husband. He put his hands up again. 'Just hear me out.'

Ena sighed. 'Go on.'

'If it was Frieda you saw, who was the man she was talking to outside the store?'

Ena frowned. 'I don't know. I didn't see his face.' Her frown deepened. 'I don't think it was her brother, Walter.'

'Of course it wasn't. Walter died in prison.'

'Did he? Are you sure? If an unknown woman was buried in place of Frieda Voight, isn't it possible that an unknown man was buried in place of Walter Voight?'

'Too far-fetched, Ena. Who would go to the trouble, and why?'

It was a warm day but Ena felt suddenly very cold. 'I don't know. But if MI5, MI6, or Special Branch went to the trouble to stage a funeral and burial for Frieda, why not do the same for Walter? Dead and buried is the best cover story in the world. Change your appearance, stay off the radar for six months, a year, and when those you worked for are satisfied you're no longer around you can go anywhere, do anything – you could work for an enemy government.'

'Okay, you win,' Henry said. 'If you think the woman you saw was Frieda–' Ena rolled her eyes. 'We'll look into it. We'll start with MI5's archives.'

'At Leconfield House?'

'No, Argyle Street. We'll go there first thing in the morning.'

Ena's face crumpled. 'Why wait until tomorrow?'

'Because I have work to do this afternoon.'

'Sorry, I wasn't thinking. I'll go to the Home Office and ask Dick Bentley if Sid and Artie can work the case too.'

'Will Director Bentley see finding Frieda Voight as important?' Henry asked.

'Of course! Well,' Ena said, tilting her head to the left and then right as she thought, 'he should. Because they died, or were killed, in 1946 that makes it a cold case – and Dick Bentley sees every cold case as important. And, because I now know it wasn't Frieda who was buried that day, Dick Bentley will be very interested. He'll agree with me that, if a woman was buried in forty-six and it wasn't Frieda Voight, a crime has been committed and there has been a cover-up.'

Ena glanced at Henry. He looked worried. 'What's MI5 and, or, Special Branch hiding? Do you know something I don't, Henry?'

Henry laughed. 'You see a conspiracy round every corner, Ena.'

Ena shot her husband an angry look. 'Someone died, or was killed, and they were buried in Frieda Voight's place. Don't you think whoever it was is worthy of their own grave, their own headstone to mark their life? It's more than likely the person had a family; a mother and father who haven't heard from their daughter in all this time. Don't they deserve to know their child is dead so they can mourn her passing?'

'Walter Voight may have died, but his sister did not!' Ena was annoyed with Henry. He was being unreasonable. 'Bentley will let the cold case office work on this because he knows I am not given to seeing ghosts.'

'I hope you are right.'

'I am! You may not believe me, but Bentley will. Besides, he's sweet on me,' Ena said, her tone lighter. 'I shall tell him that Sid and Artie are currently underemployed, which they aren't, and that this case will be something they can get their teeth into.'

'I met one of your chaps at Bletchley.'

'You never said. They both worked in decoding during the war. Cryptic analysts, I think.'

'Sidney something. He was an odd fellow.'

'Sidney Parfitt. And he is extremely bright,' Ena said in Sid's defence. 'I'll run the Voight case past him before I see Dick Bentley.'

'Before you go in all guns blazing telling Bentley you've seen Frieda King – Voight – you need proof she's alive. We need to investigate this ourselves first, get some real evidence before you get Director Bentley and Sid and Artie involved.'

Ena tutted.

'So, it's the MI5 archive, first. Agree?'

'If you say so.' Ena stood up, Henry remained seated. 'What are you waiting for?' she said, grabbing her handbag.

'I have just told you that I have to work this afternoon.'

Ena threw her bag onto the table and flopped down in the chair she had vacated seconds before. 'You're determined to make this difficult, Henry!'

'Don't be ridiculous. I'm in the middle of something that I can't just walk away from. I'll finish it today if I can get back to work, and we'll go to the records office tomorrow.'

'Whatever's best for bloody MI5,' Ena said.

Henry took Ena by the hand. 'I'm due some leave, so I'll go back to the office now, finish what I've been working on, and I'll take the whole of tomorrow off. We'll go down to Argyle Street first thing in the morning, all right?'

Ena nodded half-heartedly.

Henry looked at his watch. 'I've got to go. See you later.'

'Will you be home for dinner?'

'I should think so. I'll telephone before I leave the office. Hey,' Henry said, 'come here.'

Ena walked slowly, teasingly, over to her husband, looked up into his face and pulled on his lapels. 'Try to get home for dinner, will you?'

'I promise.'

Arms wrapped around each other, Ena and Henry left the café. Outside they went their separate ways. When she was sure Henry was too far away to hear her, Ena hailed a cab. 'Dean's Crescent, Holland Park, please.'

FOUR

Beyond the cab's windows were the tree-lined streets of Knightsbridge and Kensington. Travelling through the leafy suburbs was like being transported to another place and time. London, Ena thought, is a city of two parts. West and northwest of the Thames had an abundance of green areas: heaths and parks, large Victorian houses with small families; Nannies to care for the children, a cook to feed them and a kitchen maid to clean up after them. Most of the houses in Holland Park had garages that were built better than many of the houses in the East End. Flashy limousines, polished within an inch of their shiny lives, were driven by white-gloved chauffeurs in peaked caps and brass-buttoned uniforms.

The southeast and southwest of London had green areas. A favourite of Ena's was Clapham Common, though she rarely had time to visit it. But there were fewer in the East End. Children played on bomb sites where houses destroyed by the Luftwaffe in the war still hadn't been rebuilt, even though the war had ended thirteen years ago.

'Here will do, driver,' Ena said, when the cab turned into Dean's Crescent. She jumped out and paid the fare. She didn't want to risk anyone from number 7 looking out of the window and seeing her and walked briskly across the road to the public park.

Ena's stomach was an amalgamation of fluttering butterflies and dive-bombing tree swallows. The tarmac path ran parallel with the road. A short distance from the entrance to the park was a bench. It was dedicated to someone Ena had never heard of. She sat down. Hidden from inquisitive eyes by a cluster of rhododendron bushes she placed her arm casually along the back of the bench. No one took much notice of her. A man walking a dog pulled on its lead when it cocked its leg near the bench. A young couple with their arms entwined were looking into each other's eyes and didn't see her, and a middle-aged workman doffed his cap as he ambled past.

Leaning sideways, Ena looked over her shoulder. While pretending to admire the rich green leaves on the rhododendron bushes behind her, Ena gave her attention to the house she could see when she looked between them. On the other side of the railings was Dean's Crescent – and the other side of the crescent was number 7 a large Victorian townhouse where Self-ridges had earlier delivered purchases to Madame Romanovski, aka Frieda Voight.

The three storey residence had wide steps leading to the front door, a bay window on either side, and three large windows above – two over the ground floor bays and one above the door. Below street level narrow steps led from the main gate. They arced round to the garage on one side of the house and to the basement, or servants' quarters, on the other. The lower ground floor windows had iron bars in them. Ena chuckled. Were the bars to keep the security services out, or the servants in?

As the afternoon nudged into early evening the temperature began to fall. Ena pulled her collar up and held her coat tightly around her. Storm clouds swept across the sky as the sun went down behind the park's enormous oak trees – and the lights in the basement of number 7 came on. Soon afterwards there were lights on the first floor. Ena left the bench and followed the path until she came to a narrow wrought iron pedestrian gate. Observing the house from behind hawthorn and maple hedges, she strained to see the face of a man who appeared briefly at the first floor window. He looked across the road and into the park. If she hadn't known better Ena would have sworn he was looking at her. He pulled the curtains, became a shadow and was gone. It wasn't the man she had seen with Frieda in Oxford Street. He was taller and slimmer than the man at the window.

Ena stamped her feet and walked up and down on the spot. She was cold. As there had been no sign of *Madame Romanovski* she left the park by the narrow gate.

'Damn!' she said. Henry had promised to be home early and she had promised to cook dinner. She sprinted to Holland Park Underground, took the Central Line to Tottenham Court Road, changed to the Northern Line and alighted at Stockwell. As luck would have it, the 196 was pulling away from the stop as Ena left the station. She ran across the road, boarded the moving bus and got off two stops later at Stockwell Gardens. A hundred yards along the road she arrived at St Michael's Square and home.

Out of breath, Ena pushed open the door. The flat was in darkness; Henry wasn't back from work. She exhaled with relief, shrugged off her jacket and hung it up in the hall. Dropping her handbag onto the seat of the armchair behind the door in the sitting room, she ran into the kitchen and started to prepare dinner.

'Nothing!' Ena pushed the last of half a dozen files she'd been allowed to read across the table, stretched out her arms and flopped forward, her head resting on a pile of papers. It was hot in the archive offices in Argyle Street. She flung herself back in the swivel chair and swung round to face Henry.

'Nothing here either,' he said, and closed the last file he'd been looking through. 'Not surprising really, King not being their real name.'

'But when Freda worked with me at Silcott Engineering her work papers were in the name of King. She had a National Insurance Number so there must be a certificate. She had a medical card, food tokens, a ration book – and she could drive. Her driving licence would have been in the name of Freda King. If it had been in any other name it would have looked suspicious.' Ena picked up the files and slammed them down on the table. 'There has to be something with her name on it.'

Henry shook his head. 'There isn't.'

'But there must be, somewhere. You can't live, drive, work, without there being records. What about Walter?'

'Nothing.'

A thought struck Ena. 'They had an uncle. Look up, H. Villiers. He rented the house they lived in, in Northampton.'

'Intelligence went through the house in forty-four. They didn't find any evidence of an uncle, or anyone else other than Frieda and Walter living there.'

'But someone must have rented the house.'

'But not anyone by the name of Villiers. He was as fictitious as Freda and Walter King's papers.'

'If Freda's papers were forged they were damn good.'

'As were Walter's at university.'

'Let's get the German Nationals Department to give us what they have on Frieda Voight and Walter Voight.'

Henry raised his eyebrows at Jim Matthews, the officer in charge of MI5's archives department. 'Would you ring through for us, Jim? Ask if we can have a look at anyone between nineteen forty-two and forty-five with the surname Voight?'

'Or King,' Ena said. 'It's a long shot, but it can't do any harm to check whether the Kings are listed in the GN files.'

'They may not be together, of course.'

'But they were.' Ena looked at Henry. 'They were brother and sister.'

'We know that, but they could be Mr and Mrs in the GN files.'

Jim left the room. He was gone for only a few minutes. 'I'm sorry, Mr Green, the officer in charge of the German Nationals archive said the files on Walter and Frieda Voight are code red.'

'I have clearance for code red.'

'Sorry, sir, the files are locked. Access to them is only through the Director of Operations.'

'This is an important case, Jim,' Ena said, standing as tall as she was able.

'They all are, Mrs Green.'

'Thanks, Jim. We'll make an appointment with Director Robinson.'

'He's on sick leave,' the security man said.

'We'll put a request in for when he's back. Thanks, again.' Henry took a pack of cigarettes from his coat pocket. 'I'm going out for a smoke. Coming, Ena?' Without waiting for Ena's reply Henry took hold of her arm and steered her out of the room.

Once she was sure Jim Matthews wouldn't be able to hear, Ena pulled free of Henry's grip. 'What are you doing?'

'Leaving. Frieda's and Walter's files are locked, there's nothing more we can do until we get permission to see them from Mac Robinson.'

'Oh yes there is,' Ena said, batting her eyelashes.

'Okay. See what you can do. I'll be outside.' Henry mounted the stairs, turned to Ena and winked. Ena nodded and went back to the security officer. She gave him her sweetest smile. 'Do you know when Director Robinson will be back, Jim?'

'No, but...'

'What is it?'

'His personal assistant will. Her telephone number is in the staff directory. I'm not really supposed to let anyone other than a member of staff see it without a request in writing, but as you're with Mr Green and he has clearance, I'll get it for you.' Jim rummaged around in the drawer of the cabinet behind his desk. 'I know it's here somewhere. I showed it to a woman this morning.'

'A woman?'

'One of the secretaries. She said your husband...' Jim cleared his throat, 'I mean, Mr Green, wanted the private telephone number of the director's PA, Miss Crowther.'

'Did she say why?'

'No.'

'And you didn't ask?'

'Not my place to, Mrs Green. If the paperwork is in order...'

'What did this woman look like?'

'Very attractive she was.' Ena gave the man a weary look. 'She was, err, tall and slim. Oh, and she had fair hair, blonde you might say, curled like Marilyn Munroe.'

'How old was she?'

'You've got me there. I'm not very good on lady's ages.' Jim leaned back and squinted at Ena. 'She was older than you.'

'Ah, yes, that would have been Freda,' Ena said, casually, her heart pounding in the hopes that she may at last have proof, however flimsy, that Frieda Voight was alive.

'She didn't tell me her name.'

'What? She didn't show you her ID?'

'No, she showed me Mr Green's ID.'

Ena gasped, quickly checked herself and said, 'No matter, there are so many women in his department – young, old, dark-haired, blonde.' Ena was seething but forced a half-hearted smile. She knew exactly who had been looking at the personnel files. How the hell had Frieda Voight got into MI5's archive? More importantly, how had she got hold of Henry's ID?

'I remember now. I didn't have time to take it back so I put it in this drawer.' The security man opened the top drawer of his desk. It wasn't there. He looked in the second drawer. 'Here it is. Phew! I thought it had gone missing.' He pulled a comical face. 'I knew it couldn't have, I remember the lady giving it back to me.' He handed the directory to Ena.

Under Jim's watchful eye, Ena opened the black leather-bound book and ran her finger down the stepped-alphabet at the side until she came to the letter C. Crowther, Helen.

At that moment, the telephone rang. While Jim answered it, Ena ran her finger on, stopping at the letter R. Robinson, McKenzie, George. It was a Brighton telephone number. She consigned it to memory. When the security officer put down the telephone, Ena gave him the directory, thanked him and left.

FIVE

That evening, Henry arrived home with a folder stamped Top Secret. Ena viewed its contents with suspicion. The paper the report was written on looked new. It was too clean, there wasn't a mark or crease on it anywhere. She suspected it had been put together by some minion at MI5 for her benefit, using information that was common knowledge to anyone in the security services. She speed-read the pages. There was no mention of an uncle, or anyone else with the name Villiers.

She looked at Henry, a cynical smile played on her lips. 'This report only tells us what we already know about Frieda and Walter Voight. *At the time of the original investigation in 1944, Military Intelligence searched the house and found no evidence that a third person lived there. It is our opinion that H Villiers was invented to give respectability to a man and woman living together.*' Freda's and Walter's papers said they were brother and sister. Why they felt the need to invent an uncle was a mystery to Ena. But then McKenzie Robinson had told her after Frieda's arrest in 1944 that Frieda and Walter had been lovers. Brother, sister, lover? Ena suspected the real reason that they didn't want people snooping about was in case their covers were blown.

After reading to the end of the report Ena returned it to the folder. 'What about Oxford? Walter was at university with you. There'll be records.'

'As there will be at Silcott Engineering from when Freda worked with you in the war. Herbert Silcott's bound to have kept records. He probably still has them.'

'Of course,' Ena said, throwing her arms around her husband and kissing him. 'Why didn't I think of that? Mrs Silcott was the company's bookkeeper. She did the timesheets, put the wages in envelopes and sent off our National Insurance contributions.' Ena kissed Henry again. 'How about a couple of days in the country?'

'Okay. As soon as I can get some time off, I'll go up to Oxford, to Balliol, and you go to Lowarth, to the factory.'

To beat the traffic going into London, Henry and Ena left home at six o'clock in the morning. Turning right onto Stockwell Road, again onto Clapham Road, and left to South Lambeth took no time at all. Soon they were driving through Wandsworth to Vauxhall. They made good time and were over Vauxhall Bridge without any delays. With Victoria behind them, they drove round Hyde Park Corner and up Park Lane to Marble Arch. Once across Oxford Street to Edgware Road, it was more or less plain sailing along the A5 – give or take dozens of towns – all the way to Rugby.

When they arrived at Rugby station, Henry caught a train to Coventry, where he changed to a cross country train to Oxford. Ena, after waving him off, bought a bunch of flowers for her mother from a stall on the platform and left the station.

At the car she laid the flowers in the boot and slipped in

behind the steering wheel. She loved driving. And she loved the new Sunbeam Rapier that she had persuaded Henry they should buy. They shared the car, and because Henry did most of the long distance driving he wanted a Hillman Minx, but Ena had her heart set on the sporty blue Sunbeam with its white roof. And, as she so often did, she got her way. She gunned the Sunbeam's engine and set off for Foxden.

Outside her mother's cottage, Ena took her shoulder bag from the passenger seat, opened the driver's door and swung her legs out. The early autumn air was damp. She would take a stroll to the village of Woodcote later if there was time – and if the weather held. Leaving the car, she hitched the strap of her bag onto her shoulder and took the flowers from the boot.

She squelched through a drift of fallen leaves sodden by the recent rain and pushed on the gate. A mound of browning mulch, decaying leaves blown from the trees on either side of the lane, resisted the bottom rung of the gate. Ena put her weight behind it and levelled the soggy mass.

She knocked the front door and while she waited for her mother to answer, looked back. The afternoon sun glistened through the branches of the trees, highlighting the yellows and golds, reds and greens of the remaining leaves.

'Hello, love.' Ena's mother greeted her with a kiss. 'Are they for me?' she said when Ena gave her the flowers. 'They're lovely, our Ena, but you shouldn't go spending your money on me.' Ena smiled. Her mother's answer to any gift was always the same.

'Come in, love. You must be perished. I'll put the kettle on.' Ena followed her mother into the cottage. After taking off her coat and hanging it up, she went through to the kitchen. 'I'd just put a log on the fire when I heard your car. Sit down and warm yourself.'

Ena stretched out her hands towards the smoky flames from

the damp wood. While the kettle boiled, Lily Dudley put the flowers in a vase of water, admired her handiwork, and then placed the arrangement on the draining board. 'I'll take them into the sitting room in a bit. It's not so warm in there, they'll last longer.'

When the kettle boiled Ena made the tea. Her mother took cups and saucers from the kitchen cabinet and while Ena poured, fetched the milk and a sponge cake from the larder.

'That looks good, mam.'

'It's your favourite,' her mother said, cutting a slice twice as thick as she'd have given anyone else. 'You look half starved, girl.' She stood back and scrutinised her daughter. 'You've lost weight since you were last here. How long are you staying?'

'What?' Ena mumbled, her mouth full of cake.

'Are you staying long enough for me to feed you up?'

Ena almost choked. She took a drink of tea to help the cake go down and laughed. Her mother's conversation really didn't change. 'You always say that.'

'I suppose it's living in that big city,' Lily Dudley said, resignedly.

'What is?'

'You, being so thin. No good fresh food in those places. I don't suppose you feed Henry properly either. What time will he be here?'

'He's staying with his old professor from Balliol College tonight. If the trains are on time, he'll be back around twelve tomorrow.'

'We'll have an early lunch, then.' Lily Dudley got up and topped up the teapot with boiling water. 'I made a loaf this morning, then I popped into Mr Moore's in Woodcote and bought a nice bit of gammon, a tin of salmon and half a pound of Cheddar. Course, I've got other food, so if Henry fancies something else,' she said, refreshing their cups. She picked up the knife to cut another slice of cake.

'No more for me, mam, or I won't want my tea. That's assuming you're not keeping all that delicious food until your son-in-law gets here tomorrow.'

'Any more cheek from you, our Ena, and I'll send you up to your room *without* any supper.' Lily Dudley grinned. 'Come on, love, let's go into the sitting room. I'll take the cups and you bring the flowers.'

Ena did as she was told, opened the door for her mother to leave the kitchen and followed her into the sitting room. It hadn't changed since the last time she was home, or the time before that. The same floral-patterned covers were on the seats of the settee and chairs – and the same antimacassars on the arms. She was surprised to see the small coffee table had an ashtray on it. For Henry, Ena thought. Her mother hadn't put it there for her. She thought Ena had stopped smoking long ago. She had, almost.

On the right of the mantelshelf above the chair her late father always sat in was his pipe-rack and four pipes. He only smoked a pipe on special occasions, like Christmas and New Year. The rest of the time he smoked Capstan Full Strength cigarettes, or rolled his own. Ena picked up one of the pipes. Her father was the only person in her life, other than her oldest sister Bess, who Ena could confide in. She missed not being able to go to him with her problems or ask his advice. He was a calming influence, a strong intelligent man who never took sides and never judged.

Ena missed her siblings too. When her brother Tom came home from the army at the end of the war he moved to Kent with his wife and daughter. He managed a country estate and bred horses. Bess was the only one who lived locally. She had been in charge of an army of land girls in the war and had turned the Foxden Estate into arable land. She now owned the Foxden Hotel with her husband Frank and had adopted a daughter. Margot, Ena's second oldest sister was a singer and dancer in London during war. She was the leading lady in a number of West End shows, but left the theatre at the end of the war and moved back to the Midlands to start a family. Ena laughed remembering how on Saturday afternoons, when they were children, Margot would make her and Claire sit and watch her practice the dances and songs she had learned that morning in the village hall. Claire, closest in age to Ena, had worked with the French Resistance in the war and her work – like Ena's for Bletchley Park – was top secret. Claire, now married with a daughter, taught French and German at RAF Brize Norton in Oxfordshire.

With five women in the house, there were always disagreements. Ena smiled to herself. Her mother would often say something that made matters worse. Her father on the other hand only had to enter the room and give his daughters a stern look to silence them.

Ena set the pipe back on the rack and sat down on the settee.

'I'll take our cups out and make us some sandwiches,' her mother said, pushing herself out of her chair when they had finished their tea.

'I have a better idea,' Ena said. 'I want to see Bess while I'm here, so, in case Henry has to go back to London after lunch tomorrow, why don't we go up to the Foxden Hotel for an early dinner?'

Her mother's face lit up. 'Well, I'll have to get changed. I can't go up in this frock, I've been doing the housework in it.'

Ena laughed. Her mother loved to get dressed up. 'Go and put your glad rags on then.'

Lily Dudley moved quicker than Ena had seen her move all afternoon. 'Shan't be long,' she said, clearing away the cups and saucers.

'There's no rush, mam.' It crossed Ena's mind that there

might not be a table available in the dining room. When she spoke to Bess to tell her that she and Henry were coming to Foxden, and she hoped to see her, her sister had said the hotel was full but she would arrange cover so she and Ena could catch up with each other's news. 'I'll telephone Bess and make sure she can fit us in,' Ena called to her mother, as she headed up the stairs.

On the approach to the Foxden Hotel, Ena looked over at the car park. No longer a roped-off area in a cobbled courtyard, it had been extended and was full of smart cars. She followed her mother up the steps to the hotel's entrance and into the foyer. The main hall had been decorated since Ena was last there. The marble floor, as beautiful as ever, complimented the rich cream of the walls. The dark reddish brown stair carpet sweeping up to the first floor, the gilt light fittings on the walls – and the magnificent chandelier that hung from the ceiling – added a touch of grandeur.

Ena had seen Bess wave when she and their mother arrived. She was now heading across the hall to meet them. Bess threw her arms around Ena and they both spoke at the same time asking each other how they were and exclaiming how long it had been since they last saw each other.

With Bess in the middle, their arms still round each other, they chatted all the way to the reception desk. Ena's mother said she was going to find her granddaughter and after a quick word with the receptionist, Bess and Ena went into the familiar office behind reception. Except for a lick of paint that looked as if it had been left over after decorating the walls of the marble hall the room hadn't changed.

'How's Frank? I hope the new car park doesn't mean his menagerie had to go.'

Bess looked at Ena horrified. 'No, it didn't. Do you think I'd want a riot on my hands? Sadly,' Bess said, a mischievous glint in her eyes, 'we no longer keep pigs. But there are new sheds for the chickens and new stables for the Nancy's ponies. She'll give you the grand tour tomorrow.'

Ena pulled a face. 'I'm not sure I'll be here tomorrow.'

'Another flying visit?'

'Afraid so.'

'One of these days you'll have to stop and catch your breath, Ena.'

'I know. And I will. It's just–' She never talked to anyone about the cold cases she worked on. But she and Bess had no secrets. In the past they had told each other everything. Her eldest sister was perhaps the only person in the world, apart from her husband Henry, that Ena could really trust. Even so, she hesitated.

'What is it, Ena? Something is worrying you.'

'It's nothing really.' Should she tell Bess about the Voight case? She decided against it. 'It's just that I'm going up to Silcott's in the morning, while Henry's in Oxford. He's coming into Rugby by train, so there's no telling what time he'll get here. And, because he has to show his face at work before the end of the day, we'll probably have to leave Mam's early after-noon to miss the rush hour traffic in London.'

'Never mind, next time,' Bess said.

'I promise. Henry too. He won't even have time to see his parents tomorrow. But, as soon as the case I'm working on is finished, we'll come up for a long weekend.'

Bess looked perturbed. 'Does the case you're working on involve Herbert Silcott?'

'In a way, yes.' Ena took a breath. Since Henry didn't believe her, she would confide in Bess; tell her that she had seen Frieda Voight, who Bess knew in the war as Freda King. 'I'm looking for proof that Freda King existed.'

Bess looked confused. 'But you know she did. You worked with her.'

'Yes, I did. I also exposed her and her brother Walter as spies. They were sent to prison because of me. At least Walter was. He was in Brixton until he died.' Ena thought it best not to tell Bess Walter's death was a suspected murder. 'Sometime after Walter died, Freda is supposed to have killed herself. She was buried with him. I went to her funeral.'

'I don't understand.'

'Freda isn't dead. Her funeral was a sham. A coffin was interred and the name on the brass plate said Frieda Voight which was her real name. If anyone *was* buried that day, it was not Freda.'

'Are you sure?'

'I'm certain. Her funeral was a set-up by MI5. Being dead is the best cover a spy can have. It sounds like something you'd read in a cheap spy thriller, but I'd bet my last pound that the security services promised her anonymity if she spied for them.'

'I understand that but what makes you think after all this time that Freda is alive?'

'I saw her in Oxford Street.'

Ena and her mother dined with Bess, Frank and their teenage daughter Nancy. Over dinner, Bess brought Ena up to date with recent news of their sisters and brother.

There wasn't time to visit her sister, Margot, even though she was only fourteen miles away in Coventry, and there was no way she could visit Claire or Tom, they both lived too far away. It suddenly struck Ena that for many years it had been the tradition that the Dudley family met up at Easter and Christmas. When they had finished eating Ena said, 'Let's get everyone together and have a family Christmas this year.' She raised her glass in the hopes the Frieda Voight case would be history by then.

'That's a lovely idea. I'll telephone everyone, see what their plans are.' Bess lifted her glass to join Ena's. 'Here's to a traditional Dudley family Christmas!'

SIX

The next morning, Ena set off for Lowarth and Silcott's Engineering, the factory where she had worked in the war, and where she had shared an office with Freda King. Ena had made dials and discs for a secret location that she only knew as Station-X. After the bombing of Coventry in November 1941 it became necessary for Ena to deliver her work, which was of great importance, to Bletchley Park.

She parked the Sunbeam and ran across the road to the shop where she had bought pear drops to suck on the train when she accompanied Mr Silcott or Freda to Bletchley. She felt a sudden chill. The thought of the many times she had travelled with Freda and the danger she had been in made her shiver. She stepped into the shop and shook her head to rid herself of the memory.

She asked the young woman behind the counter, 'Has the gentleman who owned the shop retired?'

'Two years ago. Were you a customer?'

'Yes, when I worked at Silcott's.'

'Come to visit old friends, have you?'

'Yes,' Ena said, which wasn't really a lie because she hoped to see some of her old friends while she was there. She looked at her watch. 'It's almost eleven. It'll soon be tea break, won't it?'

'The factory side breaks before the offices. You'll see the men come out and light up.'

'In that case, I had better buy some chocolates.' She looked along the shelf behind the counter. A jar of pear drops caught her eye. Recalling the day she was poisoned made her stomach churn. She quickly put the memory out of her mind. 'I'll take a box of Cadbury's Milk Tray and a tin of Quality Street.'

Armed with a selection of confectionery, Ena left the Newsagents and crossed the road. The street had changed. The old two-up-two-down cottages, made unsafe when the Luftwaffe dropped stray bombs in 1940, had been pulled down. In their place were the new temporary prefabricated homes made of pebbledash slabs. The small area on either side of each front door had been cultivated and, although many of the flowers had gone over, the gardens still looked attractive. She wrinkled her nose. The metal roofs on the bungalows were anything but attractive. Still, they had solved the housing shortage after the war. And, coming from America as part of the post-war Marshall Aid plan, they had fitted kitchens and indoor lavatories that were separate from the bathrooms. The downside, Ena thought, was their ten-year life expectancy, which had ended some years ago. She wondered what the council would replace the 'prefabs' with.

As she neared the factory Ena stopped. The building was twice as big as it was when she worked there. There was now a large brick extension on the left where the old factory used to be and the offices on the right of the building had new windows and their own entrance. No more having to walk through the factory avoiding greasy machines to get to and from the offices, Ena mused.

In the car park a smart advertising board said Silcott Engineering, Lowarth. Beneath the name was a detailed plan of the factory. Arrows pointed to various parts of the building. Ena decided not to go to the offices via the side entrance. She wanted to see how improved the building was and went through the front door to reception.

The main entrance door opened into a spacious lobby. A new wall had been built after a Luftwaffe bomb had brought most of the outer wall down, leaving a huge crater in the car park.

'Ena Green to see Mr Silcott,' she said to the smartly dressed young woman behind the desk.

While the receptionist phoned through to her old boss, Ena kept an eye on the door to the factory hoping to see one of her friends come through. They didn't.

'Mr Silcott is coming out to see you now, Mrs Green.'

A second later Herbert Silcott burst through a door on the opposite side of the lobby, arms open and beaming a welcoming smile.

Before Ena could speak he threw his arms around her and lifted her off her feet knocking the wind out of her. 'Come through, come through,' he said when he put her down. 'We'll go to my office, have a chat, then I'll show you around. You won't recognise the old place.'

Herbert opened the door to the offices and almost skipped down the corridor. Halfway along he stopped. 'My secretary,' he said, over his shoulder as he opened the door. 'Telephone Frank Whittle, Miss Rose. Tell him his order is finished. It'll be going down overnight and will be with him tomorrow morning. But first, would you bring tea and biscuits to my office? Thank you.' Without waiting for a reply from the flustered Miss Rose, Herbert shut the door.

The room opposite was the small office that had played such a large part in Ena's life during the war. On the door was a brass nameplate: Herbert Silcott, Proprietor.

So Mr Silcott's father-in-law was no longer named as

proprietor of Silcott Engineering. Good for you, Herbert, Ena thought. She didn't say anything because Herbert had always led the staff to believe he owned the Lowarth factory. He pulled out a chair from beneath an ebony-wood desk for Ena and took his seat behind it.

Sitting down, Ena gave the room an approving smile. Before she could comment, there was a knock at the door.

'Come in,' Herbert called.

'Your tea, Mr Silcott.' Miss Rose put down the tray. 'Would you like me to pour, sir?'

'No, we'll manage. You get back to your post, Miss Rose.'

The secretary gave Ena a polite smile as she made for the door. 'Thank you,' Herbert called after her. Half turning back to her boss, Miss Rose smiled again.

Herbert was a kind man and fair in his dealings with the people who worked for him. Ena and Herbert had always sent each other Christmas cards. The cards often contained snippets of news, and one year Herbert told her that his father-in-law had died. He said no more than that, but Ena's mother had told her that, even though it was Herbert who had run the company successfully for many years, old Mr Williams had left the factory to his daughter. He may be the boss at work, but his wife wears the trousers at home, Ena thought. 'How is Mrs Silcott?'

'She is very well. She still does the wages and brings them in.' Herbert chuckled. 'I don't think she trusts me to add the hours up correctly. She has always been prudent, has my good lady-wife. She was brought up to be careful, where I was brought up to be... Well, put it this way, our childhoods were very different.'

Ena knew they were. Her mother had told her when Ena first went to work at Silcott's that Herbert's father had worked for Williams Engineering, working his way up from a fourteen-year-old apprentice to foreman. Lily Dudley had known Herbert's mother. She was a dressmaker. It was after a dress fitting to which Mrs Williams had brought her daughter that she and Herbert started walking out together.

'Well, they say opposites attract, don't they?' Ena poured the tea. 'Like old times, isn't it?' she said, handing Herbert a cup and pushing the plate of biscuits across the desk to him.

'What do you think of our old office, Ena?'

'It's lovely.' Ena looked round the room. 'With just one desk it appears much bigger.'

'Yes, there's a good deal more space now, than when the three of us worked in here.'

Ena looked at Herbert. This was the opening she needed. She mustn't let it pass. 'A lot has happened since then, Mr Silcott,' she said, with a sigh, 'and some of it isn't good.'

'No. I gathered it wasn't from the brief telephone conversation we had. If there's anything I can do to help, Ena, you know I will.'

'Thank you.' Ena took a deep breath. What she was about to tell Herbert she knew would upset him, but there was no way around it. She needed his help. 'You know Freda was a spy, don't you?'

'Yes.' Herbert shook his head slowly. 'I found it hard to believe, but Military Intelligence came to see me. They explained everything. They knew I wasn't involved in her treachery. They told me the investigation was hush-hush, but word got out. Even though I was cleared the business suffered for several years.' He took a drink of his tea. 'But that's by-the-by. The business recovered. Freda on the other hand... To kill herself...' Herbert looked as if he was about to cry. He put down his cup. 'Terrible, just terrible.'

'Freda didn't kill herself.'

Herbert shot Ena a look that was somewhere between relief and disbelief.

'I saw her not long ago in London.'

'Are you sure?'

'Yes, I am. It's why I've come to see you. I need a copy of her work records to help me find her.'

'But I don't have any, dear.'

'You must have, Mr Silcott. When you paid her you'd have deducted tax and National Insurance. Mrs Silcott would have kept a record. We all had work numbers. Freda must have had one because she clocked in like the rest of us.'

Herbert shook his head.

'There must be something, surely?'

'I no longer have Freda King's work details. The intelligence people took all the staff records. They took everything between nineteen forty and forty-five. They asked why there were no time sheets and I told them my wife dealt with everything to do with staff hours and wages, and they went to my house. Did the same thing there. They took everything.'

'Everything?'

'Yes. The only remaining references to Freda King ever having worked here were in the annual account ledgers at my accountant's office.'

Ena expelled a sigh of relief. She was about to ask for the accountant's address when her old boss dashed her hopes. 'Military Intelligence searched his offices too. They took several years of his records, the same as they did from here.' Hebert leaned back in his chair. 'I have no proof that Freda King ever worked for me.'

'No,' Ena said, thoughtfully, 'no one does. It's as if she never existed.'

'Except we know she did.'

'*Does*,' Ena corrected.

'Yes, of course, does. I'm sorry I can't be of more help, Ena.'

'Don't be!' Ena dashed the idea of Freda King away as if she was swatting a fly. 'How about showing me around. I want to see all the changes you've made since I worked here.' In truth, it was the last thing Ena wanted, but she was not about to offend her old boss. Military Intelligence might have erased Freda King on paper, but they had not erased her from Herbert's memory, or hers. Ena decided not to pursue the subject and followed Herbert out of his office.

Her heart wasn't in the tour of the factory but she put on a smile and listened to Herbert as he explained the capabilities of each new machine. She stopped to speak to a girl from Lowarth who she had been at school with, and two old friends that she had worked with in the war. When the lunch bell rang she went back to the office, collected her bag and the chocolates, and joined the women in the canteen.

Without touching on Bletchley Park or Beaumanor, the women talked about the war work they did in the factory, the dances they went to, who was walking out with who, and who ended up marrying who. One of Ena's friends showed her photographs of her husband and children and asked her when she was going to come back to Lowarth, settle down and have a family.

'I'm too busy at the moment,' Ena said, 'but one day.'

Another asked her about the work she did. Ena managed to bat-off most of the questions about her job, and ended up saying she was a clerk in an office in Covent Garden. After that, the conversation changed. A couple of the women said they had been to Covent Garden when they visited London.

The time flew by. It felt as if the morning was over before it began. When the bell rang at the end of the lunch break, Ena promised to visit again when she next came up to Foxden. As the women returned to their machines, Herbert Silcott arrived to walk Ena out of the canteen and into the reception.

'Be careful, Ena,' Herbert said. He took her hand in his and shook it gently. 'Keep in touch, will you? Let me know what happens to Freda?'

Before Ena could answer, the receptionist appeared at Herbert's side. 'There's a telephone call for you, Mr Silcott.'

Herbert looked uncomfortable about leaving Ena. 'It's Mr Whittle at Bristol Aero Engines. He'll only speak to you, sir.'

'I shall have to take this call, Ena. I won't be a minute.' Herbert followed the young woman to the reception desk and picked up the telephone. Without taking his eyes off Ena he greeted Frank Whittle.

Ena waved goodbye. She had no intention of involving Herbert further in the web of lies and deceit that his ex-employee Freda King had woven. To do so would be dangerous.

Closing the door of Silcott's Engineering, Ena became overwhelmed by a feeling of loss; of not belonging. At the car, she looked back at the factory. It had once been the most important part of her working life, but now? Now, it wasn't. She had moved on.

SEVEN

On the way back to Foxden, Ena stopped at a garage to put petrol in the Sunbeam for the return journey to London. The attendant came out of the garage with a baby in his arms. He handed the child to a young woman who Ena assumed was the child's mother.

'Six gallons, please.' While the young man filled the car, Ena watched the woman jiggle the baby up and down in her arms. She had never thought it unusual not to have a child, until today; until her friend at the factory showed her photographs of her children. She wondered if her family thought she was unusual too. Her sister Bess had been desperate to have a child, wasn't able to conceive, so she and Frank adopted their daughter. Her brother Tom, and her older sisters Claire and Margot had children, so the family probably did think it a bit unusual that Ena didn't. Because Henry was ten years older than her, Ena had thought when they first started courting that he would want to start a family as soon as they were married. He didn't. Nor did she for that matter.

'... shillings, miss.'

'Sorry?'

'For the petrol. Nine shillings.'

Ena had been miles away, lost in thoughts of babies. She apologised, paid the attendant, and set off again to Foxden.

'I'm back.' Ena took off her coat, hung it up in the hall, and went through to the kitchen. Her mother wasn't there. 'Anyone home?'

'In here,' Henry called from the sitting room.

'You're back early,' Ena said, greeting Henry with a kiss. 'Where's Mam?'

'Gone up to the hotel. I'm surprised you didn't see her, she has only just left.' Henry lit a cigarette. 'Want one?'

'While the cat's away...' Ena removed the cigarette from Henry's lips and took a drag. He lit another. 'So, what did you find out in Oxford?'

'Nothing that I didn't already know. I told the admissions officer at Balliol I was thinking about organising a get together with my old alumni but couldn't find the addresses of Jack Heyhoe-Bloom or Walter King. He was more than happy to look up both names.'

'And?'

'Jack's dead. I knew he was. He was killed in a car accident, which is why I used the poor chap's name. And there was no record of Walter King. The admissions officer was thorough. He asked me if I was sure Mr King came up to Balliol. I made a bit of a meal of thinking about it and said, now you mention it I'm not sure he did. I said perhaps I'd known the chap socially, or I had worked with him during the war. I apologised for wasting his time and left.'

'So, Walter King doesn't exist.'

'It appears not. What about you? Did you have any luck?'

'Same as you. Herbert and I know Freda King existed because she worked with us for four years, but there is no record of her ever having been there. But then you already knew that, didn't you, Henry?'

Henry gave Ena a look she couldn't decipher and said nothing.

'There is no record because, after Freda's arrest in forty-four, your lot commandeered every scrap of proof that she ever existed. You could have saved me the trouble of going up to the factory and worrying poor old Herbert Silcott. Why the hell didn't you tell me?'

'Because I didn't know.'

'I don't believe you.' Ena jumped up, took the keys to the Sunbeam from the sideboard and left the room. Grabbing her coat she hurried down the hall and made her exit, slamming the door.

Henry ran after her. 'Where are you going?'

'To the Fox in Lowarth for a drink.'

'I'm coming with you,' he said, jumping into the passenger seat.

Ena ignored him, turned the key in the ignition and put her foot down hard on the accelerator. By the time she pulled into the car park of the Fox, she had calmed down.

Ena headed for the log fire while Henry got the drinks: gin and tonic for Ena and a pint of bitter for himself.

They sat in silence for a while, then Henry said, 'I knew Five had been up to see Herbert Silcott, but I had no idea they'd confiscated any staff records, Ena.'

'Okay. I thought that because you didn't believe I'd seen Freda, you were trying to put me off investigating her case. I'm sorry I blew up at you.'

'You'd have had every right to blow up at me if I had known.' Henry took a swig of his pint. 'Curious!'

'What is?'

'That I wasn't told.'

· · ·

Ena and Henry left for London after lunch. Ena dropped Henry at Leconfield House and drove on to the Church of St Leonard in Brixton, where Walter Voight and his sister Frieda were supposed to be buried.

The four spires of the old church cast shadows like daggers across Walter and Frieda's grave. Ena read the inscription on the headstone. At Peace. Walter Voight. And beloved sister Frieda Voight.

As the sun went down it took with it the meagre amount of warmth it had shared with the world that day. Ena left the churchyard of St Leonard in darkness.

Lights were coming on in the buildings along Long Acre as Ena turned into Mercer Street. She parked the Sunbeam on the derelict ground opposite and let herself into the office.

'Director Bentley telephoned while you were away,' Artie said, 'we're opening up the Frieda Voight case.'

'Good!' Ena sat down and exhaled loudly.

'You look all in. Want a cuppa?' Tea was Artie's answer to every ill. He got up and put on the kettle without waiting for Ena to answer.

'Find out anything we don't already know about Voight, while you were up north?' Sid asked.

Ena shook her head. 'As far as the world is concerned, Freda King never existed and Frieda Voight is dead.'

Artie brought in three mugs of tea, plonked them down on Ena's desk, and pulled up a chair. 'So, what do we do now?'

'We find her, that's what we do.'

Ena made an appointment to see Commander Dalton, the Head of Operations at Bletchley Park during the war. He had retired but still lived in the town.

Commander Dalton had been kind to Ena. Knowing how she felt about Henry when he worked at Bletchley, the commander had instructed his driver to take her to see Henry before he went undercover; before he went on the run with Walter Voight in the hopes of gaining Voight's trust and infiltrating the spy network that he and Frieda belonged to.

'I don't have much,' the commander said, 'but what I have you are welcome to see.'

There was nothing Ena didn't already know about Frieda's trips to Bletchley, the work she delivered and the worksheets she took back to Silcott's.

'Nothing new here,' Ena said. Then a document stamped Classified caught her eye. Flicking through it, Ena saw it was a detailed account of Frieda Voight's arrest.

'Can I take this?'

'I'm afraid not. But, you're welcome to stay here for as long as it takes to read it.'

Ena glanced through the first half-dozen pages of typed script. Freda's capture had happened pretty much the way she had been told at the time.

'Oh?' Ena looked up at Commander Dalton. 'Frieda's death certificate.' A feeling of sadness mixed with anger swept over her. 'I've never seen this.'

'They have a copy at MI5.'

'And I bet it looks authentic too.'

'Why wouldn't it?'

'Because Frieda isn't dead. At least she wasn't when I saw her in London in August.'

Commander Dalton pushed back his chair, stretched out his legs, and clasped his hands behind his head.

'You don't look surprised, Commander.'

'I'm not. The death of Frieda Voight, as we now know her, was too sudden and too convenient.'

Ena laid her hand on top of the papers Commander Dalton had given her to read. 'These are false. Frieda Voight's death was fabricated by MI5, her funeral staged by them. Which,'

Ena said, contempt creeping into her voice, 'is why her file is locked and the spooks at Five are tight-lipped about her.'

Commander Dalton's eyes widened. 'Including Henry?'

'Yes.'

'I have something you can take with you that will help,' Commander Dalton said, going to his bureau and taking a manila envelope from it. 'This was given to me by McKenzie Robinson at MI5. Mac's the man you need to speak to.'

Ena took the envelope. 'Director Robinson is on sick leave.'

'He is,' Commander Dalton said, with a sad smile. 'And when his sick leave is over he will retire; put out to grass like me. Harold Macmillan's lot have no use for old warhorses like Mac Robinson and myself. Gaitskell's no better,' the commander said, skimming through a large black telephone book. 'Mac moved out of London. I've got his address somewhere.'

Ena opened the envelope, took out a couple of pages and glanced through them.

'I expect your husband is kept busy,' Commander Dalton said.

Ena lifted her head from the sheet of paper she was reading. 'I rarely see him these days. He works in the German office – but is occasionally seconded to the Russian desk.'

'Bloody Russians. You can't see your enemy in this damn cold war. You don't know who he or she is, or where he or she is coming from. It's a rum game. The Russians were on our side five minutes ago, now they're our greatest threat.

'Ah, got it!' Commander Dalton took a lined notepad from the drawer in his desk and wrote Mac Robinson's address down. He tore off the page and gave it to Ena.

'Get him to show you the archived files, spies, agents, double agents! Tell Mac I told you he would help you. Tell him what you told me and say, Dalton said the situation could end up damaging National Security.'

Ena returned the documents to their envelope, put it in her

bag and picked up her coat. 'Thank you,' she said, turning to leave.

'Keep me up to date with the Voight enquiry.' Commander Dalton put out his hand. 'And give Mac Robinson my best, will you?'

'I will, sir.' Ena took the commander's hand. His skin felt dry. She looked into his face. He had aged. But then it had been fourteen years.

EIGHT

'I thought you were cooking dinner?'

'I am.' Ena got up from the table and went to the kitchen. 'I didn't hear you come in.' She took two lamb chops out of the oven. 'Don't touch anything. It's in chronological order,' she shouted over her shoulder.

'The vegetables need another minute,' she said, dashing into the sitting room and stacking the files and documents – one straight, the next sideways, the third straight, and so on until she had a brick-pattern of papers. 'Set the table, darling,' she said, quickly moving the envelope Commander Dalton had given her to the sideboard and putting the papers on top of it before returning to the kitchen. 'Clean tablecloth, second drawer down in the sideboard; below the cutlery.'

She grabbed the handle of the saucepan and took off the lid. The potatoes had boiled dry and had stuck to the bottom of the pan. She put the spatula under them. They weren't burnt. Exhaling with relief, Ena took half a pound of butter from the cupboard, sliced off a wedge, and dropped it into the potatoes. After straining the greens she mashed the potatoes and made the gravy. A minute later she set two delicious smelling dinners on the dining table.

While they ate, Ena told Henry that Dick Bentley had given her permission to open a cold case file on Frieda. 'He was fascinated by the idea. And Sid did some digging. Apparently, Frieda was a double agent. He said MI5 would definitely have files on her.' Ena looked up from her meal. 'Was she, Henry?'

'What?'

'Frieda? A double agent? Sid said Dick Bentley told him she broke the Official Secrets Act and was rapped well and truly over the knuckles. He said it was then that she began working for the Russians. Is he right? Did she? I mean, does she work for the Russians?' Henry didn't answer. 'She does doesn't she?'

'You know I can't confirm that.'

'Good God. What happened to her that was so awful that she went to work for the Russians? The Germans, yes. East Germany with her coming from Berlin, but Russia, her country's greatest enemy?'

'Ours too.'

'That's why her file is locked.' Ena was itching to tell Henry about her afternoon, but he didn't appear to be interested.

'Is tinned fruit and Nestlé's cream all right?' she asked when they had eaten their chops. It was a rhetorical question that didn't warrant an answer. 'And, cheese and biscuits,' she said, putting a dish of fruit salad in front of Henry, and a plate with cheddar, stilton and savoury biscuits in the middle of the table.

When they had finished eating Ena took the dishes into the kitchen and washed up. By the time she returned to the sitting room, Henry was looking through the first pile of papers that Ena had brought home.

'Worth his weight in gold is Sid,' she said, taking the papers from him.

'What was that?' Henry asked. 'Missing Women 1944 to 1958.'

Ena hadn't intended Henry to see the files. Sid had persuaded a chum of his at Scotland Yard to let him borrow it. He shouldn't have taken it out of the building and promised to have it back at the Yard within twenty-four hours.

'Not for your eyes. Sorry.' Ena hated going behind Henry's back and felt the blush of embarrassment colour her cheeks. 'I thought, as Frieda isn't dead, she couldn't have been buried in a double grave with Walter, so whoever was buried that day had probably been reported to the police as a missing person.'

'I'm going for a walk,' Henry said.

'I'll come with you. We could call in the Hope and Anchor for a drink.'

'I thought you wanted to crack on with that lot?'

'Fine! If you don't want me to come.'

'Of course I want you to come. I just thought–' Henry went to the hall, put on his coat and returned to the sitting room. 'Well, come on, then.'

Ena put up her hands. 'Forget it. You go on your own and I'll *crack on*.'

Ena was in bed by the time Henry came home. She wasn't asleep but didn't respond to him when he crept into bed and put his arm around her. If she'd have said anything it would have been, take your freezing arm off me. Knowing that would upset him, Ena lay still, her breathing even and rhythmical.

The next morning, Henry left for work while Ena was in the bathroom.

She sauntered into the kitchen, felt the kettle, it was cold. Yawning, she flicked it on and spooned tea leaves into the pot. Cutting two slices of bread she put them under the grill and made the tea. By the time the tea was mashed the bread was toasted. She buttered both slices, poured a cup of tea and took it through to the sitting room.

Unable to ignore the paperwork on the dining table, Ena pulled a sheet from a pile she hadn't yet looked at and began reading a statement from the Russian Embassy.

The body of Russian diplomat Sergei Romanovski was found in his Holland Park residence on August 28, 1958. After an investigation by Scotland Yard and the Soviet Union's premier security agency, Madam Frieda Romanovski was cleared of any involvement in the diplomat's death. A spokesman from the Russian Embassy called Mr Romanovski's death – a heart attack causing him to fall down a flight of stairs – a tragic accident.

'Good God!' Ena said aloud. Was Sergei Romanovski the man she had seen Frieda talking to outside Selfridges in Oxford Street? She'd go to the library and look at the newspapers printed on August 29. If she couldn't find what she was looking for locally she could go to the British Newspaper Archive. But what would be the point? Even if there was a photograph of the diplomat, Ena wouldn't know whether it was him she had seen in Oxford Street, she hadn't seen his face.

Fortified by a second cup of tea, Ena dressed, put on her make-up and gathered up the papers she hadn't had time to read. She put them back in the envelope and placed them in her satchel next to the papers Commander Dalton had given her.

She tidied her hair and went into the hall. That morning the weatherman on the wireless said it was going to be another cold day. Ena grimaced. Henry had the car today. She tied a scarf around her neck, and put on a thick coat, hat and gloves. With her satchel over her shoulder, she set off for the railway station at Clapham Junction to catch a train to Brighton.

NINE

Making herself comfortable next to the window in the first empty compartment she came to, Ena took the remaining sheets of paper that Sid had given her from her bag and began to read. *Notes to clarify*, Sid had titled the last half dozen pages. There was nothing new, nothing that she hadn't already read. Sid was meticulous in his work. He had done a thorough job but he had repeated several things that Ena presumed he thought were important.

She looked again through the papers Commander Dalton had given her. After scrutinising every page she had a niggling feeling that she had missed something, but couldn't put her finger on it. What made it worse, everything after Walter Voight's arrest was sketchy.

Closing her eyes Ena brought to mind what Commander Dalton had said. She shook her head. Again, most of what he had told her only confirmed what she already knew. Frieda Voight had been arrested in 1944 whilst trying to escape to Ireland. He hadn't said what had happened to her after that and Ena hadn't asked because she assumed she would be reading

the details in the envelope he had given her. She had assumed
wrongly.

Five words defined Walter Voight's trial. *Guilty. Brixton
Prison. Maximum Security.*

Curious that there was no mention of Frieda at the trial. It
was not, however, the court transcript Ena was reading. Even so,
Frieda was an equal partner in everything Walter did. She was
equally as clever as her brother, and might well have been the
instigator of much of what they did. Ena flicked back and forth
through the pages but found no mention of Frieda. In fact, there
was nothing about her after she had been arrested. Ena sat back
in her seat, frustrated. She read the last page again. It ended
with PS. She turned the page. There was no postscript.

Ena took the first taxi outside Brighton station. 'Victoria
Crescent, Hove.' The short journey cost five shillings. She
didn't tip the driver. You could travel three times the distance
for five-bob in London, or buy a roast dinner on Sunday at the
Hope and Anchor. Thinking about their local pub brought
Henry to mind. She hated it that he had left the flat while she
was getting dressed. Hated it even more that he hadn't said
goodbye to her. Ena couldn't remember the last time they had
fallen out. In the ten years that they'd been married, they had
hardly ever argued. They had made up for it since she'd seen
Frieda Voight. She sighed. It seemed to Ena that they had done
nothing but argue for weeks.

Ena left the taxi and crossed the road. The two-storey
detached house faced the sea. She walked up the curved tarmac
drive and mounted the steps to the front door. A gusting wind
whistled around the corner of the house. Turning her back on it,
Ena held her coat closed with one hand and rang the bell with
the other.

She could see movement through the glass panels in the top of the door, but it was several minutes before the door was answered. 'Is Mr Robinson at home?' Ena asked a woman in her mid-to-late fifties, with salt-and-pepper hair, wearing a pinafore and holding a duster.

'He isn't, I'm afraid,' the woman said, 'he is in hospital.'

'Perhaps I could speak to Mrs Robinson?'

'She's gone to visit him, madam. She's been gone almost two hours. I'm expecting her back any minute. The hospital is only a ten-minute walk along the front.' The woman pointed to the right.

The sea was rough and the sky looked darker than it had when the train pulled into Brighton. 'Looks like it's going to rain.' Ena nodded in agreement. 'Are you a friend of Mrs Robinson, do you mind me asking, madam?'

'We've met, but it's Mr Robinson who I know. We worked together in the war.'

'Then I'm sure it would be all right if you came in and waited for Mrs Robinson.' Ena made no attempt to move. 'Or I could tell her you called when she gets back.'

'Ten minutes along the seafront, you said?'

The woman nodded. 'No more than ten, I'm sure. The Robert Bevan. It's a big white building.'

'In that case, I'll risk the rain and go to the hospital. Thank you for your help.'

Ena heard the door close as she walked down the drive. She lifted her face to the sky. The wind was bracing, the tangy salt air refreshing, but it was cold.

The Robert Bevan Hospital came into view in less time than Ena had anticipated. The early 1930s Art Deco style building, sleek and geometric in design, was painted white. Three circular steps led to wide double doors with windows on either side.

A private hospital, Ena thought. It would be expensive, but

then as director of MI5 Mac Robinson would be the highest paid person at Leconfield House. Ena entered the white entrance lobby with doors to the left and right of a white reception desk. She crossed the pristine black and white tiled floor and asked the receptionist if she could tell her which ward Mr McKenzie Robinson was in.

'Room one, ward seven, on the first floor.'

Ena took the lift and walked the short distance along the corridor to the ward. She looked through the glass pane in the top half of the swing doors.

'Excuse me?' she said, to a staff nurse who was leaving the ward as she arrived. 'Could you tell me how Mr Robinson is?'

'Are you a relative?'

'No, I'm a friend of the family. A close friend,' Ena added, which was a gross exaggeration. 'I've dashed down from London, you see–'

'He is responding well. There is no reason why he shouldn't make a full recovery. Complete rest is what he needs. Now, if you'll excuse me, it's time for the doctor's rounds.'

'Of course. What time shall I come back?' Ena asked, expecting the nurse to say in half an hour or this evening.

'Next week.'

Ena began to protest.

'As you are a *good* friend, I'm sure Mrs Robinson will keep you up to date with her husband's recovery.'

'Yes, of course. Would you give Mr Robinson a message, please? I wouldn't ask, but it's rather important. Would you tell him I came to see him?'

The staff nurse took a pen and a small notebook from her uniform pocket and nodded.

'Ena Green. Wife of Henry Green.'

The staff nurse wrote down Ena's name.

'Would you say, *Commander Dalton* referred me.' Ena watched the staff nurse write down the commander's name, and then snap the notebook shut and returned the book and pen to her pocket. At that moment a doctor wearing a traditional white coat, with an unlit pipe in his mouth, breezed around the corner followed by several junior doctors. The staff nurse left Ena and followed the party into the ward.

TEN

'Ena?'

'In the kitchen.'

She carried in two plates of sausage and mash, peas and gravy. It was what they usually had for lunch on Saturday because they went to the cinema most Saturday nights and afterwards stayed in town for a bite to eat. Tomorrow, however, Ena was going down to Hove to see McKenzie Robinson, and Henry had to work, so they were having Saturday's lunch on Friday night.

Absent-mindedly, Henry reached for the mustard and spooned a line along each sausage.

'Pick up a joint for Sunday on your way home from the office tomorrow, will you, darling? I won't be back from Hove before the butcher closes.' Ena cut off the end of a sausage and speared it with her fork. 'Visiting time in the afternoon is from two till four.'

She looked at Henry. 'What is it? You've hardly said a word since you got home.' Henry didn't reply, but gave Ena a sad smile.

'Darling, what's wrong?'

'I'm sorry to have to tell you, Ena, but Mac Robinson is dead.'

Ena put down her knife and fork with a clatter. 'How? When? What happened? The nurse said he was doing well when I was there last week. She said he only needed rest. He'd had a stroke, yes, but it was a mild one. Did he have another stroke?' Tears filled her eyes.

'No one knows. The section manager came into the office and said Director Robinson's PA, who had been at the director's bedside at the time – with his wife – phoned to say the director had died suddenly and would the section manager let us know. She didn't elaborate,' Henry said. 'Everyone's in shock.'

Ena got up from the table without speaking and took their dinner plates into the kitchen. On her way back she took a bottle of Teacher's Whisky and two glasses from the sideboard.

Henry poured them both a double. 'To the director,' he said, raising his glass.

'Director Robinson,' Ena whispered.

Ena went back to the hospital in Hove as planned and asked to see the staff nurse who was on duty the week before. She hadn't arrived she was told by a middle-aged woman who introduced herself as a friend of The Robert Bevan Hospital. Giving Ena a patronising smile she said, 'Perhaps I can help you?'

'I'd be grateful if you could. I've come from London, you see,' Ena said, taking a handkerchief from her pocket and putting it up to her nose. 'I was hoping to ask the staff nurse how my friend McKenzie Robinson had died. It was such a shock. I hope he didn't suffer,' Ena said, with despondency in her voice.

'No dear, be assured that your friend didn't suffer, he just slipped away in his sleep.'

'Oh? I mean that's good. That he didn't suffer. Strange

though,' Ena said, 'I was told he was getting better, that all he needed was rest.'

'He was. But you never know with strokes. I've been a volunteer here for many years, since my dear husband passed, and I've seen it all. As I said to Mr Robinson's daughter–'

'Daughter? I didn't know he had a daughter.'

'Yes,' the woman said, 'a lovely lady. I was going into Mr Robinson's room with the book trolley as she was leaving. She asked me not to tell her mother she'd been to see her father. They are estranged you see. Her mother disowned her over the man she married. The poor lady said even though it was more than ten years ago, her mother had never forgiven her.'

'How sad,' Ena said, 'but I'm not surprised. Mrs Robinson, good woman that she is, can be...' Ena searched her mind for a word that wouldn't sound too harsh. Evelyn Robinson was the epitome of the phrase, behind every big man is a bigger woman. 'Strict,' Ena said eventually.

'She specifically came out of visiting hours, so her mother wouldn't see her.'

'Did she. And how long was Mr Robinson's daughter with him?'

'Not long. It was a shame she wasn't able to stay longer. She told me she had travelled down by train from somewhere in the Midlands. I can't remember where she said now, but I remember thinking at the time that she'd come a long way.'

'Did Mr Robinson say anything about his daughter when you took the books into him.'

'He was asleep by the time I went back.'

'Thank you for the chat,' Ena said, taking the woman's hands in hers. 'I feel much better knowing my friend wasn't in pain when he died.'

As she was leaving, Ena heard someone call her name. She turned to see the staff nurse she'd spoken to the week before walking briskly along the corridor. 'I told Mr Robinson you had been to see him, Mrs Green, and I gave him your message.'

'Did you tell him that it was Commander Dalton who suggested I spoke to him?'

'I did. I also told him you were coming back today.' The staff nurse looked embarrassed. 'I am sorry you didn't get to see him.'

'So am I,' Ena said.

Getting back to London earlier than expected and bursting to tell Henry that she'd discovered McKenzie Robinson had a daughter, Ena went to Leconfield House. 'Would you tell Henry Green I need to see him. It's important.'

The receptionist picked up the telephone and dialled Henry's internal number. She gave Ena a smile and raised her eyebrows. 'No reply.' She looked at the clock on the wall. 'He won't be at lunch. I'll try one of the secretaries.' She dialled again. 'Janet, is Henry Green in the office today?' The receptionist shook her head at Ena. 'Thank you, Janet.' She put the receiver down.

'Mr Green isn't in the office today.'

'He's probably working from home,' Ena said, doing her best to hide the shock in her voice. 'I'm sorry to have troubled you.'

'It isn't my place to tell you this, Mrs Green, but...'

The word *but* sent Ena's heart into a tailspin.

The receptionist looked to her left to make sure her colleague on the other side of reception couldn't hear her. 'Janet said Henry is out of the country and she doesn't know when he'll be back.'

Ena didn't know whether to be angry that Henry hadn't told her he was going abroad, or worried for his safety.

'Janet shouldn't have told me, and I shouldn't have told you, so—'

Ena nodded that she understood. 'I won't say anything.

Henry would have told me himself, but I've been away on business and only just arrived back.'

'Ships that pass in the night. That's what my mum used to say about my dad.'

'Something like that.' The telephone rang and the receptionist picked up the receiver. Ena whispered thank you and left.

ELEVEN

Ena held onto her hat with one hand and the ornate railings that separated the beach from the path – and a six feet drop – with the other. The wind, thick with salt and minute particles of shell, stung her face as it growled along Brighton's seafront. Shop assistants from the newsagents, fish and chip shop and souvenir shops, battled the blustery weather to retrieve advertising boards that had been blown over. And café owners, their aprons billowing like ship's sails, took long poles with metal hooks on the end and pushed back striped awnings that in the summer gave shade to holidaymakers lunching at tables in the window.

Shutters were quickly pulled together and padlocked to keep out the tempest and out of season visitors to the popular East Sussex resort hurried along wet pavements to their hotels.

Ena watched the sea crashing onto the pebble beach, pushing the shingle into ridges and covering it with seaweed only to recede and suck the shingle clean again. She buttoned her coat and pulled up the collar. The clock on the pier said one o'clock. There was plenty of time before she needed to be in Hove.

Mac Robinson's death didn't sit easily with Ena. He'd had a stroke, but he was recovering. How then could it be that he had died? Inhaling the cold damp air, Ena wiped away her tears. The director's funeral was at two. It would take her half an hour at the most to drive to Hove and find the church. She kept walking.

When the funeral service ended, the vicar said, 'Mrs Robinson has asked me to say, if anyone would like to go back to the house after the interment there will be refreshments.' Ena didn't like funerals, who did? She had attended too many in the war. She joined the procession of mourners walking behind Mac Robinson's coffin out of the church. She didn't go to the graveside. She wasn't family, she wasn't even a friend. It had been fourteen years since she first met *Mr* Robinson in Commander Dalton's office at Bletchley Park. She hadn't known then that he was the head of MI5. Ena was miles away when she noticed the mourners leaving the grave.

There was a queue to go into the Robinson's house. Eve Robinson was at the door.

Ena smiled sympathetically. 'Hello, Mrs Robinson.' Her greeting was met with stony silence.

The widow of the head of MI5 put out her right arm and barred Ena from entering. She picked up a nondescript cardboard file from inside the door and said, 'My husband's last words to me were, make sure Ena Green gets this.' She thrust the file into Ena's hands. 'I hope what you find in there was worth my husband's life. If you hadn't come to the hospital to see him, he would still be alive.'

Ena opened her mouth to ask Mrs Robinson what she meant but wasn't able to speak.

'My husband admired you, Mrs Green. He told me once

you were a clever young woman who wanted to make the world a better place.'

'Did he?'

'I didn't agree with him then, and I don't agree with him now. I told him I thought you were hard and selfish. And, like him, you would go to any lengths to prove you were right.' Eve Robinson burst into tears. Ena took a step towards her. Eve backed away. 'You remind me of my husband when he was your age. He wanted justice at any cost. He was an idealist in those days. He thought he could make the world a better place.'

Ena put her hand on Eve Robinson's arm. 'I'm so sorry.'

She snatched her arm away. 'No, you're not. Not really. As my husband would have been, you're sorry you've lost someone that could have been useful to you, someone who could have helped you.'

Ena looked away from the angry wife of the man she had respected, who she knew would want her to find Frieda Voight for the sake of justice.

'You have what you came for. Take it and go. You are not welcome here, Mrs Green.'

Ena couldn't move. Her legs felt like jelly. She looked into Eve Robinson's tear-stained face, lost for something to say that the grieving woman wouldn't throw back at her. 'Thank you,' she whispered.

'Don't thank me,' Eve Robinson spat. 'Find out who murdered my husband. You owe him that much!'

Shocked that Eve Robinson believed her husband had been murdered, Ena was again unable to speak.

'Goodbye Mrs Green. Don't come back.' Turning her back on Ena, Eve Robinson went into the house and closed the door.

Reeling from what she had just heard, tears falling onto her cheeks, Ena walked shakily down the steps.

'Mrs Green?' someone called from the door Eve Robinson had just shut in Ena's face.

Ena stopped, hastily wiped her tears with the palm of her hand, and turned again.

'Helen Crowther,' the woman said, catching up with Ena. 'Helen! I was McKenzie's personal assistant. I work with your husband.'

'Of course. How do you do, Miss Crowther, Helen,' Ena said, taking her outstretched hand.

'You're not leaving, are you?'

'Yes.'

'But why?'

Ena burst into tears.

'Come now.' Helen put her arm around Ena's shoulder. 'You're shivering. You need something to drink, something to warm you up. Why don't you come back to the house?'

'Mrs Robinson has made it very clear that I am not welcome in her house. Besides, I should be getting back to London.'

'You must forgive her. Losing McKenzie like that was a terrible shock. She wasn't prepared for it. None of us were.'

Ena smiled warmly. 'It was a shock to everyone, not least to me.'

Helen nodded. 'McKenzie liked you, you know. He thought you were very brave going undercover in forty-four. He liked Henry too.' Helen looked around. 'I thought Henry would be here.'

'He's working.'

Helen raised her eyebrows.

'He isn't *just* working, he's... away.' Ena didn't need to tell Helen that. As McKenzie Robinson's PA she would have known.

'I expect someone at the office will let him know about Mac's death.'

'Yes, I'm sure they will.' Ena looked down. She felt ashamed that Henry wasn't there. He knew about Mac's death before he went away. It was Henry who had told her. He should have been at the funeral.

'Mac told me you had seen Commander Dalton and that you were looking into the death of Frieda Voight.' Helen glanced over her shoulder. There were a couple of people smoking cigarettes on the veranda, but no one near enough to hear their conversation. 'At the time the official line was Frieda had killed herself when she heard that her brother had died. Potassium cyanide pills.'

'Whatever the official line, Frieda did not commit suicide then, or at any other time after Walter's death, because I saw her not long ago in London. Frieda Voight is as alive as you and I.'

'You are right, Ena. Mac knew Frieda Voight wasn't dead.'

And so did you as his personal assistant, Ena thought. 'But her brother Walter is dead.'

'Yes, Walter died in prison. Call me,' Helen said, 'I'm at Leconfield House three days a week. When I'm not there, you can get me on this number.' She gave Ena a business card. 'Mac would want me to help you, so if I can, I will.'

Ena stared at the card. Miss Helen Crowther. The telephone number was not a London number. She turned it over in her hand expecting to see Helen's address. It was blank.

'I live in Brighton now. My guest room has a sea view. Come and visit. It's quiet at this time of year. We have holiday-makers from Easter through to September, but the season has finished now.'

Ena put the card in her handbag.

'I must get back to the house. I promised Eve I would pass round sandwiches and pour cups of tea.'

'Thank you, Helen.'

'And don't blame yourself for Mac's death.'

Ena did blame herself but gave Helen an assuring smile as she shook her hand again.

'Don't forget, anything you need to know, just pick up the telephone. Better still, let me know what time your train gets into Brighton and I'll be on the platform to meet you. You look as if you could do with some sea air.'

The conversation between Ena and Helen was interrupted by Eve Robinson who opened the door and glared at Ena.

'I'd better get back. Goodbye, Ena. Keep me posted.'

'I will. And, thank you.' As Helen made for the steps leading to her late boss's house, Ena braced herself against the cold wind coming off the sea and set off for the car.

How could someone murder a patient in a hospital, a private hospital at that? She would have to go back to the Robert Bevan and talk to the staff. She also needed to talk to Henry. Or did she? Every chance he got, Henry tried to stop her from investigating Frieda Voight.

Ena put the file Eve Robinson had given her in her satchel and smiled. Henry may not want to help her, but Mac's personal assistant of thirty-plus years did. Helen Crowther in your corner was almost as good as having McKenzie Robinson himself.

Ena decided not to go to the office. Instead of driving to Mercer Street, she drove to Lambeth, crossed the Thames on Westminster Bridge, and drove up to Whitehall and King Charles Street.

TWELVE

'Director Bentley is in a meeting, Ena. It's due to finish at half past four. He was going straight into another meeting, but you're in luck. The person has just telephoned to say he has been delayed and will be late. If you don't mind waiting, and you don't keep the director too long, I'll put you down for four thirty. Is that all right?'

'It is. Thank you,' Ena said, 'I won't take more than ten minutes of his time, but it is important that I see him today. If it wasn't, I'd have gone through the proper channels.'

Director Bentley's secretary waved her hand in the air. A gesture that told Ena it didn't matter. 'Take a seat. I'll let you know as soon as he's free.'

Ena plucked a magazine from the pile in front of her and flicked through it to pass the time. She put it down when two men came out of the director's office. She looked up expectantly when the telephone rang.

The clock on the wall behind the secretary's desk made a dull thudding sound. Ena looked up again. It was half past four. She was thinking about asking the secretary if Director Bentley was free yet when the telephone rang and the secretary beckoned her.

'Director Bentley will see you now, Ena.'

She knocked on the director's door. He shouted, come in.

As she entered the large wood-panelled office, Dick Bentley came from behind his desk to meet her. 'Good to see you, Ena,' he said, shaking her hand and leading her to a chair. When Ena sat down, he returned to his own chair. 'How are you getting on in Mercer Street? Have there been any more sightings of Frieda Voight?'

'No, sir. No sightings recently. But I'm not here about Voight or the work we do at the Mercer Street office, sir.'

'Go on.'

'I've just got back from McKenzie Robinson's funeral.'

'I know. I saw you in the church. Unfortunately, I had to leave after the service. I had a meeting that couldn't be rescheduled, or I'd have gone to the house to pay my respects to Eve.'

'I went to the house but Mrs Robinson didn't invite me in. In fact, she did the opposite.' Ena felt tears pricking the back of her eyes and swallowed. 'I'll get to the point, sir. I went to see McKenzie Robinson about Frieda Voight while he was in hospital after the stroke. Unfortunately, I wasn't able to see him. However, the staff nurse told me he was on the mend and suggested I came back the following week.'

'And by then Mac was dead.'

'Yes. And today Mrs Robinson told me that her husband had been murdered.'

Director Bentley got up and walked slowly to the window. He looked out for some minutes before turning back and facing Ena. 'Do *you* think Mac was murdered?'

'I don't know. It's possible.'

'Of course, it could have been grief talking. Losing her husband so suddenly must have been a terrible shock for Eve.'

Ena shook her head. 'It wasn't grief talking.'

'Are you sure?'

'Yes, I am.'

'Then we have a problem.' The director returned to his chair.

'She gave me this.' Ena took the file that Eve Robinson had given her from her satchel and showed Director Bentley.

'I don't have time to read it now. I have another meeting to go to.' He drummed the top of his desk with the fingers of his right hand and picked up the telephone with his left. 'There are . some documents here that I need copying,' he said 'Mrs Green will give them to you when she leaves.' He put the receiver down.

Frowning, Bentley passed the file back to Ena.

'Sir, I would like your permission to investigate Director Robinson's death.'

'It isn't a cold case, Ena. You concentrate on finding Frieda Voight. If Mac Robinson was murdered the investigation will be done by MI5.'

'Sir, Mrs Robinson accused me of being responsible for her husband's death. She said if I hadn't gone to see him about Frieda Voight he would still be alive. The papers,' Ena nodded in the direction of the file, 'she said were what her husband wanted me to read. The last thing she said to me before slamming the door in my face was, "Find who murdered my husband, you owe him that much!" Please let me make some enquires.'

Deep in thought, Director Bentley rubbed his chin.

'At least give me permission to speak to the hospital staff.'

'Two days, Ena. If you haven't got anything conclusive in forty-eight hours, the case goes to MI5.'

Sid and Artie got to their feet as Ena entered the office.

'Well?' Sid said.

'How was the funeral?' Artie asked.

Sid gave Artie a sideways glance. 'You're late getting back.'

'That's because I've been to see Dick Bentley.' Ena sat down at her desk and taking in both men said, 'Eve Robinson thinks McKenzie was murdered.'

'Good God!'

'How?'

'Why?'

'The how, I don't know. The why, well,' Ena inhaled and exhaled slowly, 'Eve Robinson said it was because of me; because of what's in this file. Mac must have told her that Commander Dalton at Bletchley had asked him to help me with the Frieda Voight case, or he wouldn't have given her this to pass on to me.'

Ena took the file from her satchel and threw it across her desk.

'Can we read it?' Sid asked.

'Of course. It's the original, so don't spill coffee on it. And while you read it, I'm going to work out an itinerary for the next forty-eight hours.' Both men looked quizzically at her. 'That's how long Dick Bentley has given us to find Mac Robinson's killer. If we don't come up with something by five o'clock the day after tomorrow, Bentley is going to give the case to MI5.'

'I feel it's going to be a long night. Have you eaten anything?' Sid asked.

'Not since breakfast.'

'Right, Artie, put the kettle on. I'll nip to that new café on Langley Street and get some sandwiches. Any preferences?' Already pawing over the first few pages, neither Ena nor Artie replied. 'Whatever they've got left then. Artie? Artie!' Sid's young colleague lifted his head. 'Kettle!'

By the time Sid returned, Ena had moved the file and other relevant documents to the conference table and Artie had made the tea. Sid put the food next to the teapot and poured himself a cup. 'Found anything?'

Artie shook his head. Concentrating on what he was reading, he reached across the table and grabbed a sandwich. The pages she and Artie had already read Ena passed to Sid. While she read she drank tea, ate sandwiches and drew up a plan of action for the following day. When she had finished, she began checking files.

At midnight, Ena put to one side the files she thought important to their investigation, yawned and rubbed her eyes. 'That's it!' she slammed the last file shut. 'I've just read the same paragraph three times. Come on,' she said to Sid and Artie, 'it's time to go. We'll come back to this lot in the morning. The car's across the road, I'll drop you off on my way home.'

'I'm going to walk,' Artie said, 'I'm as stiff as a board.' He tilted his head from side to side and rolled his shoulders. 'And I need some air.'

'I'll take you up on a lift, Ena. Mum will wonder where I've got to.' Ena gave Sid a concerned look. 'Don't worry, she isn't on her own. My sister brings her dinner round every evening and stays until I get home. She only lives a few doors away, so it works out well.'

It took a quarter of the time to get home after dropping Sid off without the daytime traffic. Ena put her key in the lock and turned it. The mechanism didn't engage properly. There was no pressure on the key that usually needed a firm twist to push back the double locking system. It wasn't on. Relief swept over her. Henry was back. She turned the key once and pushed open the door. She put the straps of her satchel and handbag over a coat hook in the hall, shrugged off her coat, and hung it on top. She was about to call out to Henry when she heard the sound of breaking glass. A loud crash followed by several tinkling sounds. Ena strained her ears.

She tiptoed across the hall and poked her head round the sitting room door. The table lamp was on and the wireless was playing jazz. Henry didn't like jazz, he preferred classical music. A draught coming from the direction of the kitchen cut across her ankles. She peered through the door and exhaled with relief. She had left the kitchen window open. The curtains, blowing inwards, had caught a drinking glass and swept it off the work surface.

Laughing and trembling at the same time, Ena crossed to the window to close it. Closer inspection revealed the window had not been left open, it had been smashed from the inside. Her stomach lurched. Someone had been in the flat when she arrived home.

Shaking with anger she ran out of the kitchen and into the sitting room. Nothing had been disturbed as far as she could see. She went to the bedroom and flicked on the light. Nothing was out of place. The few pieces of good jewellery she owned were still in the jewellery box. As far as she could tell the bedroom hadn't been touched. On her way back to the sitting room she looked in the spare bedroom. Nothing out of place in there either. She had come home before the burglar had time to steal anything.

Ena poured herself a whisky and took a drink. She rummaged through the drawers for a cigarette. Henry always kept a pack in the house, but she couldn't find them and went into the bedroom again. She searched the pockets of his jackets and found a packet of Players. Returning to the sitting room she noticed the door to the street was ajar. She took the key from the lock on the outside and kicked the door shut. Not feeling safe with only the lock on, she slid the bolt across.

Still shaking, Ena looked in the rooms again and when she was sure there was no one hiding in the wardrobe or under the bed, she checked the windows were closed and drew the curtains.

Satisfied that no one could now get into the flat, Ena poured herself a second whisky and lit a cigarette. She flopped onto the settee. Cold air whipped through from the kitchen window causing a draught and bringing the temperature in the sitting room to below bearable. Stubbing out the cigarette she went into the kitchen.

After brushing up the broken drinking glass, Ena leaned over the work surface and pulled on the window's ornate handle. The wind was strong, forcing the window back against the wall. It took several minutes and some swearing before she managed to close it. There was only one pane missing so as a temporary measure she took an old tea towel from the drawer, a hammer and nails from Henry's toolbox under the sink, and nailed the towel to the wooden frame. Finally, she jammed the breadboard under the handle. Standing back, Ena looked at the distance between the smashed pane and the handle and doubted anyone had long enough arms to reach down and open the window. To be sure, she lined up all the pots and pans she could find along the work surface. 'If anyone gets in now there'll be a hell of a racket when that lot is knocked off,' she told herself.

Ena fetched her satchel from the hall and settled down in the sitting room to look over the plans for the next day. She groaned. Before she did anything tomorrow she needed to telephone the landlord about getting a glazier. He was a tight-wad. He'll probably do the job himself to save money. Ena didn't care who repaired the window as long as it was done. Pouring another drink she decided not to go to bed. She couldn't be certain whoever had broken in wouldn't come back. They say criminals don't return to the scene of the crime. Ena wasn't going to risk it.

. . .

Unlocking the door on Mercer Street, Ena entered what was once a courtyard. She closed the door and stuck her hand into the metal basket under the letterbox that caught the post. It was empty. She crossed to the cold cases office, and through the panels of frosted glass in the top of the door she saw the lights were on. Someone was early. Pushing open the door she found Sid and Artie on their knees peering at the contents of the bottom drawer of the filing cabinet. 'What are you two doing?'

'We've been burgled,' Artie said.

'Not burgled, exactly,' Sid corrected. 'As far as I can see nothing has been taken. There were fifteen files to go through when we left here last night.' He nodded towards the stack of files on the table. 'There are still fifteen.'

'I noticed the bottom drawer of this cabinet was slightly open when I arrived, so we're checking each file against my inventory, see if any selected for investigation are missing.'

'Ena went across to her desk. Do we know how they got in?'

'No. You locked up last night, I saw you,' Sid said.

'I did.' Ena slowly pulled open the top drawer of the desk, then the second and the third. 'My drawers have been gone through. It isn't obvious and nothing seems to be missing, but... Good Lord!'

'What is it?' Sid asked.

'Someone broke into my flat last night. A bit of a coincidence, don't you think?' She took off her coat and threw it over the back of her chair. 'As I opened the front door they left by the kitchen window.'

Artie gasped. 'Are you all right?'

'Yes, I'm fine. I daren't go to sleep afterwards in case they came back, so I'm tired.'

'I'm not surprised,' Sid said.

Ena took her notebook from her satchel. 'I was scared, I don't mind telling you, but if someone, or some organisation, thinks they are going to frighten me off investigating–' She stopped speaking mid-sentence and waved her hands about frantically.

Sid looked bewildered. 'What?'

Ena put her forefinger to her lips. 'Would you like a coffee, Sid?' she asked, putting her thumb up and nodding.

'Yes, I would. It's your turn to make the coffee, Artie,' he shouted.

Ena scribbled a note and pushed it across the table. *BUGS*. Sid nodded.

When Artie brought in the coffee, she showed him the note and said, 'How about some music, Artie?'

Artie put down the tray of hot drinks, went to the wireless and turned it on. Singing along with Pat Boone and 'Ain't That A Shame', he took a screwdriver and removed the panel on the back of the wireless. Shaking his head he replaced it. Still singing he joined his colleagues at the conference table and entered into a conversation of no importance.

When they had finished their coffee, Artie took the dirty cups back to the small kitchenette and washed them up making sure he made a loud clatter picking up and putting down every item of crockery. Ena pointed to the telephones on their desks and Sid put up his thumb. Starting with her own telephone she unscrewed the mouthpiece, and then the earpiece.

Singing even louder to Bill Haley and 'Rock Around The Clock', Artie checked everything in and around the drink-making area. There was nothing.

Having found no listening device in her telephone, Ena ran her hand along the underside of her desk. She mouthed the word *nothing* to Sid who was on his knees doing the same. Ena checked the typewriters while Sid looked under the conference table and chairs.

'Well?' Artie called.

Sid shook his head and joined his colleague at the store cupboard on the far wall. When they had looked everywhere they thought was possible to conceal a bug, Artie put up his hand. He pointed to the only window in the room. Not a window at all, but a kind of priest hole that had once looked out onto the courtyard before it had glass in it.

Sid lifted up his several dictionaries. Nothing was hidden behind them. Nor was there anything secreted between the old blackout blind and the new curtains.

Ena raised her shoulders and let them drop. Where would I put a listening device, she mused. She cast her eyes slowly around the room and suddenly a thought materialised. 'I checked the letter box when I came in but there was nothing in it. Did either of you collect the post before I arrived?'

'The postman hadn't been when we got here this morning,' Artie said, 'I'll see if there's anything in the box now.'

Ena followed him out the office. There was no post. 'We only have until tomorrow at five to get something on Frieda Voight, so go to the HO, pick up a telephone van and drive up to Holland Park. See if there's any movement in Dean's Crescent. I want to know if Frieda is living there. If she hasn't shown up after three hours, give the door a knock. You know the drill. Say several residents in the Crescent have reported clicking noises on their telephone line. They're bound to think it's bugs and ask you in. Once you're inside keep your eyes peeled for photographs of Frieda and the man I told you about, the man I saw her with outside Selfridges.'

'Will do.'

'It's a big place. There's bound to be a cook and a house-maid, as well as a manservant, which means there'll be tele-phones downstairs. If the cook, or anyone else, asks if you'd like a cup of tea say yes and get them talking. Cooks and house-maids love to gossip.'

'And if the Russian is there?'

'Ask him if he's had any trouble with his line. If he says no, don't push it, apologise for disturbing him and leave. If he looks

unsure, ask him if he would like you to test the main house telephone to be on the safe side. If he says yes, check it, thank him,
and get out.'

When they went back to the office, Ena wrote a note and
gave it to Sid along with her house keys. 'What time is your
mother's hospital appointment, Sid?'

Sid understood what Ena meant straight away. 'Eleven.' He
looked at his wristwatch. 'I'll have to leave in ten minutes if
that's all right?'

'Of course.'

Sid read the note. *Go to my flat. Check for bugs. If none, fine.
If you find any, dismantle. Stay and work from my place today.*

Sid winked. 'I don't know what time I'll be back. It's a
nuisance having to go to the hospital today. I should be checking
these files.' He brought his fist down heavily on top of the metal
filing cabinet.

'It's important your mother keeps her appointment. Artie
will stay here and go through the files, won't you, Artie?'

Artie said yes.

'Okay, thanks,' Sid said, then mouthed, *You.*

'If you don't get away from the hospital until late in the
afternoon, take your mum home and we'll see you in the morning.' Ena took the piece of paper out of Sid's hand and wrote on
the back. *Me – Nurse, Hospital, Hove. See you at mine – PM.*

Sid was first to leave the office taking half a dozen unread
files with him – and Ena's house keys. Artie left next, wearing
overalls and carrying a telephone engineer's toolbox. Ena
checked the window was fastened and the kettle was unplugged
but left on the lights and the wireless.

THIRTEEN

There was no one about. Ena walked along the first floor corridor until she got to the room where Mac Robinson had died. The pulse in her temples started to throb and her heart was beating like a drum. She poked her head around the door. The room was empty, the bed had been stripped and the curtains were drawn.

Two young nurses appeared and without acknowledging Ena went into Mac's room.

'Excuse me?' Ena said, following them in. 'A friend of mine was in this room until a couple of weeks ago. I was wondering if either of you had been on this ward when he was here.'

The nurses looked at each other and shook their heads.

'His name was McKenzie Robinson?'

Ena could see they were worried by her questions and said, 'I'm not asking about him because he died. I'm asking because Mr Robinson's daughter is a friend of mine and I would like to send her a sympathy card. The thing is, I can't remember her address. I was wondering if either of you met her?'

'No,' the fair-haired nurse said.

'We don't have anything to do with patients or visitors,' the darker of the two girls added. 'We're only probationers.'

'Trainee nurses. We change beds and things.'

'This is our first week on this ward.'

'The ward sister's office is along the corridor,' the fair-haired nurse said, 'Sister Walker will be able to tell you who nursed your friend.'

Ena saw a flash of navy out of the corner of her eye. 'Thank you.' She left the trainee nurses to get on with their work and headed off down the corridor. She knocked on the door of the ward sister's office and waited until she was called in.

'Mrs Green, isn't it?' Ena looked surprised.

'Reception told me you were here. What can I do for you?'

'I'd like to speak to the nurse who was with Mr Robinson on the day he died?'

Sister Walker stiffened and frowned. 'Is there a problem?'

'No, not at all. The nurse was excellent. All the staff were.' Sister Walker didn't volunteer any information as to the nurse's whereabouts. Ena thought, she is waiting for an explanation from me. 'She may have met Mr Robinson's daughter and I wanted to ask her if–' Ena had a split second to think of a name, 'Frieda had left a forwarding address.'

'Mr Robinson's daughter's name was not Frieda, Mrs Green.'

'Oh, I thought–' Ena felt her cheeks colour. Why had she said Frieda?

Sister Walker consulted the ward's visitors book. 'Robinson? Robinson?' she said, flicking back through the pages. 'Ah, here we are. Mr Robinson's daughter's name is Ena Dudley.'

Ena stared at her maiden name. Bile rose from her stomach and stuck in her throat. She swallowed to clear it. 'Excuse me.' Turning away from Sister Walker, Ena held the back of a chair and began to cough.

The sister crossed to a small sink in the corner of her office, turned on the tap and poured a glass of water. Ena took the glass in shaking hands and drank its contents down in one. 'A tickle in my throat,' she whispered, unbuttoning her coat. 'It's hot in here.'

'Hospitals are always warm. With sick and vulnerable patients the temperature has to be kept constant.'

'Are you sure Ena Dudley was the name of Mr Robinson's daughter?' Ena asked, regaining her composure.

'Oh yes, Dudley was her married name. She said she dropped Mrs when she got divorced.'

'But you can't be sure that was her name, can you?'

'I can actually. I saw her driving licence.'

Ena's eyes widened in disbelief.

'One of the nurses went in to check on Mr Robinson and found someone she hadn't seen before standing at his bedside. She quite rightly reported back to me and I went to investigate. You can't be too careful these days, especially as Mr Robinson held an important position in... Well, never mind. I asked the woman who she was and she showed me her driving licence. A lovely young woman.' The sister's eyes narrowed. 'Did you say Miss Dudley was a friend of yours?'

'Er, yes. I haven't seen her for years, which is why I didn't know she had been married, but yes, Ena and I go back a long way. I don't suppose you have her address, do you?'

'There was no need to take her address. Now, Mrs Green, if that is all, I really must get on.' The sister walked briskly across the room and opened the door.

'Could I ask you one more question?' Ena said, drawing level with her. Sister Walker looked down at the fob watch on the breast pocket of her uniform. 'Just one question, and then I'll go.' The sister nodded. 'Thank you. Was Mr Robinson's daughter here on the day he died?'

'I'm sure I don't know why you're asking all these questions. It's most inappropriate...'

'I work for the same agency as Director Robinson.' Ena paused to let the significance of what she had said sink in. 'It is important, or I wouldn't ask.'

'No. She was here the day before her father died, but not on the morning he died.'

Driving past Eve Robinson's house, Ena was consumed with guilt. She put her foot down and soon Hove and Brighton were behind her. She hoped Sid had found the bugs in her flat, if there were any, so they could speak freely. She hoped too that the landlord had found a glazier to repair the kitchen window. If he hadn't it would mean another sleepless night.

Ena yawned. Her eyes felt heavy. She closed them, telling herself it was only for a second. Suddenly her head jerked back and she sat up with a jolt. Feet away from the car in front of her, Ena slammed her foot on the brake. She wound down the Sunbeam's window and breathed in the cold air.

Driving with the window open made her teeth chatter. It also stopped her from falling asleep.

She glanced at her wristwatch. It was five o'clock. She was ravenous and pulled up outside Comstock's Fish and Chip Shop in Stockwell. There was no food at home so Sid would be hungry too. 'Fish and chips twice please.'

Her mouth watered watching Mr Comstock dip the cod fillets into a bowl of batter and drop one after the other into a large pan of boiling fat. While the fish sizzled and spat he scooped enough chips for half a dozen people onto sheets of paper. When the fish was cooked he took a long-handled fish turner, lifted each portion of crispy battered fish out of the bubbling fat, and tipped them on top of the chips. He then sprinkled both mounds of piping hot food with a generous helping of salt and vinegar. 'Anything else, love?' Ena shook her head, and Mr Comstock wrapped both meals in several sheets of newspaper.

Ena paid Mr Comstock three shillings and left. She laid the steaming parcels on the passenger seat and drove home. Pulling up outside the flat she saw the sitting room light was on. She blew out her cheeks, relieved that Sid was still there.

Grabbing the fish and chips, she left the car and locked it, ran up the steps and knocked on the door. 'I hope you're hungry,' she said when Sid let her in. She thrust the fish and chips into his hands, dropped her bag on the floor and hung up her coat. Closing the door she followed Sid into the kitchen.

'I was going to stop at the chippy on my way home,' Sid said. 'I brought a cheese sandwich for my lunch, but as usual, I ate it at eleven. I was beginning to feel hungry.'

'Well, we have a feast here.' Taking two trays from the cupboard beneath the window in the kitchen Ena noticed the glass had been replaced. 'The glazier came then?'

'Your landlord did it.'

'Oh cripes.' Ena gave the new pane of glass a prod. 'He's a skinflint, a Jack-of-all-trades, but that feels solid enough.' Unwrapping what felt to Ena like a week's worth of newspapers, she popped a chip into her mouth. 'Hot!' she gasped, breathing fast and fanning her mouth with her hand. 'I'm going to eat mine out of the paper, do you want a plate?'

'No. It'll spoil the flavour.'

'Come on then,' Ena said, handing Sid a knife and fork and leading the way to the sitting room. 'You've built a fire! I thought the flat felt warm when I came in.'

'I hope you don't mind.'

'Mind? Of course I don't mind, I'm delighted. I was bitterly cold last night...' Ena put her tray on the table and went back to the kitchen. 'I'm going to have a beer. What would you like,' she shouted, 'Guinness or IPA?'

'IPA, please.'

'We've earned this,' Ena said, pouring half a bottle of beer into each glass. 'Cheers!' Twisting round in her chair, Ena stretched out her hand and picked up the notepad and pen from beside the telephone. While they ate she scribbled. *Did you find any listening devices?*

Sid nodded and pointed to the telephone and the overhead light.

FOURTEEN

Ask me how I got on at the hospital. Ena scribbled on the notepad.

Sid nodded. 'How did it go at the hospital? Was the woman who visited McKenzie Robinson his daughter?'

'According to the ward sister I talked to she was,' Ena said, shaking her head and mouthing, no.

'What do you think?'

'Well, if the woman who visited Mac was his daughter, and I've no reason to think she wasn't, she visited him the day before he died, so she couldn't have killed him.'

Sid looked surprised. 'Then who did?'

'I don't think anyone did. I don't think Mac was murdered. It's more likely that Eve Robinson won't accept her husband died of natural causes. The woman has lived with intrigue and conspiracy all her married life. She probably sees murder and treachery around every corner. Or, as Commander Dalton said, it was grief talking.'

When they had finished eating Ena took the trays to the kitchen, returned with another bottle of beer and replenished their glasses. 'What kind of day have you had?'

Sid pointed to the overhead light and then to his ear. 'Same old, same old.'

'That good, aye?'

He laughed. 'When we've finished these,' he picked up his glass of beer, 'do you fancy a drink at the pub?'

Looking up at the light fitting, Ena said, 'Some other time, Sid, but not today. Damn it!' she shouted. 'Can you take the bloody thing down?'

'Yes, but–'

'Then take it down, will you? I'm not having some bloody Russian spy listening to my conversations in my own home, nor will I let him chase me out to the pub every time I want to talk to a friend.'

Sid switched on the standard lamp at the side of the settee, then flicked off the ceiling light at the door. 'I'll give the bulb a couple of minutes to cool down.' He went over to the telephone, lifted the receiver, and unscrewed the mouthpiece. 'That's one,' he said, handing Ena a small black object.

'Thank you.' Ena examined the back of the device. 'Mm... Smash it or put it somewhere safe for Henry to take to MI5?'

'Okay.' Sid took down the light shade and gave it to Ena. 'Put this one with it,' he chuckled, swapping the listening device for the shade.

Ena took both pieces of invasive equipment to the bathroom, put them in the hand basin and tuned on the cold tap.

Returning to the sitting room she said, 'It was Frieda who visited Mac Robinson.'

'So she could have killed him?'

'Not according to the ward sister. Only his wife and his personal assistant were there the day he died.'

'You don't think either of them killed him do you?'

'No. Eve worshipped Mac. And Helen Crowther had been his PA for as long as Mac had worked for MI5. I think Helen was a little in love with him too.'

'Sure it couldn't have been Helen? A woman scorned and all that?'

Ena laughed. 'I think the scorn would have manifested into murder a long time ago if Helen Crowther was *the other woman*. She wasn't only Mac's PA, she was his right hand at Five for thirty years. No, neither Eve nor Helen had reason to kill him. Besides, they were the only visitors Mac had that day, it would have been too obvious. What about you. What kind of day have you really had?'

Sid sighed. 'I've gone through every one of these files and, nothing. None of them should take precedence over what we already have. If we're going to prioritise, there are a dozen files at the office with profiles of more suspicious characters than anyone in this lot. It's the dodgy rogues in the files back at the office who we should be investigating.'

'Okay. I'll leave you and Artie to sort them out tomorrow. Which reminds me, have you heard from Artie?'

'No. He hasn't phoned here.'

'Mmmm... He would have done if he'd had anything to report, wouldn't he?'

'I'd have thought so.'

'Time enough to find out about Madam Romanovski of Holland Park tomorrow,' Ena said, 'or is there?'

Sid gave her a quizzical look. 'What's on your mind? Now we can speak freely, what did you find out at the hospital in Hove?'

'That McKenzie Robinson's supposed daughter's name wasn't Frieda or Romanovski.'

'How do you know?'

'What I said about the ward sister at the hospital and Mac's supposed daughter was true. A woman claiming to be Mac's daughter did visit him.'

'Then we've got her!'

'No. It was the day *before* he died.'

'Could the ward sister have made a mistake about the day?'

'No. She was positive. She said a nurse had found a woman in Mac's room the day before he died, reported it to her, and she had gone along and asked the woman who she was. The woman said she was the director's daughter. She told the ward sister some cock and bull story about not wanting her mother to know she'd been in to see her father because, according to *the daughter,* she had run away from home when she was young and married a man her mother didn't approve of. Anyway, the daughter signed the visitor's book.'

'And you saw the book?'

'Of course.'

'I still don't understand how you knew the woman was Frieda.'

'Because, the phoney daughter also showed the ward sister her driving licence. The name in the visitor's book and on the licence was, Ena Dudley.'

'But– How–'

'When I went up to Silcott's Engineering there were no records of Freda King or of me ever having worked there. MI5 had taken them in forty-four. God knows why they took my records...'

'Unless whoever Freda was working for took them, and not MI5.'

'There's a thought. Mr Silcott called them the intelligence people and Military Intelligence. He didn't actually say they were from MI5.' Ena knew Freda had done a deal with MI5 when they arrested her. Because her file was classified, she didn't elaborate.

'No,' Sid said, shaking his head. 'That would be too much of a stretch.'

'Would it? She's using a driving licence with my name on it, what other explanation is there?'

'Oh no!' The colour drained from Sid's face.

'What?'

'Dudley! You said your name was Dudley before you were married, and you worked in engineering?'

'Yes, I worked on the design side. What of it?'

'I remember seeing a cold case file where a woman was suspected of stealing designs from a nuclear power plant. I'm going back to the office. I need to find that file.' Jumping up, Sid flew to the sitting room door and opened it.

'I'll drive you, Sid. Have you finished with these files?'

'Yes. Leave them. I won't need to look at them again.' Sid put on his coat and hat and yanked open the outside door.

Locking it, Ena followed him down the steps. At the car, a flicker of what looked like a cigarette lighter from the driver's side of a large saloon car parked along the road caught her eye. She jumped into the Sunbeam, reached across the passenger seat and opened the door. When Sid was seated, Ena switched on the car's headlights and gunned the engine. She looked in the rear-view mirror. There were no vehicles behind her. But as she pulled out, the headlights of the car at the end of the road came on.

Ena drove quickly out of St Michael's Square and turned into Stockwell Gardens. She brought the Sunbeam to a halt on Stockwell Road and waited for a gap in the traffic. Before there was space enough to safely pull in between two cars, the saloon car from the end of her road had caught up with her. When she turned onto Lambeth Road he must have hung back. She spotted him again going over Waterloo Bridge and a few minutes later on Long Acre.

When Ena turned into Mercer Street the car that had been following her drove on. No need to follow me down here, she thought, the driver knows where I work.

Sid shot out of her car and ran across to the office. Ena bumped the car up the kerb and onto the derelict piece of ground where a pub had once stood. The Covent Garden

Tavern and the house next to it had been bombed during the war. Like a lot of London bomb sites, the ground had been cleared, but there was no money to rebuild. She parked the car, locked it and crossed the road.

The wireless was still blaring out when Ena entered the office. Sid was on his knees frantically going through files in the bottom drawer of the big filing cabinet. 'Can I help, Sid?' He shook his head.

Artie came in from the kitchen. 'What are you looking for, Matey?'

'A file.'

'Silly question,' Artie said to himself.

'I can't remember the name on it, but I'll know it when I see it.'

'Sounds a bit rum, don't you think, Ena?'

'If you've nothing constructive to say, Artie, bugger off and leave me to get on with it,' Sid shouted.

'In that case,' Artie said, 'I'll take Ena to Lyons Corner House for a cup of tea. She can buy me a cake and I'll tell her how busy I've been organising the files into date order just so you can sling them about all over the place.'

Sid lifted his head and gave Artie a withering look. Artie giggled.

FIFTEEN

'How many listening devices did you find?' Ena asked, as she and Artie walked through the stalls in Covent Garden market to Southampton Row and down to the Strand.

'Two. Shall we leave them and feed the Ruskies false information?'

'No, get rid of them. Sid found two in my flat.' Artie's eyes widened. 'I neutralised them under cold water. Whoever planted them will know we've found them by now and assume we've done the same at the office. If we leave them, they'll know we're feeding them rubbish.'

In Lyon's Corner House, Ena gave Artie a pound note and told him to get something to eat. Having just eaten fish and chips, Ena only wanted a pot of tea.

Looking around the spacious café and seeing no one she'd seen before, Ena did her best to relax. The door opened and she gave the man entering special attention. She didn't recognise him either. She sighed. Not much chance of relaxing when you know you're being followed, especially when you have no idea who it is following you.

'That was a big sigh,' Artie said, plonking a tray down with tea for Ena, and coffee and two rounds of sandwiches for himself. 'Your change,' he said handing Ena a ten-shilling note and couple of coins.

She absent-mindedly took the money and dropped it into her handbag.

'Right, what's going on? Sid came back like a whirlwind and you appear to be in another world.'

'It's a long story.'

'I've got all night.'

While she drank her tea and Artie ate his sandwiches, Ena told him everything she had learned at the Robert Bevan hospital.

'What about you?' she asked, as they walked back to the office. 'How did you get on in Holland Park? Were you able to get into the house?'

'Yes, it was a doddle. When no one had come or gone from the house in two hours, I decided to try my luck as a telephone engineer. I took my tools, knocked on the door, and was let in by a bruiser of a fellow. He was over six feet tall, almost as wide, with a thick foreign accent. I assumed he was the diplomat's manservant.'

'His butler I expect.'

'Whatever he was he happily took me to three rooms on the ground floor of the house that had telephones.' Artie grimaced.

'What's the face for?'

'He stood next to me and looked over my shoulder while I checked each of them, so I wasn't able to do any snooping.'

He took a box of Players from his overcoat pocket and offered Ena a cigarette. She took one and Artie took out a box of Swan Vesta. He struck a match, cupped his hands around the flickering flame and Ena leant into it and sucked. Once her cigarette was alight, he lit his.

'Any evidence to suggest Frieda lived there?'

'No.' Artie blew a long stream of smoke into the cold air. 'I purposely clocked the photographs. There weren't many; a couple on the mantelshelf of one room and one on a side table under a standard lamp in another room. You know the thing.'

'No women?'

'No women under the age of sixty. I wasn't taken upstairs to the bedrooms, where I know there were telephones because I could see the wires from the street. If there had been photographs of a wife or lady friend, they were probably up there.'

'And that was it?'

'Not quite. There was a telephone in a room off the kitchen. It was a small room; a large pantry kind of room with a wooden desk and a chest of drawers on one wall, and an armchair at the side of the fire on the other. Very masculine. I expect it was the manservant's room. Four telephones in four rooms. I know there were more, but I wasn't shown them.'

'Except for the manservant, no staff?'

'Yes. A barrel of a woman with wiry grey hair in her late fifties and a young girl who looked about fourteen.'

'The cook and the kitchen maid.'

'They were eating their midday meal when I was in the small room with the desk in it, so I didn't get the chance to talk to them. The manservant was friendly enough. He smiled a lot, but didn't say much. Probably didn't speak English beyond hello and come in. I took my time checking the telephones, but once I'd finished, I had no reason to hang around. The manservant showed me out and I went back to the van.'

When they got back to the office Sid was in a bad mood, angry with himself for not seeing the similarity between Ena Dudley who works in nuclear research and Ena Dudley who had worked in engineering.

Ena told him he couldn't have known about the work she did in the war because no one knew. Eventually, she ordered him to leave the office with her, and on no account was he to return until the following morning.

Sid's house – or his mother's house, Ena had never worked out who actually owned the place – was on her way home. If she hadn't insisted on giving him a lift, he would probably have stayed in the office and worked all night.

Ena liked Sid. She liked Artie too. But Artie was apt to cut corners where Sid was old school, steady and responsible – and stayed at work until the work was done. She admired him for his dedication but worried that he sometimes became obsessed with a case. That's what Henry said she was, obsessed. Ena brought the Sunbeam to a halt outside Sid's house. 'See you in the morning. I'll pick you up at seven thirty.'

'No, don't worry about me. There's a couple of things I need to do before I come into the office, so I'll be leaving home really early. Besides which, my sister is coming down at the crack of dawn. When she and Mother get yacking, I get out of the way.'

Ena laughed. 'All right, if you're sure.' Sid left the car, slammed the door, and tapped the roof. 'See you at the office,' she shouted, and drove away.

As she turned into St Michael's Square Ena spotted the dark-coloured surveillance car. Its sidelights were on. She wound down her window as she approached and slowed to a crawl. If she wasn't mistaken the car's engine was ticking over. Her first thought was her tail had kept the engine running for a quick getaway. But it was more likely that, on a cold night like tonight, it was to keep the heater on and him warm.

By the glow of the streetlight, she saw the large saloon car was a green Austin Cambridge. Not an MI5 vehicle then, she thought. And not a car from the Home Office's pool of vehicles either. The cars of both arms of the intelligence service were black.

Ena parked in her usual place in front of the flat. She opened the door, swung her legs out, and pushed herself up until she was standing. She reached into the back of the car and took her handbag and satchel from the back seat. After locking the driver's door she went round to the passenger door and locked that. Satisfied that the Sunbeam was secure she climbed the steps to the flat. At the top, she looked back. The green Austin was still there. She was desperate to know who was watching her but having been awake the entire night the night before she was more desperate to get some sleep. She would confront the driver of the Austin another time. Tonight, she was going straight to bed.

The smell of stale fish and chips and vinegar-soaked newspaper met her as soon as she stepped into the hall. Closing the door she groaned. For a second she thought about taking what was left of the cold fish meal to the dustbin. The second passed. She was too tired. All she wanted to do was fall into bed and sleep.

She took off her coat and hung it up. As she turned to go to the bedroom she heard the sitting room door open. She squealed and spun round. 'Henry?' Stumbling sideways she caught her head on a coat-hook. 'Damn it, Henry, what are you doing back?'

'Nice to see you, too, Ena.'

'Is it?'

'Of course it is. Here.' Henry put his hand under Ena's chin and lifted her face to his. 'Let me look at your forehead.'

Ena flicked his hand away.

'What is it?'

'What is it? You have a bloody nerve, Henry. Where the hell have you been?'

'You know I can't tell you that.'

'No. But you could have told me you were going off grid. I've been worried sick.'

'I'm sorry, darling, it was very last minute.'

'It always is.'

'You know how these things work,' he said, kissing her forehead.

'All right. But next time...'

'I'll tell you, I promise.' Henry pulled Ena to him and put his arms around her.

She rested her head on his chest. 'It's been a very long day.'

'You're freezing,' Henry said.

Holding her hand, Henry led Ena into the sitting room. He went to the cupboard and took out a bottle of Teacher's Whisky and Ena knelt in front of the fire.

'Here.' Henry handed her a glass of Scotch and sat down beside her. He took a drink and exhaled with appreciation.

With her head on Henry's shoulder Ena watched the orange and red flames jump from one lump of coal to another.

Henry put his glass on the hearth and wrapped his arms around her. Rocking her gently he kissed the back of her neck. Then he nibbled the lobe of her ear and, breathing heavily, said, 'I've missed you, Ena.'

Ena, almost asleep, snuggled into her husband. 'I've missed you too,' she mumbled, stifling a yawn.

Henry took the glass of whisky Ena was about to spill out of her hand. He put it on the hearth next to his empty glass and helped her to her feet. With her arms around Henry and her eyes shut, stumbling like someone who'd had too much to drink, Ena let her husband guide her out of the sitting room and into the bedroom.

She fell onto the bed exhausted, turned over and sighed heavily. Henry took off her shoes and kicked off his own. By the time he had taken off his shirt, Ena was fast asleep. Lifting the eiderdown from his side of the bed he folded it over her.

Putting his shirt back on, he returned to the sitting room and finished Ena's drink.

SIXTEEN

When she opened her eyes the following morning, Ena sprang out of bed and went into the sitting room. 'I thought I'd dreamed you were back,' she said, throwing her arms around Henry. 'Why didn't you ring the office and tell me you were coming home?'

'I didn't know I was until yesterday. I got a last minute flight. Besides, I wanted to surprise you.'

'Flight? So you were overseas when Mac Robinson was buried?'

'Of course.' Henry looked shocked that Ena could think he had lied. 'If I'd been in England I'd have been at Mac's funeral, you know I would.'

'I know. That's what I told Helen Crowther.' Ena hoped her voice didn't reveal the disappointment she felt and changed the subject.

'Tea and toast?' she said, leaping out of her chair and going into the kitchen.

'The tea might be a bit stewed by now.'

'I'll make a fresh pot.'

'How about we do something today?' Suddenly behind her,

Henry put his arms around her waist and held her close. 'We could go back to bed,' he whispered, blowing warm air on her neck. Ena felt the flutter of butterflies in the pit of her stomach as she became aroused. 'This afternoon we could see a film at the Ritz, have an early dinner somewhere and,' he buried his face in her hair, 'we could have an early night.' He lowered his hands and began to caress her.

Ena swayed with desire. She wanted Henry. She needed him, but not today. Today she had important work to do. 'That sounds perfect, darling, but I can't take today off. Today is the worst possible day...' She felt Henry's hands leave her. 'Tomorrow. We can do all that tomorrow.'

Without saying a word, Henry left the kitchen.

When she had made the tea and toast, she took it into the sitting room. Henry was sitting on the settee reading the newspaper. He had turned the wireless on, the volume up.

'Can we talk?' Ena said, putting the breakfast tray on the table.

Henry lifted his head from the paper. 'Do we have anything to talk about?'

'Henry, please don't be like that. I know how you feel about the cold case investigation into Frieda Voight.'

Henry folded the newspaper and lobbed it at the coffee table. Leaning his head on the back of the settee, he closed his eyes and sighed.

'It's now a live case.'

Henry's eyes shot open. They were bright. Ena wasn't sure whether they were shining with anger or interest.

She poured two cups of tea. She didn't ask if Henry wanted toast, she just gave it to him. While she drank her tea she told him about the funeral, that Eve Robinson was convinced her husband had been murdered and that she had blamed Ena. She also told him that Mac Robinson's daughter had visited him in hospital.

'Mac doesn't have a daughter,' Henry said, 'the hospital must have made a mistake.'

'They didn't make a mistake, Henry. Mac may not have a daughter but a woman posing as his daughter visited him the day before he died.'

Henry slowly shook his head. The lines deepened on his forehead and his eyes flashed. This time it was anger that Ena could see in them. In the ten years that they had been married, Ena had never seen Henry so annoyed.

She drank her tea and forced herself to eat some toast. When she had finished, she said, 'The name of the woman who visited Mac in the hospital was Ena Dudley.' Henry remained silent, his face blank. Because she couldn't read him, Ena said again that she needed to go to the office.

'Dick Bentley has given me forty-eight hours to find proof that the woman using *my* name and *my* driving licence is Frieda Voight. That's why I have to go to work today. When I told Sid, he remembered seeing the name Ena Dudley in one of the cold case files. He thinks Frieda is working as an engineer in a nuclear research facility somewhere. He knew I'd worked in engineering, but he didn't know my maiden name so he didn't make the connection. We're hoping when we find the file, we'll be able to prove that Frieda is working in nuclear research. And, because her address is the same as a Russian diplomat in Holland Park, I think she is spying for the Russians.'

Henry stood up and looked out of the window. 'I want you to drop the Voight case, Ena.'

Ena took a sharp breath. 'No!'

'It's dangerous.'

'Don't you think I know that?'

'Did you know you're being watched.'

'Yes. By someone in a green Austin Cambridge. He – or she – was parked along the road when I got home last night.

Whoever it is followed Sid and me when we left here yesterday afternoon.'

'Why was Sid here?'

'He worked from here. The office was broken into during the night, so, as Artie was going out on a surveillance job, I didn't want Sid to work from there on his own.' Henry's eyes widened and his brow furrowed. 'Don't worry, it was only to bug the place.'

'What?'

'The flat was bugged too.'

'When? How?' Henry left the window. 'Christ, Ena, what the fuck have you got yourself into?'

'If you stop shouting and swearing at me, I'll tell you.'

Henry threw his arms in the air and fell backwards onto the settee. 'Go on.'

'Someone, I presume it was a man, was in the flat when I got home the night before last. When he heard me come in, he high-tailed it out of the kitchen window.'

'Did you get a look at him? Did you see his face?'

'No. I heard someone in the kitchen, but by the time I got in there he had escaped.'

'Thank God for that!'

'Thank God for what? That a thief, spy, or a murderer, got away scot free?'

'No. That you didn't see his face. If you can't identify him, chances are he won't come after you. Is anything missing?'

'No. Nothing. I thought I'd scared him off before he'd had time to steal anything. When I got to the office it had been broken into as well. Nothing missing there either, but it had been bugged. Artie was going out so I brought Sid and the files he was working on back here. He oversaw the repair of the kitchen window while I went down to the hospital in Hove.' Ena thought it best not to tell Henry that Artie had spent the day poking around in the house of a Russian diplomat in the hopes of finding something incriminating against Frieda.

'When I got back from Hove, Sid had found two devices. One in the overhead light and one in the telephone.'

'That's it!' Henry stormed out of the room.

Ena ran after him and grabbed him by the arm. 'Where are you going?'

'To find out who the bloke in the surveillance car is working for.'

'No, Henry. Don't confront him. He's probably armed.'

Henry returned to the sitting room, opened the second drawer of the sideboard and reached into the back. Removing assorted dining table paraphernalia, he took out his gun.

'Oh no you don't, Henry! Please don't take your gun,' Ena begged.

'I'm not having anyone following you, frightening you.' Ena ran into the hall. Arms outstretched, she stood with her back against the door.

Henry put the gun in his jacket pocket, gripped the top of Ena's arms and lifted her out of the way. Pulling the door open he took the steps to the street two at a time. Ena ran after him. He ran between the front of the Sunbeam and the car next to it. Ena cut round the back of the Sunbeam arriving in the road at the same time as Henry. She put her hands on his chest. 'Stop! Take the registration number. Give it to MI5. Get someone there to find out who the car belongs to. But please,' Ena pleaded, 'don't challenge the driver.'

Henry ignored her.

'You said it was good that I hadn't seen the face of the man who broke into the flat. Well that's the same for you. If you approach him – if you see his face – you'll be in danger too.'

While Ena was pleading with Henry, the engine of the green Austin Cambridge roared into life. Ena saw it heading towards them and screamed. Henry pushed her out of the way and as she fell he threw himself on top of her. The Austin raced past, missing them by inches.

They lay in the road, Henry shielding Ena, her arms wrapped around him so tightly they ached.

'Come on,' Henry said, getting to his feet and pulling Ena to hers. 'Are you hurt?'

Ena shook her head. 'No, not really. My elbows feel sore, and I expect my bottom will be bruised, but I'm fine. You?'

'I'm all right. Blast!' he shouted, 'I didn't get the car's damn number.'

'I've got it in the flat. Come on.'

'I don't understand you. You've had the registration number of that damn car for however long and haven't taken it to Five. I give up, Ena, I really do.'

When she was ready for work, her hair dressed and her make-up on, Ena picked up her bags. 'I'll see you later.' Henry ignored her. 'Henry, I am seeing this thing through. At least I shall do as much as I can before I have to go into the HO and give Dick Bentley my findings.' Henry didn't reply. 'You can be bloody exasperating sometimes,' she said, taking a piece of paper out of her handbag. 'Here. This is the registration number of the car that's been following me. Will you take it to Leconfield House, or are you going to sit and wallow in what *might* have happened all day?'

'You take the bloody biscuit, Ena. You're so damned pig-headed.'

'I don't have time for this, Henry, nor do you. Take the registration number and get one of your giggling secretaries to check it out with Motor Licensing. I'd put money on it being owned by the Russian Diplomatic Service. I'll see you after I've seen Director Bentley.'

Ena left the flat, tears streaming down her face. Her legs felt weak. Henry was right. She could have been killed outside their home. So could he. A loud sob escaped her throat. She wanted to run back to the flat, tell Henry how much she loved him, thank him for throwing himself on top of her, for pushing her out of the way and saving her life.

She took in a lungful of air and cried out. Henry might have been killed saving her. She opened the door of the Sunbeam, dropped onto the drivers' seat, and leant her head on the steering wheel. When she had recovered, she looked up at the sitting room window. Henry was looking out. I love you, she mouthed, but he wasn't looking at her.

Ena turned the key in the ignition and started the engine. She looked up at the window again. Henry had gone.

SEVENTEEN

'Not again,' Ena said, seeing open filing cabinets, files, folders and sheets of paper strewn all over the floor.

'It was like this when I got in this morning,' Artie said. 'Twice in two days! What the Dickens is going on?'

'They obviously didn't have time to search the place when they bugged it.'

'All that damned work for nothing.' Artie threw a file onto the table, it slid across the polished surface and fell onto the floor. 'Argh!' he shouted. 'I'll have to sort this lot out again.'

'And I have to write a memo on what we've got on Frieda Voight to give to Director Bentley at five o'clock this afternoon. Before I start I need to know what Sid remembered about Frieda Voight's latest alias. Where is he?'

'I don't know. I thought he was coming in with you.'

'No. When I dropped him off last night he said he had things to do before he came to work, but he would be here early because he needed to find a file.'

'Then why isn't he here?' Artie stopped what he was doing. 'Did he say which file?'

'No, he said he'd know it when he saw it.' Ena looked at her watch. 'He always rings if he knows he's going to be late.'

'Shall I telephone the house?'

Loud knocking on the street door interrupted Ena before she could answer.

'This'll be him now,' Artie said, putting down the telephone. 'Forgotten his keys,' he sighed, jogging across the room and out into the courtyard. When Artie returned it was not with Sid. 'Ena? There's someone here to see you.'

Two men, one in a police uniform, and a policewoman followed Artie into the office. 'Mrs Green?'

'Yes.' Ena left her seat and met the grim-faced visitors in the middle of the room. 'What can I do for you?'

'Detective Inspector Powell,' the older policeman wearing civvies said, offering Ena his hand. She shook it and gave him a brief nod.

'Sergeant Thompson and WPC Jarvis,' the inspector added.

'What's this about, Inspector?'

'A man's body was found in the early hours of this morning beneath Waterloo Bridge. We'd like you to come down to the station to answer a few questions.'

'Me? What has this unfortunate man got to do with me?'

'From the identification found in his wallet and from subsequent enquiries, we believe the man is a work colleague of yours, Sidney Parfitt.'

Ena's heart thumped in her chest. 'Sid? You must be mistaken, Inspector.'

'The sooner we can establish Mr Parfitt's whereabouts last night, the sooner we'll be able to get his death cleared up.'

'He was at home last night. I drove him there myself. When I dropped him off he said he'd see me here this morning.'

The sergeant opened the office door and stood beside it. The policewoman walked across the room and stood next to

Ena. 'If you come with us, Mrs Green? I'm sure we'll get the matter sorted out in no time.'

'Yes, of course.' Ena grabbed her coat from the back of her chair and picked up her handbag. 'Artie, telephone Henry.' She glanced at the clock on the office wall. 'He should still be at home. Tell him—' Ena looked at the inspector. 'Where are you taking me?'

'Bow Street police station.'

'Tell him to come quickly, will you?'

WPC Jarvis took Ena's coat out of her hands and held it up. 'It's chilly this morning, Mrs Green.'

Near to tears, Ena let herself be led out of the office by the policewoman. She looked back as the door was closing. Artie had already picked up the telephone. He nodded at Ena and she smiled through her tears. The tears were not for herself, but for her colleague and friend, Sid Parfitt.

From Mercer Street to Bow Street police station was a short walk, but there was a black Wolseley waiting outside. WPC Jarvis opened the nearside rear door and Ena slid onto the back seat.

Sergeant Thompson opened the door to interview room one. 'Take a seat, Mrs Green, Inspector Powell won't be long.'

Two minutes later DI Powell arrived. WPC Jarvis followed him in. The DI pulled out a chair from beneath the table for himself and one for the constable. The policewoman took a notebook and pen from the top pocket of her uniform, opened the notebook and placed it on the table in front of her. The pen she held in her hand, poised to make notes.

'Was it an accident, Inspector?'

'It *appears* so.'

'Poor Sid. Did he drown?'

'We can't be sure until after the autopsy, but the coroner doesn't think so.'

'But if he fell into the Thames?'

'He didn't fall into the Thames, he fell onto concrete steps that were once part of a jetty. The tide was out, so his body wasn't carried downriver. I shall know more when I get the coroner's report, but it looks as though your friend had one too many and fell to his death.'

'But Sid didn't drink,' Ena said. 'He had the occasional glass of beer, but beyond that... No, Inspector, he wouldn't have been drunk.' Suddenly the file Sid wanted to find came into her mind. She felt the heat of anger rise up her neck to her cheeks. 'Could Sid's death have been foul play?'

'That's what we're here to find out, Mrs Green.'

Shocked that the inspector could think she had anything to do with her friend's death, Ena gave him a contemptuous look. 'What do you mean, that's what we're here to find out?'

The inspector put up his hand and Ena stopped speaking. 'We understand from Mr Parfitt's mother and sister that you telephoned him last night at around ten fifteen.'

'What?'

'And asked him to meet you at the office in Mercer Street.'

'I did no such thing!' Alarm bells began to ring in the back of Ena's mind. She was being set up. 'I didn't telephone Sid. I told him he'd done enough for one day, drove him home and said I'd see him this morning at the office. I neither spoke to him nor saw him after that.'

The inspector consulted his notebook. 'Did Mr Parfitt spend the day with you at number seven St Michael's Square?'

'Yes. Actually no. He was on his own for most of the day. I was in Hove on business. I didn't get back until mid-afternoon. I was having the glass replaced in my kitchen window and Sid, Mr Parfitt, said he would work from my flat to make sure the work was done. His work is – was – investigatory. He was working his way through a box of files and didn't need to be in the office.'

The inspector consulted his notebook, again. 'And you're sure you *didn't* telephone Mr Parfitt at ten fifteen or thereabouts last night?'

'How many times? No! I did not telephone Sid last night. I had no reason to.'

'Were you and Mr Parfitt having a relationship?'

'What? For goodness' sake! No, we were not having a *relationship*, as you call it. Other than a working relationship. I am happily married.' Ena felt her cheeks colour. She and Henry were happy, weren't they? They had been until recently. It was only the Frieda Voight case that they argued about. Suddenly a realisation hit her. Apart from Frieda Voight using Ena's identity to get a job in nuclear research, Sid had remembered something about her, or someone connected to her, that had worried him. Thinking about it, Sid was on edge. He said he was desperate to get to work the next day and go through the files to remind himself what it was. Did he go back to the office? If he did, he'd have crossed the river on Westminster Bridge, not Waterloo.

'Mrs Green?'

'What? Sorry, I– No. Sid and I were good friends, work colleagues, as my other colleague in the office and I am. To suggest that Sid and I were having some sort of sordid affair is not only preposterous, but it's offensive to me and an insult to my late colleague. Besides,' Ena spat, 'my husband was at home last night, all night. He will confirm that I neither telephoned anyone nor went out to meet anyone. We were together until I left for work this morning.'

Sergeant Thompson opened the interview room door and poked his head in. 'Excuse me, sir. Could I have a word?'

DI Powell glared at him. 'Can't it wait?'

'No, sir. There's someone here who you will want to see.'

'This had better be good,' the DI barked.

The constable stood up when the DI did. 'Would you like a cup of tea, Mrs Green?'

Ena shook her head. 'I'd like a glass of water.'

The policewoman crossed the room to where a glass jug and half a dozen tumblers stood on the top of a wooden cabinet. She poured Ena a glass of water and took it to her.

No sooner had the policewoman returned to her seat than the inspector burst into the room. 'You have friends in high places, Mrs Green. You are free to go.' He banged his notebook on the table as if he was stacking bricks.

Ena leapt out of her chair.

Ignoring her, the inspector looked at WPC Jarvis. 'Show Mrs Green out of the station, Constable.'

EIGHTEEN

With less than five hours until her meeting with Director Bentley, Ena should have gone back to the office and written a report. Instead she hailed a cab.

'Embankment, Waterloo Bridge.'

'No can do, miss!' the cab driver said, 'Waterloo Bridge is closed. Some bloke's gone and committed harry-carry.'

Ena's hackles rose. She bit her tongue. 'Could you get me there via Westminster Bridge?'

'Not sure, miss. I can try.'

'Don't bother, I'm in a hurry.' Ena was running out of patience. 'Drop me off on the corner of the Strand and Lancaster Place, I'll walk across the bridge.'

The cab driver looked at Ena in the rear-view mirror and jerked his head in annoyance. Not as long a journey as he would have liked, Ena thought, as he spun the cab's steering wheel to the right at the end of Wellington Street.

'Stop!' Ena shouted, as the cab cruised past Lancaster Place and down the Strand. 'Now!' she ordered. The cab driver stood on the brake at the corner of Savoy Street, the momentum propelling Ena from the back seat.

Ena slapped a half-crown in the driver's hand and left the cab giving him a surly look. She walked back to Lancaster Place. Six policemen stood in a line across the road. Two were waving vehicles on down the Strand.

'Sorry, miss. There's not access to Waterloo Station or South London, from here. You'll have to go to Charing Cross if you want a train, Westminster Bridge for a bus south.'

'The man who fell from Waterloo Bridge was my associate.' Ena took her Home Office identification from her handbag and showed it to the officer. His brow furrowed. He clearly hadn't seen a Home Office ID card before. 'I have just come from Bow Street police station,' which was true, 'if you telephone Detective Inspector Powell, he will confirm I have clearance,' which was not true. Ena held her breath. If DI Powell thought she had something to do with Sid's death, which Ena was sure he did, he'd be the last person on earth to help her.

The policeman looked bewildered. 'I shouldn't tell you this,' Ena said, conspiratorially, 'but the man found dead on the embankment,' she nodded to the end of the bridge, 'and I were working on a matter of vital importance to the country. I wish I could tell you more, but our work is classified. *Top secret*,' she whispered. 'I'm bound by the Official Secrets Act, so... I'm sure you understand.'

The bobby didn't look convinced. 'If you'd like to telephone the director of military intelligence, or, better still my boss at the Home Office, Director Bentley, he will confirm what I have told you.' Ena was sure Dick Bentley would back her up, but not until he'd had the request in writing – and in triplicate. She flashed her Home Office ID at him again. 'I'm sure either high-ranking man, even though they are up to their eyes keeping our country safe, would make time to get in touch with your superior at Scotland Yard.'

The policeman looked terrified at the idea, nodded at Ena's

ID card and shouted to his fellow officers, 'This lady has clearance.'

'Thank you, Officer. You have done the Home Office an important service.' Ena held up her ID card – so the policeman opposite could see it – and set off past Somerset House to the south side of Waterloo Bridge.

Until today, Waterloo Bridge had been Ena's favourite place in London. She would often stop halfway across the bridge and look towards Westminster; to Big Ben and the Houses of Parliament. Today she was on the north side of the bridge. As she walked she looked to the left, to Blackfriars Bridge, the City of London and St Paul's. The winter sun reflected off the Cathedral's dome and ships sailed to and from the docks. Even on a day as sad as this one had become, the sight of ships and boats heading for the docks pleased her. London's docks had been heavily bombed in the war, they seemed to be thriving now.

It was always slightly windy in the middle of the bridge at this time of year, but today the wind was fierce. It cut across the bridge causing Ena's eyes to run.

Twenty yards short of the police cordon on the south side of the bridge she stopped and took out her identification card. She looked over the wall at the river. There was nothing to see. The tide was in. She needed to stand in the spot directly above the place where Sid's body was found; the place where the police thought he had been standing before he fell. Not for a second did Ena believe Sid had accidentally fallen from the bridge onto the riverbank. Nor did she think he was drunk.

Prepared to go through the same rigmarole as she had at the other end of Waterloo Bridge Ena held up her ID card to the approaching policeman.

'I was expecting you, Mrs Green. Sergeant Havers,' the policeman said, with a sideways nod to the north end of the bridge. 'I'll take you to where your colleague's body was found. There isn't anything to see now, I'm afraid,' the sergeant said, as they reached the end of the bridge and began walking down the steep slope to the embankment. 'Tide's in, you see. The evidence has been washed away.'

Forcing herself not show she was upset, Ena looked over the railings. She was five feet eight inches tall and there was no way she'd be able to fall over the railing. Sid was six feet tall. But she couldn't see how even at six feet, he would have fallen into the river from here. 'How tall are you, Sergeant Havers?'

'Just over six feet, Mrs Green.'

Ena took a couple of steps back to get a full picture of the sergeant and the railings. 'How easy would it be for you to fall over this rail?'

The sergeant turned and faced the river. Ena placed her hand on his back and gently pushed. He leant forward until his chest pressed against the railings. 'It wouldn't be easy at all. In fact,' he leant forward again, 'I'd say it would be impossible.'

'Even if you were drunk?'

'Not even then. You'd have to be six inches taller than me to fall over this,' he said, slapping the top of the railing with the flat of his hand.

'Did you see Mr Parfitt's body?'

'Yes, ma'am.'

'Any marks to suggest he fell from Waterloo Bridge, and not from down here?'

'Yes, ma'am. Your colleague's head was badly injured. The right side of his head and–' Ena nodded for the sergeant to continue. 'Half of his face had been smashed in. The kind of injuries he sustained couldn't have been done falling from these railings. Not even if he climbed on them and threw himself off.'

Ena walked along the pavement until she came to a length of rail that had a slight dent in it. She called the sergeant.

'There's blood on the top of this section of railing. And this,' Ena said, crouching until her eyes were level with the top of the rail, 'is hair.' She swallowed hard. 'And skin.'

'Over here!' the sergeant called to two men who were taking off white coats and packing a large medical bag as if they were getting ready to leave.

'This lady is a work colleague of the victim,' the police sergeant said.

'Sandy Berman, Police Surgeon.' The older man put out his hand and Ena shook it. 'And my assistant, Dan Peters.' The younger man nodded.

'Ena Green.' Ena moved out of the way to let the men see the railing.

'Good God!' Sandy Berman said, scraping dried blood and skin from the handrail with a piece of equipment that looked like a narrow cake knife and putting it into a small white envelope. 'Thank God you spotted this blood, Mrs Green.' Sandy Berman looked embarrassed. 'I'm ashamed to say we didn't look this far along the railings. We didn't think it possible for anyone with that kind of head injury to move after they'd fallen–' He looked up at the bridge.

Ena followed his eyeline. Sandy Berman didn't believe Sid fell from the embankment railings either. No, it wouldn't have been possible, she thought. Someone must have moved Sid's body. It was the only explanation. Ena shivered. If the blood on the railings was Sid's, she had earlier been standing where he had stood before he jumped, or was pushed. Convinced it was the latter, she looked along the path, and again at the bridge. If Sid had fallen from that height onto concrete, even if his fall had been broken by the railings, there was no way on earth he would have survived. No one would have.

'I need to get back to my office, write a report on what I know about my colleague's death. Thank you for bringing me down to the scene of the–' she was about to say crime, but since the police were adamant Sid's death was a drunken accident, she said, 'accident.'

Both medical men looked at her, their brows lined with worry.

'My report won't say anything about the police investigation or missed evidence, but it will conflict with the police report in the respect that I believe my colleague's death was caused by falling off Waterloo Bridge onto these railings, not from falling over them on the embankment. Now,' Ena looked from the Police Surgeon to his assistant, 'I think your findings will support that.'

'Odd that he wasn't wearing any shoes,' Sergeant Havers said.

Ena spun round. 'What did you say?' her eyes wide and questioning.

'Your colleague wasn't wearing his shoes when he was found.'

'His shoes were ten yards further along the embankment,' Sandy Berman said. 'It looked to us as if he had decided to end his life, taken off his shoes, and thrown them over the bridge first.'

'Why would a man with suicide on his mind take off his shoes?' Ena looked from one medical man to the other.

'Maybe he didn't. Maybe someone pushed him off the bridge,' the assistant said, 'and threw the shoes after him?'

'Why would they do that?' the police sergeant asked.

Unless Sid had something hidden in the heel of his shoes, Ena thought. Or whoever pushed him off Waterloo Bridge *thought* he had something in his shoes and made him take them off. If they didn't find anything, they might have thrown them after Sid in frustration. 'Where is Mr Parfitt now?'

'St Thomas's morgue,' Sandy Berman said.

'And that's where his shoes will be?'

'No, ma'am,' the police sergeant cut in. 'Detective Inspector Powell took his shoes. They'll be at Bow Street. If they're not, the inspector will know where they are.'

NINETEEN

Ena walked back across Waterloo Bridge. For the first time since she had lived in London, she did not stop halfway across the bridge to marvel at the view. At Aldwych she decided against getting a cab; she needed to walk, to think. Twenty minutes more or less wasn't going to be enough time to write a report for Director Bentley. Besides, out of respect for Sid, Ena wanted to tell the director what she had learned about their colleague's death in person. She also wanted to tell him about the file Sid was desperate to find. A file that would help in the Freda Voight investigation. Which, in Ena's opinion, would be the only reason for Sid returning to the office last night, if indeed he did. And the reason he was killed.

Approaching Bow Street police station, Ena couldn't help but wonder why Sid wasn't wearing shoes when he was found. It could only mean he'd put something important in one of them, or in one of the heels. Was it a message? A name perhaps? And did his killer find it? Her gut feeling was they hadn't, and they had thrown the shoes in frustration.

Sloppy work, she thought. If Sid's killer had put his shoes back on him after finding nothing in them, Sid's death would have looked even more like a suicide. Ena wondered why they hadn't. She needed to see Sid's shoes and there was only one way she was going to do that.

She opened the door of the police station and went to the enquiries window. 'Would you tell Detective Inspector Powell that Ena Green would like to speak to him?'

'If you'd like to wait over there, Mrs Green.' The desk sergeant pointed to a row of chairs lined up along the far wall. Ena walked over and sat down on the only vacant seat.

It was a sparsely furnished lobby-type entrance. Except for the chairs where she was sitting there was no other furniture. But then, a police station was not the place where most of the characters brought in would want to stay. Not for long anyway. There was a glass panel on the right of the enquires window. Ena could see doors to the interview rooms and stairs leading to the first floor. If Detective Inspector Powell had time to see her he would probably come from that direction.

The man on her left nudged her. Ena turned to face him and he gave her a toothless grin. She could smell the stale earthy odour of clothes that were wet and had started to dry. Her neighbour, a man-of-the-road, had probably come into the station to get warm. Ena smiled at him and his face, weather-beaten and so dirty she was unable to tell his age, softened into deep brown creases. When he smiled his old rheumy eyes lit up. He chuntered to himself. Ena didn't catch what he was saying, then he turned to her again. 'They said the war was a war to end all wars. But it weren't. They made us go through it again, in this last lot.' He shook his head and nudged Ena a second time. 'And that Yank and my Sheila walking out together.' He lifted his arm and wiped the sleeve of his coat across his face. 'It weren't right,' he said, sniffing. 'Did you hear what I said, woman? I said, it weren't right.'

'No,' Ena said, sympathetically, 'it wasn't.'

The girl on the other side of the man giggled. Ena gave her a critical look, which clearly went over the girl's head because she put her hand up to her face and pinched her nose. Ena gave a slight nod to let her know she knew the man smelled and hoped that would be the end of the girl's antics. It wasn't. The girl giggled again.

'Mrs Green?'

Hearing her name, Ena stood up. Detective Inspector Powell was walking across the room. 'What can I do for you?'

'Can we speak in private?'

'Of course.' Ena heard the sound of surprise in his voice. 'This way,' he said, opening the door leading to the interview rooms. The DI opened the door to room one and ushered Ena in. Shutting the door he motioned to her to sit down.

'I've just come from Waterloo Bridge,' Ena said.

The inspector half smiled. 'Well?'

'Well, drunk or not – and I don't believe Mr Parfitt was drunk – it wouldn't have been possible to fall over the embankment railings and do that amount of damage. It's obvious that he fell from the bridge.'

'Fall or jump, the outcome is the same.'

'I don't believe he jumped either. I don't think his death was an accident.'

DI Powell took a box of Senior Service and a lighter from his jacket pocket. He offered Ena a cigarette. She took one and he lit it. Taking a cigarette for himself the inspector walked over to the window before lighting it.

Deep in thought he smoked his cigarette looking into the busy street. Ena wondered what he was thinking. The inspector took the last drag, inhaled deeply, and stubbed the cigarette out in an ashtray on the windowsill that was overflowing with dog-ends.

'I don't think he fell off the bridge either,' the inspector said. Turning, he leant against the wall, one leg bent behind him with his foot on the wall to keep his balance, and faced Ena.

'Someone was looking for something they thought your colleague had. They'd pat him down and look in his pockets and wallet.'

'And his shoes,' Ena added. 'And when they didn't find what they were looking for they pushed him off the bridge.'

'Or they killed him on the bridge, searched him, and threw his body off to make it look like he was drunk and fell, or committed suicide.'

'If they were trying to make it look like suicide, why didn't they put his shoes back on him. Why throw them after him? And why so far away from his body?'

'That's what I've been asking myself,' DI Powell said.

'And that's why I came to see you, Inspector.'

'To ask if you could see Mr Parfitt's shoes?' DI Powell pushed himself off the wall. 'His shoes are in my office,' he said, striding across the room and opening the door. He held it for Ena and followed her out. 'Upstairs,' he said, 'end of the corridor.'

'Take a seat,' the DI said when they were in his office. He pulled open a metal four drawer cabinet, took out a pair of men's shoes and put them on the desk in front of Ena.

'They are Sid's shoes. He was wearing them the last time I saw him.' Tears came into the corners of Ena's eyes. She cleared her throat. 'Have you got a sixpence?'

The DI looked surprised by Ena's request, but he didn't question her. He put his hand in his trousers pocket and took out a handful of change. He dropped a sixpence onto the desk.

'Thanks.' She picked up Sid's left shoe and tapped the heel. 'Hollow.' She laid the shoe upside down on the desk and took the sixpence between her forefinger and thumb. Carefully she pushed the side of the coin into a minute gap between the sole and the heel and twisted it. The heel separated from the sole to reveal a cavity. 'Nothing. There won't be anything in the other heel either, but I'll look anyway.' Ena did the same to Sid's other shoe. Nothing there either. 'Where are his clothes?'

'On his body the last time I saw them. They'll be at the mortuary.'

Ena looked at the inspector and bit her bottom lip. 'Could I see them?'

DI Powell picked up the telephone on his desk and asked for Sergeant Thompson. After holding for a minute, he told the sergeant to bring the car round, they were going to St Thomas's.

Inspector Powell led Ena down two flights of stairs to the mortuary. She immediately noticed a difference in temperature. Neither the cold air, the atmosphere, or the décor was welcoming. The walls had been whitewashed over bare bricks. The room looked more like a public lavatory than a pathologist's laboratory, Ena thought, as they passed through it.

In the adjoining room, there was a large square stone sink on the right with one dripping tap, and one with a green hose attached to it. On the far side of the room was a row of three stainless-steel tables. Two with empty trolleys at their side and one displaying an assortment of surgical instruments.

The pathologist was bending over the third table attending to a body partially covered by a white sheet. He had a scalpel in his hand. Ena caught her breath. He was performing an autopsy on her friend Sid. She was near to tears. Suddenly, as if he had only just realised someone had entered the room, he lifted his head. He peered at the newcomers over the top of his glasses and wiped his bloodstained hands down his white apron. Ena wasn't squeamish, but the thought that the man being cut open beneath the sheet was Sid brought the toast she'd eaten at breakfast into her throat.

She turned away. Only the hair on the dead man's head was visible, but from the description the police sergeant on the embankment had given her, the man on the stainless steel table in the cold sterile room could only be her friend and colleague, Sid Parfitt.

'His clothes are in my office,' the pathologist said, drawing the white sheet over Sid's head. 'They're all yours if you want them. I've finished with them.'

The inspector steered Ena out of the mortuary and into the pathologist's office.

Ena went to the portable clothes rail where Sid's clothes hung. She didn't expect to find anything of interest in any of the pockets. She looked anyway. She took down his overcoat, turned it inside out, and laid it across the table. Taking a narrow blade from a tray on the desk she slid the point between the silk lining and the coat's woollen fabric. There was nothing hidden in the lining. She did the same to the sleeves of the coat and the same to Sid's suit jacket and trousers. 'Nothing,' she said, 'nothing at all.'

Emotionally exhausted, Ena flopped into a chair. 'It looks like whoever killed Sid found what they were looking for.'

'Or your colleague didn't have what they were looking for.'

'In which case he died for nothing,' Ena said, putting her head in her hands.

Suddenly the door flew open and a voice boomed, 'Found something that might interest you.'

Ena looked up to see the pathologist beaming her a smile. 'This was in the fellow's cheek. Didn't notice it before. Trapped in his smashed jaw, stuck behind teeth that had been–'

'Thank you!' Inspector Powell interrupted. 'Mrs Green doesn't need to know the ins-and-outs of your findings in graphic detail.' The inspector took the tiny square of paper, protected by an equally small piece of glassine out of the pathologist's hand.

'Right you are. Sorry. No need for that sort of information.

Quite unnecessary,' he said, reprimanding himself. 'Interesting though,' he offered, leaving the office.

Inspector Powell took his handkerchief from his pocket and wiped the glassine covering. It was clean. At least the pathologist had been sensitive enough to wipe the blood off it. He handed it to Ena.

She looked closely at the transparent cover. It looked like a miniature envelope. Turning it over in her hand, Ena found the flap and gently lifted it. The glassine separated to reveal a square of paper no bigger than a postage stamp.

'But there's nothing on it,' the inspector said.

'Nothing written on it, no.' Ena looked around the pathologist's office. Her eyes settled on his desk and a magnifying glass propped up in a pipe-rack. 'Pass me the magnifying glass will you, Inspector?'

The inspector's eyes followed Ena's. He took the magnifier from between the row of pipes and passed it to her. 'Have you found something?'

'Maybe.' She laid the piece of paper on the desk and, leaning over it, saw what she had hoped to see.

She stepped back to let the inspector look. 'Pinpricks?'

'Look closer.'

'C O L L I N S.' The inspector laughed. 'Pinpricks. Minute perforations that you can hardly see that spell Collins. Do you know anyone by the name of, Collins?'

'No,' Ena said, 'I don't.'

TWENTY

In the black Wolseley going back to Bow Street, DI Powell told Sergeant Thompson to drive on to Mercer Street. 'We'll drop you off at your office,' he said, smiling at Ena sympathetically.

'That'll be a help. I have a meeting this afternoon and I need to pick up some papers before I go to it.'

'What did you say you did there?'

'Administrative work. We check files, make sure names and dates are correct.'

'Government files?'

'Some are, yes.'

'For the Home Office?'

Ena felt her cheeks redden. 'We're connected to the Home Office, yes.'

'I see.'

Did the inspector *see*? Ena hoped not. She looked sideways at him. He smiled. She smiled back.

They sat in silence for a while, and then the inspector said, 'And you don't have any idea who this Collins character is?'

'No.'

When the police car pulled up outside the office in Mercer

Street, DI Powell said, 'You've had a shock. Will you be all right? If you'd like me to come in with you?'

'No! I'll be fine. My other assistant, Artie, will be there. I would like to break the news of Sid's death to him on my own.'

DI Powell walked her to the door. 'I want you to know you can trust me, Mrs Green.'

Ena looked into his eyes. 'Thank you.' She held his gaze. By doing so she hoped he would know that she trusted him. Unlocking the door, she said, 'When I find out who Collins is, I'll let you know.'

'Ena?' Henry strode across the room to meet her.

'Are you all right?' Artie asked, near to tears. 'Was it Sid's body they found?'

'I'm sorry, Artie, I'm afraid it was.'

Artie slumped into his chair.

'Where have you been for the last four hours?' Henry asked. 'I went to Bow Street police station. They told me you'd left. What's going on? Where have you been until now?'

'You went to Bow Street and I'd already left? Wasn't it you who got me released?'

'It was Director Bentley,' Artie said.

'What?'

'I'm sorry, Ena, but the first time I phoned Henry at home there was no reply. I panicked and phoned Director Bentley.'

'Oh hell,' Ena said. 'God knows what Dick Bentley will say when I see him, but thank you, Artie, if you hadn't telephoned him I'd probably be locked up by now. At first, the inspector thought I was involved in Sid's death.' She looked at her watch. 'Damn! It's half past four, I'm seeing Bentley at five. I'd better get a move on,' she said, gathering papers and files.

'I'll run you down to Whitehall,' Henry said, 'you're in no fit state to drive yourself.'

'Okay, thanks, I do feel a bit shaky.'

'Have you eaten anything since leaving the flat this morning?'

Ena looked at her husband and pulled a face. Except for the breakfast she had almost brought up in the morgue, she hadn't even thought about food. Her thoughts were only about Sid lying on the sterile mortuary table with his head... 'I don't think I could eat anything.'

'We'll pick something up on the way.'

Ena grimaced. 'I'll be back in an hour, Artie. Will you be all right on your own?' Artie sighed. 'Why don't you go out for a walk? I don't suppose you've had any lunch.' Artie shook his head. 'I didn't think so. Go and get something to eat. You'll feel better with something inside you.' Ena put her arms around her colleague. 'And don't forget to lock up.'

'So, what's this about, Ena?' Henry asked, when she had thrown her handbag and shoulder bag into the back of the Sunbeam, settled down in the passenger seat and closed the door.

'I'll tell you everything at home tonight, I promise. But I need this ten minutes in the car to collect my thoughts and decide what I'm going to say to Director Bentley.' Ena leaned back and closed her eyes.

Arriving at the Home Office, Henry said, 'I'll park round the back and leave the keys for you at the front desk. Will you be all right to drive yourself home?'

'Of course. Where are you going? I thought you were taking the day off.'

'I was, but I telephoned Leconfield House from your office and they want me in this afternoon.'

'What for?'

'Didn't say. It'll be something and nothing I expect.' Henry grabbed Ena's bags from the back seat and leapt out of the car. 'See you tonight,' he said, handing them to her.

Ena kissed him. 'I love you.'

Henry looked into Ena's eyes. 'I love you too.' She began to leave, but Henry pulled her to him. 'Promise me that, if you feel unwell after the meeting with Dick Bentley, you'll leave the car here and get a cab home?'

'Promise,' she said, shaking her head.

'I mean it,' Henry shouted. 'And be careful.'

'I will!' Ena blew him a kiss and ran along King Charles Street to the Home Office.

Waiting in the small reception area outside Director Bentley's office gave Ena time to think. She needed to relate the key facts of the investigation into Frieda Voight, including her most recent alias, Ena Dudley, as well as tell him about Sid's death. Dick Bentley didn't go in for small talk, so she needed to get to the point and be specific. But how? There was so much to tell him. And not only that, much of what she wanted to say needed explaining. She inhaled and exhaled slowly a number of times while she watched the black second hand on the clock above his secretary's desk tick around the clock's white face. Finally, it got to the twelve and juddered. It was five o'clock.

'Director Bentley will see you now.'

Ena jumped. 'What?' She had been miles away. Fear of what the director would say about her being taken to the police station, and him having to get her out, had dried up every drop of saliva in her mouth. She licked her lips and pushed on the already open door.

The director looked up as she entered. He motioned to the chair in front of his desk, and Ena sat down. Taking the files she had brought with her from her satchel she placed them on the desk. Then her mind went blank.

'Are you all right, Ena?'

'Not really, sir,' Ena said. 'Quite honestly, so much has

happened in the last forty-eight hours it's difficult to know where to start.' She took a deep breath and let it out slowly. 'First of all, thank you for getting me out of Bow Street police station.' Bentley gave a sharp nod. 'I believe Artie Mallory told you that a man's body had been found under Waterloo Bridge and that the police, finding his wallet, identified the man as our colleague, Sid Parfitt.'

'Yes, Mallory told me. What I don't know is why you were taken to Bow Street.'

'I'm sorry, sir, I wasn't sure how much Artie had told you. I'll get to the point.' Bentley nodded. 'I was taken to Bow Street because Sid's mother told Detective Inspector Powell that Sid had received a telephone call from Ena Green at ten o'clock last night and he left the house soon afterwards. Naturally, she assumed it was me, so the police came to the office and took me in for questioning.'

'But you didn't telephone Parfitt?'

'No, sir. I didn't telephone anyone last night. And I didn't go out. As I told the police, I didn't leave the flat until this morning to go to work.' Ena felt dizzy. Her stomach was empty. She wished now she'd let Henry buy her a sandwich. 'I think Frieda Voight used my name to lure Sid out of his house.'

'You think this, because...'

'Because when I went to the hospital the ward sister told me McKenzie Robinson's daughter had visited him, she told me the daughter's name was Ena Dudley. She said she had seen Mac's daughter's driving licence. Anyway, when I got home I told Sid and he said he remembered seeing the same name on a list of employees at a nuclear research facility.'

'Home? Was Sid Parfitt at your house?'

'Yes, sir.' Ena felt her cheeks flush. It was hot in Bentley's office. 'The truth is–'

'That would be good.'

'I'm sorry, sir, but today has been horrendous. I was trying to itemise the most important events of the last forty-eight hours, but it's too complicated. I'll start at the beginning.' Director Bentley nodded again. 'Someone broke into my flat. I must have scared him off when I arrived home because he escaped out of the kitchen window. It swung back and a pane of glass got broken. Sid was working on some low priority files and offered to work from my flat and oversee the repair of my window so I could go down to Hove.'

'Was anything stolen in the burglary?'

'No, sir. I assumed I had come home before the burglar had time to take anything, but Sid thought it was suspicious. And it was. While I was in Hove, he checked for listening devices and found two.

'I am also being watched, followed. I was almost run down by a surveillance car and now, Sid.' Ena did her best to stave off her tears. She took her handkerchief from her handbag and blew her nose. 'May I?' she said, pointing to a jug of water and several glasses.

'Of course.' Director Bentley stood up and poured them each a glass of water. 'Take your time.'

When Ena had quenched her thirst, she continued. 'When I told Sid my name was Ena Dudley before I was married and that I'd been an engineer, he said he had seen the same name and job title in one of the cold case files. He was adamant that it was a file connected to Frieda Voight. He wanted to go to the office and look for it. I said no, he had done enough for one day and took him home. I told him I'd see him in the morning.' Ena shook her head. 'But this morning...' She blurted out: 'He didn't fall from Waterloo Bridge, sir. Nor did he commit suicide. Sid was murdered. He was killed for a piece of paper with the name Collins on it.'

'Good Lord, Ena, how do you know this?'

'Sid's shoes were not with his body. It's an old spy tactic, as you are well aware. My sister Claire and her husband worked with the French resistance in the war. When they acted as couriers they hid money or information in their shoes. They walked on it. Sometimes information was hidden in the heels, in hollow compartments, but there was nothing in Sid's shoes. I thought because his shoes had nothing in them that whoever had killed him had found what he was hiding. But I was wrong. Detective Inspector Powell at Bow Street took me to the mortuary at St Thomas's for me to see if anything had been hidden in the lining of Sid's clothes. It was while we were there that the pathologist found this trapped between Sid's teeth and his cheek.' Ena passed the square of paper to the director.

He placed it on his black diary, lowered his head until his eyes were level with it and squinted. 'Collins?' He lifted his head. 'Do you know who Collins is?'

'No, sir.'

The director got up and paced the room. When he sat down again, he said, 'Parfitt thought there was something in one of the files that was important to the Voight investigation, you said?'

'Yes, sir.'

'Then you'd better stay with it. Go through the files Parfitt would have gone through if he hadn't been killed, and find this bloody chap Collins.'

'I will, sir.'

Director Bentley walked round his desk and put out his hand. 'Good work, Ena.'

'Thank you, sir.'

'I needn't tell you how important it is that this business with Sid Parfitt is kept in-house.'

'No, sir.'

'Good. Who else knows about Collins?'

Ena began to panic. She didn't want to lie to the director, but she couldn't tell him the truth. 'Inspector Powell took me to the mortuary, but it was the pathologist who found the piece of paper in Sid's mouth. I'm sure neither man knew the name Collins was stencilled on it.'

Director Bentley held Ena's gaze, as if he was looking for signs of doubt. 'Good,' he said at last, 'keep it that way. Any information comes straight to me, understood?'

'Understood.'

Ena left Director Bentley's office shaking. She felt guilty that she had lied to him when he had been so understanding. It was true that the pathologist hadn't seen the name Collins, but the inspector had. She needed to see him; ask him not to tell anyone. She blew out her cheeks. How the hell do you tell a Detective Inspector in charge of a murder enquiry not to do his job?

TWENTY-ONE

Ena and Artie spent the following week trawling through the boxes of cold case files that Sid had classified as urgent, important and unimportant. They even looked through closed and dead files. They found nothing. No mention of Frieda Voight, any of her aliases, or anyone called Collins.

Ena brought the last dozen boxes from the store room, giving Artie six and putting six on the cupboard at her end of the conference table. 'Wipe that frown off you face, Artie. It's boring, but it has to be done.'

'I know,' he sighed, 'and I don't mind really. Not if we find something that will help us catch the bastard that killed Sid.' Artie reached out and pulled a box nearer and cut through the brown tape that held it closed. 'Catch,' he said, giving the scissors a gentle shove that sent them spinning effortlessly to Ena at the other end of the table. 'What time is it?' he asked, taking out a file, dropping it on the table and laying his head on it.

Ena looked at her watch. 'Gone six; time we had a break.'

'Wake me when I can go home,' he mumbled.

'You look as if you've had enough. I know I have. My eyes are seeing words that aren't there,' Ena said, yawning.

'Sod's law what we're looking for is in this box,' Artie said, lifting his head. 'Let's have a wager. A quid says Collins is hiding in this box.'

'Do you want to go on, then?'

'Yes. No. I ought to for Sid, but I need sustenance.'

Ena hauled herself out of her chair. 'Let's go to the pub. I'll buy you a pint and a sandwich.'

'What about *Mr Collins*?'

'He isn't invited,' Ena said, in an attempt to lighten Artie's mood. It didn't work. 'If Collins is in this lot,' she said, bringing her hand down on top of the box she had been about to open, 'he will still be here in the morning.'

Artie put the file back in its box and taped it up. Pretending to drag himself to his feet, he gave Ena a cheeky grin. 'I'm a bit short of the old readies. I'll be your slave forever if you buy me a pint.'

Ena laughed. 'I'll buy you two if you get a move on.' It was the first time she and Artie had shared a joke since Sid's death.

Ena was working, had been for a couple of hours, when Artie arrived the following morning. She had returned the files she had gone through to their correct boxes, writing *checked* in black ink on them and had stacked them on top of the cupboard that ran along the wall. At the far end of the table were the remaining dozen files, their empty boxes under the table.

'Good morning,' Ena called as Artie passed her heading for the kitchen and the kettle.

'Not so loud, Ena, please.' He scowled. 'There are several wee workmen with hammers and drills in my head.'

'Can't take it, eh?'

Artie turned and gave her an exaggerated frown. 'Do you ply all your young gentlemen friends with alcohol?'

Ena laughed. 'You didn't have to stay on, you could have left when I did.'

'I felt obliged,' he called from the kitchenette. 'One of the chaps was a friends of Sid's. Coffee?'

'I'd love one.'

'Where are we up to with this lot?' Artie asked, bringing in Ena's coffee and setting it down on the table in front of her.

'The boxes behind you contain the files where the person investigated is either dead or was found not guilty. Those we've already been through can go back into storage. The files Sid had marked as less important, I went through this morning but found nothing. These,' Ena pointed to the files on the table, 'I haven't looked at yet. If we get a wriggle on we should get through them by the end of today.'

Artie took a file from the top of the pile and sighed. 'I suppose the sooner we get it done, the sooner we'll know who Collins is.'

'And when we do, we will know who killed Sid,' Ena said.

Stimulated by endless cups of coffee, Ena and Artie worked through the morning. Because of Artie's hangover the wireless wasn't blaring out. Only the sound of paper being shuffled, the occasional tut, and the thud of empty boxes as they were thrown under the table could be heard. By lunchtime the pile hadn't reduced as much as their hard work deserved. Artie stood up and stretched.

'Why don't you go out and get us fish and chips, Artie?'

He at first turned up his nose, 'The old tum does need something inside it, and I could do with some fresh air, but fish and chips, again?'

'Yes. There isn't time to make anything for lunch and the chip shop is near. Here.' Ena gave him the money. 'I'll keep going until you get back.'

Ena watched Artie put on his overcoat and wind his old university scarf around his neck. He saluted her, his way of saying thank you because she was buying him food. A minute later a draught swept into the office when the street door opened and closed. Artie had gone.

Ena yawned. It was after one. She had been working since six. Leaning back in her chair she closed her eyes. Her stomach rumbled. The last time she had eaten was at five o'clock that morning, and then it was only a slice of toast. She felt dizzy with hunger, opened her eyes and sat up straight. Turning in her chair Ena looked at Sid's empty desk. 'Who the hell is Collins?' she asked out loud. To go to the trouble to perforate a piece of paper with the name Collins and wrap it in glassine to keep it dry meant Sid knew he was in danger.

Praying that Sid hadn't suspected he was going to be killed that night, Ena suppressed her tears. Why hadn't he told her he was in trouble the day he worked from her flat? He must have known something was wrong. She could have helped him. If only... Words used too often and often too late.

Another cold draught shook Ena from her sad contemplation. 'Mm, something smells good,' she said, as Artie returned with a bag of fish and chips. He put it on the table and went into the kitchen, bringing with him a bottle of tomato ketchup.

They opened the newspaper and tucked in with their fingers. Artie smothered his chips in ketchup, sucking the red sauce from his fingers every now and then. When they had finished eating, Ena took the greasy pages of newspaper to the dustbin and Artie made them each a cup of tea.

They giggled like teenagers elbowing each other out of the way as they washed grease and newsprint – and in Artie's case, tomato ketchup – from their hands in the small sink.

Afterwards, their hunger satisfied, they drank tea and discussed where they were in the search for Mr Collins. Or, as Ena pointed out, the person they were looking for could be Miss Collins. When they had finished their tea they went back to work.

The pile of boxes decreased, the mound of folders diminished, and the day drew to a close.

'So,' Ena said, 'that's it!'

'Yep!' Artie agreed.

'And no sign of Mr or Miss Collins.'

Artie looked around the room, then suddenly stopped. 'We've missed one,' he said, pointing to a red folder on top of the furthest cabinet.

Ena went over and retrieved it. 'This is the Voight file,' she said, returning to the table. 'I've seen it. Have a look.' She threw it onto the table. 'It makes very interesting reading.'

'Good God, the cheeky mare. Does she really think she can get away with using your name and ID?'

'She did, until now,' Ena said. 'And, thanks to Sid remembering he'd seen the name Dudley – my maiden name – somewhere in the cold case files, Henry and MI5 will now have to take our investigation into Frieda Voight seriously.'

Artie yawned and rubbed his eyes. 'All right if I go? My eyes feel like they're on stalks.'

'Yes. Go home and get some sleep. I'll see you tomorrow.'

Dragging on his coat, Artie called, '*Mañana*,' and left.

Ena got up from the table and walked over to Sid's desk. 'Who is Collins, Sid?' she asked, lowering herself onto her dead colleague's chair. 'Who the hell is Collins?'

TWENTY-TWO

Sitting at Sid's desk, Ena's eyes settled on his dictionary. It was a beautiful old illustrated Collins. 'What the–?' Her heart pounded as she got up. Taking it from the window sill, she carefully opened it. She leafed through the pages. Between the first and second page of the letter E was a narrow strip of paper. She took it to her desk, tore a page from her notepad, picked up a pencil and wrote down the letter E. A second slip of paper was at the beginning of letter I, a third in N, fourth in P and the fifth in S. She leaned back in Sid's chair and read, 'E I N P S?' Then, a sneaky smile crept across her face and she punched the air. She was looking at an anagram of the word Spine.

Ena laughed out loud. 'You clever old thing, Sid. Collins is not a person at all, it's your beloved dictionary.' Sid had used the dictionary almost every day for something. When he wrote a letter he would look up the definition of an ordinary word to find a lesser known or more unusual one. He never needed the dictionary to do a crossword, but he did occasionally look a word up to confirm he had put in the correct answer. He often quoted from it, correcting Artie if he used a slang word from a song he'd heard on the wireless. 'That word is not in the Collins dictionary, Artie my boy,' Sid would say. And he would berate him if he used his precious dictionary without asking.

Ena closed the dictionary and turned it until its spine was facing her. Holding it firmly with her left hand, she ran her right thumb down the side of the dictionary's spine. Her heart beat fast with excitement as her thumb moved deftly over something small and hard that was hidden beneath the book's fabric. Using both thumbs she gently eased it up until she saw the bow of a key. Applying a little extra pressure, the blade appeared and the dictionary gave up its treasure. Ena gasped with surprise. With the key was a green ticket. She turned the ticket over in her hand. Printed on one side were the words Waterloo Station, Left Luggage. On the other side, in Sid's handwriting, 1/6d will solve the case.

Ena was laughing, enjoying her find, when she heard a noise. She caught her breath and, keeping an eye on the office door, slipped the key, the paper with the anagram, and the left luggage ticket into her skirt pocket. She put the dictionary back on the window sill between Erskine Childers *The Riddle Of The Sands*, and *Red Harvest* by Dashiell Hammett. After putting Sid's chair under his desk she ran to the lavatory where she kept a cricket bat. Armed with the bat, ready to swing it at whoever was outside, Ena crept to the door.

A loud knock made her jump. She opened the office door a couple of inches and peered out. She shivered. It was cold in the covered courtyard. With the bat raised above her head, she crossed to the street door and yanked it open. 'Inspector?'

DI Powell looked at the cricket bat on her shoulder and fabricated a frown. 'Do you always greet visitors wielding an offensive weapon?'

'It's for self-defence. I wouldn't beat anyone over the head unless I had to,' she said, laughing. 'But seriously, you can't be too careful these days, not at this time of night.' She was rambling. 'Never mind that. What can I do for you, Inspector?'

'I don't want to delay you leaving, but we've had a break-through in the death of your colleague, I thought you'd like to know.'

'You're not delaying me. And yes, I would like to know. Come through.'

Ena closed the outer door and led the inspector into the office. Pulling the door shut, she shivered again. 'It's cold,' she said, rubbing her hands together. 'This old building wasn't designed to house humans.' She realised she was rambling again. 'Sit down, Inspector.' Ena returned to her chair. 'You said you have some news?'

'When the pathologist first examined Mr Parfitt, because of the damage done when his head hit the railings under Waterloo Bridge, it wasn't easy to ascertain the actual cause of death. Today, however, he found a circular wound that could only have been made by a bullet.'

Ena struggled to speak. 'Sid was shot?'

'Yes. When I saw the pathologist this morning he was adamant that it was a bullet that killed Mr Parfitt. So, I took the forensic chaps back to Waterloo Bridge and we found this.' He took an envelope from his pocket. Ena put out her hand and the inspector dropped a small calibre bullet into her palm.

Shock took her voice. Her mouth fell open as she turned the compacted piece of brass over in her hand.

'It is the pathologist's opinion that your friend was shot and then thrown over Waterloo Bridge.'

Ena wiped tears from her eyes with the back of her hand.

'If it's too upsetting, Mrs Green—'

'It isn't. Go on.'

'The pathologist believes Mr Parfitt was shot in the ear at close range and the bullet went through his brain. In his opin-ion, because there was no visible entrance wound, he believes Mr Parfitt's murder was an execution carried out by a profes-sional killer.'

Ena had suspected Sid's killer was a professional, but shot through the ear? 'So Sid would have been dead before he hit the railings on the embankment?'

'Yes. The pathologist said he would have died the instant he was shot. He wouldn't have known anything about falling from Waterloo Bridge.'

'I suppose that's something,' Ena said, doing her best to see something positive in Sid's death. 'Thank you for taking the time to come and tell me, Inspector. I appreciate it. I'm happy, if happy is the right word, that Sid didn't suffer. His mother and sister will be too. Do they know yet?'

'If it isn't too late, I'm going to see them when I leave here.'

'I don't know which is worse, a son committing suicide, or being murdered.' Ena put her hands palms down on the desk, a gesture that she hoped would convey to the inspector that she wanted to go home. It didn't.

He looked at the stack of boxes on his left. It had become a habit that, at the end of each day, boxes that were finished with were turned to face the wall. That way any information written on them wouldn't be seen by late or early visitors. Ena hadn't long finished looking through the last of the files when the inspector arrived. She followed his gaze. From where he was sitting stencilled information, names and dates – and block capital letters saying Top Secret were not visible.

Ena didn't want the inspector looking too closely at the boxes and tried to distract him. 'My colleague Artie will be relieved to know Sid didn't suffer when I tell him tomorrow.'

'I'm sure he will,' the inspector said, still not showing any signs of leaving.

'If that's all, Inspector, it has been a long day, I should like to go home.'

'Yes of course.' The inspector started to get up, and then sat back down. 'Could Mr Parfitt's death have anything to do with the work you do for the Home Office?'

'I... I suppose it's possible.'

'And what exactly is it that you do here, Mrs Green?'

'As I said before, we–' Ena stopped. She had decided she could trust the inspector at the mortuary. She wondered why she hadn't told him the truth about the work they did then. She took a breath. 'I'm in charge of a small team of investigators who look into cold cases.'

He tilted his head, as if to hear her explanation better. 'Cold cases?'

'Yes. Cases that were brought against people during the war that weren't investigated. Files opened on people suspected of a range of crimes that have gone cold, if you like. Our job here is to go through the files to make sure they were satisfactorily dealt with at the time. If they weren't, or if the original investigator missed something, we start a new investigation.'

'In which case the cold file becomes a hot file,' the inspector said.

Ena laughed. 'Something like that. Most of the old cases are people suspected of spying for Germany in the war. The Cold Case department was set up to research people who were thought to have been involved in betraying the county, espionage, or committing treason.' Ena sighed. 'You won't believe the number of anonymous citizens who reported innocent people in the war because they looked or sounded different.

'Take this box of files,' she said, her hand on the lid, 'until today it contained a dozen cases that had been left open, cases that may or may not involve the Russians. Most of them have now been examined and closed.

'There are some cases, not many, but some, that overlap. The military are calling the race for nuclear power the cold war. There's a race on between us, the Americans and the Russians, to see who can make the biggest and most destructive nuclear bomb first.' Ena shook her head. 'If anyone involved in nuclear research or development is suspected of working for the Russians, their details are sent here for us to investigate.'

'And are there any?'

Ena laughed, nervously. She thought of Frieda Voight and said, 'We haven't found any – yet. There are other investigators in other locations who do similar work but we're given what military intelligence call Code Ones. High security cold cases.'

'Part of what you told me was true, then?'

'Yes. I didn't tell you everything because our work here is top secret. I needed to get to know you first, make sure I could trust you.'

Inspector Powell looked at Ena with surprise. 'And do you... trust me?'

'Yes. I do.'

The policeman gave her a friendly smile. 'The feeling is mutual, Mrs Green, which is why I told you about the pathologist's findings. I trust you will keep the details of Mr Parfitt's death to yourself for the time being?'

'Of course. And, please keep what we do here to yourself, Inspector.'

'Goes without saying.' The inspector stood up.

Ena stood too. She wondered whether she should share finding the key and the left luggage ticket with him. She decided not to, for the time being. 'Inspector, would you keep the name Collins to yourself too, just until we find out who he is.'

'Of course. There's something else,' the inspector said.

'Yes?' Ena's heart sank. She was desperate to go home, to get some sleep, and stifled a yawn.

'I have a friend who was at Hendon with me. When we left, I joined the Met and he joined the Sussex Constabulary. He's the head of Brighton's murder squad at John Street.'

Ena wondered what the Inspector from Brighton had to do with her, *unless Mac Robinson's death was on his patch.*

'He's an expert when it comes to guns, especially small arms like the one used to kill Mr Parfitt. So, I sent the bullet down to him when the pathologist told me your colleague was shot in what looked like an execution. It came back this afternoon. The bullet that killed Mr Parfitt was fired from the same gun that killed McKenzie Robinson, the Director General of MI5.'

'McKenzie, shot?' Ena's head began to spin. Her legs felt as if they would buckle beneath her. She caught hold of the desk to steady herself.

'Because Director Robinson was the head of MI5 and Mr Parfitt's work – your work – is connected to MI5 through the Home Office I thought you'd like to know.'

'Yes, of course. I didn't know the director well.'

'Well enough to visit him in hospital.'

The DI's attacking tone caught Ena off guard. 'Yes, I er, visited him the week before he died.'

'And well enough to go to his funeral.'

'You sound as if you're accusing me of something.' The inspector didn't reply. 'Director Robinson was my husband's boss. Henry wasn't able to go to his funeral so I went in his place.'

DI Powell gave Ena a knowing smile. 'Thank you, Mrs Green, I thought it would be something like that, but I needed to hear it from you.

'Director Robinson's death certificate says he died from an intracerebral haemorrhage. It may stay on record as a stroke for ever. But I assure you, the director was executed in the same way, and with the same gun, as your colleague, Sidney Parfitt.'

TWENTY-THREE

Ena took the key and the ticket she'd found in Sid's dictionary to Left Luggage on Waterloo Station. 'Excuse me,' she said to an elderly man sitting on the other side of a glass hatch. 'I'd like to collect a–' What was she there to collect? She said, 'bag.'

'Got a ticket?' The old man asked, hauling himself out of his seat with a groan. 'Arthritis,' he complained.

Ena handed him the ticket and the old man turned it over and laughed.

'I remember this. It's the one and six written on the back that's reminded me. I'd not long locked up. The fella that left it said it were important. Life and death he said. So, I took the case for him and he gave me ten bob for my trouble.' The old man gave Ena a tobacco stained grin and ambled off. A minute later he returned with an old brown briefcase that looked like a doctor's Gladstone bag. 'That'll be one and six, then.'

Ena delved into her handbag, took out her purse and extracted two shillings from it. She waved away the sixpence change, lifted the briefcase from the ledge of the hatch, thanked the man and left. She felt vulnerable leaving Waterloo Station with Sid's briefcase. It wasn't until she was in the Sunbeam and the case was locked securely in the boot that she felt safe.

Driving home in a state of nervous excitement, the last thing Ena thought about was the green surveillance car. But there it was. Parked in its usual place. 'Damn!' She drove on. She looked in the rear-view mirror. It was nowhere to be seen. She relaxed a little. Where to now? She couldn't go home; the goon in the Austin Cambridge would see the case when she took it from the boot – and it wasn't safe to take it to the office.

She turned into Stockwell Gardens and found the perfect place. With not a green car in sight, Ena drove into the car park at the rear of their local pub, the Hope and Anchor. The sign in the window said Bed and Breakfast – Rooms Available.

The landlord knew her. He had been in military intelligence during the war and wouldn't question why she wanted to rent a room for a couple of hours. He didn't.

Returning to her car she took her scarf and gloves from the passenger seat and locked the door. Standing for some time at the back of the Sunbeam, Ena looked for movement in the cars already in the car park. Then she watched the entrance. Satisfied that she hadn't been followed, Ena unlocked the boot and took out the briefcase. She walked swiftly to the pub's back door, went up the stairs to the first floor and into the first bedroom.

Shortly afterwards, the landlord arrived with a mug of coffee and a plate of ham and pickle sandwiches. 'A drop of Teacher's,' he said. Winking at Ena he put a tumbler with a good three measures of whisky in it on the table. 'Let me know if you need anything else,' he said, and leaving the remainder of a quarter bottle of Scotch, he left.

Ena took off her coat and dropped it on the bed next to her scarf and gloves. She went over to the small table, to the mug of coffee and took a sip. It was hot and strong. She was hungry and took a bite of a sandwich.

With the second sandwich in her hand, she kicked off her shoes, and picked up the briefcase. Eyeing it with suspicion, Ena put down the sandwich, and took the key from her pocket. Holding her breath she inserted the key into the brass keyhole. She turned it, pressed, and the finger-lock sprang open. Lifting the leather flap, her stomach churned in anticipation of what she might find.

From the first compartment in the briefcase she pulled out a large brown envelope with *1936* written across the front. Extracting a number of 8 by 10inch type written pages from the envelope, a hand-written note fell to the floor. She picked it up.

Dear Ena, I hope one day you will be able to forgive me. Perhaps when you read the contents of this envelope it will go some way to helping you understand why I did what I did.

Ena didn't finish her sandwich. Instead she picked up the glass of Scotch, sat back and began to read.

I wasn't always a grey man; someone who went home every night to a pipe and slippers; a bachelor who lived at home with his elderly widowed mother. I was once a good-looking chap with an eye for the girls – and the girls liked me too. I had a sharp wit and an inquisitive mind. I wanted to know everything and experience everything. That need in me contributed to my downfall. I understand moderation now. My God ,Ena, I am now the most moderate man I know. But in those days, university at the age of seventeen – a year younger than my peers – I had it all, or thought I did. I had a rotten childhood. Not that I'm apportioning any part of the mess I find myself in directly to my parents. Some chaps had a far worse time of it than me and got on with it. No, my parents did their *poor* best. Perhaps I should explain...

TWENTY-FOUR

My father was in the Diplomatic Corps stationed in Berlin and, not that you would know it now, my mother lectured in Politics and Humanities at the University of Berlin. Mother hated Berlin with a passion. She disliked most things. She didn't appear to like my father much, or me for that matter. When I was twelve and my sister eight, my mother walked out on my father. I didn't mind her leaving him. They hadn't spoken for months, unless it was to argue. What I did mind was, she returned to England, took my sister with her, and left me in Berlin with Father. My father was wrapped up in his work and Mother didn't have a maternal bone in her body. I suspect she only took my sister to England with her because of how it would look if she hadn't. I didn't know that at the time. I thought she had taken my sister because she was a good child and left me behind because I was bad.

My parents were ambitious and enormously competitive. It's no wonder their union was an unhappy one. But I digress. My father was too busy to look after me, so I was packed off to boarding school outside Berlin on the River Spree.

While I was there I met Walter Voight. It was spring half-term and my father was going to be away on business. Walter said I could spend the half-term with him and his family and I jumped at the chance. That was the first time I met Frieda and it was love at first sight, for me at least. I was thirteen, a teenager, and thought I was a man. In Frieda's company I felt like a man.

Walter and Frieda were an odd brother and sister. She was very possessive of him. Of me too. It was as if we were both *her* friends. For the most part the three of us had fun together. It was around that time that Walter introduced me to Hitler Youth. We now know how insane those chaps were, but when I was a kid at school, it all seemed a bit of a hoot. I didn't understand what the youth movement stood for. I was just happy that at last I had friends; I belonged.

As I said, Walter introduced me to his chums and they became my chums. They told me Adolf Hitler was going to get Germany out of the financial trouble it was in. They said he was going to make the Fatherland great again, that the Jews where crippling the country, and they were going to be sent to live and work elsewhere. Elsewhere? I was naïve, or stupid – or both. Either way, I didn't understand the implications of any of it, then.

In 1930 my father became ill with a nervous disorder. He told me it was because he had been over-working. I didn't realise how serious it was until he resigned from his job. That year we returned to England. Father and Mother lived in the same house, our original family home, but kept to their own quarters as Father called them. Again I felt like the odd one out, the one in the middle who was always in the way.

My parents lived together for appearance's sake. My sister didn't understand, or if she did she didn't care because both my parents lavished attention on her. I, on the other hand, was lonely. I had experienced friendships and love and was utterly miserable. I couldn't wait to get to university and live in rooms.

I was President of the Students' Union in my final year at Cambridge and a regular contributor to the Varsity newspaper. Because I had a knack of writing witty narrative and of spicing things up by exaggerating slightly, the readership grew. When I finished at Cambridge, in the summer of thirty-five, I got a job with *The Times*. My mother was amazed and for the first time in her life she bragged about me to her friends. I think she was actually proud of me. I didn't tell her that I was only a court reporter and the job was as boring as hell, because I was enjoying being the favoured child for a while. Again, I digress.

I can't remember how it came about, but after I'd been working at the paper for about six months I told my section editor that I hoped one day to be a foreign affairs correspondent. He laughed and said I would have to wait ten years. However, it wasn't long afterwards that I was writing up a story about a shoplifter, or some other petty criminal, when the editor-in-chief called me into his office.

He was reading a file. I could see my name on it. He put down the first page and I saw my mother and father's names on the second. His eyebrows rose. That Father had been in the Diplomatic Corps and Mother had lectured at the University of Berlin had obviously impressed him.

I told him I was educated in Berlin – at a boarding school – and that I spoke fluent German.

He had my *curriculum vitae* in front of him, so he already knew I had been a reporter and editor of the Varsity newspaper at Cambridge.

When he said my section editor had told him I wanted to be a foreign correspondent, I could only nod. The nerves in my stomach were as tight as violin strings. He said he liked a man with ambition. I tried to smile at the compliment, but the muscles in my face had turned to stone. Then he said my wish may be granted sooner than I thought because the eleventh Olympic Games were being held in Berlin next year.

The editor-in-chief sat back in his plush leather chair and
stared at me. I didn't know what to say. My throat felt like a
desert and my breathing came in short excited gasps. My mouth
was open, so I closed it. I tried not to show too much enthusi-
asm, but I could hardly believe what I was hearing. He slapped
his hand on the file and said he would get his secretary to sort
out the practicalities. He said with forty-nine countries
competing she would need to find me a hotel pretty soon, or
there would be no room at the inn. He laughed at his own joke.
He said I would not be residing in a five-star hotel off Alexandr-
erplatz, but I'd be down-town with the other newspaper men.

He asked me if I had any plans for next August. I said I
hadn't but if I had I would un-plan them. He put up his hand,
shook his head slowly, and said I mustn't do that because that
kind of thing would get me noticed. It was then that I tuned in
more seriously. He said it was vital that I treated the Olympics
like any other sports tournament. He told me to read every
sports report I could find, especially the reports covering the last
two Olympic Games, because when I got to Berlin I had to be a
hard-nosed sports hack – a fanatic.

I needed to be there in advance of the opening ceremony, to
get acclimatised the chief said. He also said he was waiting for
information on the political situation with Herr Hitler before he
agreed for me or anyone from *The Times* to go. He warned me
that Hitler was stirring up trouble and asked me how I felt
about going into a situation that could be dangerous. He said as
a newspaper reporter the danger will be less, but said I needed
to be fully aware of the potential danger.

The chief stood up and looked me in the eyes. My cue to
leave, I thought, and held his gaze. I got to my feet. I wanted this
job. I wanted it badly and I told him so. I reiterated that I was
fluent in German and told him that because my hair was fair
and my eyes blue, I was often taken for German when I was at
boarding school. I could see by the frown on his face that I

hadn't impressed him by telling him what I now realise he already knew. I put out my hand to let him know I was leaving. He shook it and told me we'd speak again nearer the time, and said the conversation we'd just had was strictly between the two of us.

Three months later, the longest three months of my life, I was called into the editor-in-chief's office again. He said, as for *The Times* foreign correspondent reporting on the eleventh Olympic Games, the job was mine and the flight to Berlin had been arranged. His secretary had organised my press pass and ticket, which I would be given in due course. He also told me I would be briefed by someone from military intelligence before I left.

REPORT WHAT'S HAPPENING IN THE GAMES – AND WHAT IS BEING SAID IN THE BARS AND RESTAURANTS ABOUT THE NAZI PARTY – TO RUPERT HIGHSMITH. IF YOU HEAR ANYTHING AT ALL ABOUT CHANCELLOR HITLER GET IT TO HIM IMMEDIATELY. (A DROP WILL BE ARRANGED BEFORE YOU LEAVE.) KEEP YOUR EYES AND EARS OPEN. FREQUENT THE PLACES STUDENTS, MILITANTS, EXTREMISTS AND RADICALS DO. USE BITTE AND DANKE – AND THE GREETINGS TOURISTS USE – BUT DON'T LET ANYONE KNOW YOU SPEAK THE LANGUAGE. THEN YOU WILL HAVE THE ADVANTAGE. YOU WILL KNOW WHAT THEY ARE SAYING, BUT THEY WON'T KNOW IT, SO THEY'LL SPEAK FREELY IN FRONT OF YOU.

DESTROY THIS NOTE. ENJOY THE GAMES.

BERLIN 1936

TWENTY-FIVE

DAY ONE. ARRIVE IN BERLIN

(Sidney Parfitt's Journal 1936)

Waiting to leave the plane I had a feeling of foreboding. It was like going back to my childhood. I was overwhelmed by sadness and loneliness, which was what I had felt for most of my young life. I was excited too. For the next few weeks I would be working alongside journalists from all over the world. A year ago at Cambridge I played at journalism, scraping together enough news to fill the Varsity newspaper. Now, I am a foreign correspondent; a sports reporter in Berlin about to cover the eleventh Olympiad. A wave of trepidation surged through me. I loosened my tie and the collar of my shirt.

Wide eyed and with all memories of my childhood consigned to the back of my mind, I gazed in awe at the modern steel structure: the hangar arch of the new Tempelhof Airport, the biggest building I had ever seen. I wondered if I was in the right country, let alone city, but then this was the dream child of Chancellor Hitler and his Nazi party. The aeroplane hangar that had purported to be an airport when I left Berlin as a teenage boy had been replaced by a magnificent building shaped like a giant eagle made of natural stone cladding, steel and glass.

'Papers?' an airport official, the height and size of a heavyweight boxer, bellowed.

I was miles away, lost in the splendour set before me. Fishing in the inside pocket of my overcoat I provided the official with passport, travel permit, job permit and ID from *The Times* that said Sports Journalist to cover the 1936 Olympic Games. He waved me on. I smiled at him. He didn't smile back.

A low truck with an equally low but long trailer carrying cases sped past. I felt a riptide of air whoosh past me and I darted out of its way. A sign saying luggage collection had an arrow pointing to the left and I followed it with the rest of the aeroplane's twenty passengers.

I found my cases quickly and set off to passport control. A burly man with staring eyes, his face devoid of any emotion scrutinised my documents and asked me half a dozen times why I was in Berlin. Pretending not to speak the language other than schoolboy German, I kept pointing to the pass that said Olympic Games – Journalist. Unimpressed, the oaf patted me down, stuck his plate of a hand between my legs, and then rummaged through both of my suitcases. Finally he gave me a sharp nod. So much for paying my sister a small fortune to iron my shirts, I thought, as I stuffed them back into my cases.

I nodded back at him and hauled the bulging cases to the new arrivals hall where a sign said *Wilkommen zu Berlin*.

'Sidney?' I jumped. I could have sworn I heard someone call my name. I looked around but saw no one I recognised. It couldn't have been me they were calling, no one knew I was in Berlin except the paper's editor-in-chief and my section editor. It had taken an age to get a visa. Confirmation of my secondment to Berlin had been a last-minute thing. I only knew myself a few days before I left.

'Sidney?' Someone called again. '*Hier drüben*. Over here,' they shouted, as I headed towards the taxi rank.

I turned again, this time irritated because I was eager to get to my hotel. Then I saw him. I had to look twice. To my astonishment, standing and waving at the front of the crowd of people waiting at the arrivals barrier, was Walter Voight, my old school chum, with a beautiful woman on his arm.

'Good Lord!' I said, heading over to him. 'It's Walter, isn't it, Walter Voight?'

'Yes,' he said, ducking under the barrier and flinging his arms around me. When he had finished hugging me, he took a step back and looked me up and down. 'You look well, my friend. You look very well.'

'I am... Thank you,' I said, as the gorgeous creature that had been standing with Walter arrived at his side.

'You remember Frieda, my sister?'

'Frieda?' Frieda smiled at me and put out her hand. When I took hold if it, I thought my heart would burst out of my chest. It was love at first sight all over again. I managed to say hello and I shook her hand for rather longer than was necessary or decent. One look at Frieda Voight and I was back to being an adolescent school boy. I cleared my throat.

'It's good to see you, Sidney Parfitt,' she said huskily.

I stood in the middle of Arrivals with my mouth open. 'I think I am in shock,' I said, when I eventually found my voice. I muttered something indistinguishable which ended with, 'to see you too.'

Frieda laughed. 'Come, Sidney, let us go to your hotel. We will first drop off your cases, and then we will go out and have fun.'

'My car is parked twenty metres away,' Walter informed me, as we left the airport, 'I shall fetch it and you will wait here with Frieda,' he said, taking my cases out of my hands as if he was lifting two feathers. Leaving me blushing and tongue-tied with Frieda, he strode off to get his car.

Walter returned in a sporty looking red and black Horch cabriolet. My suitcases were on the front passenger seat, so Frieda and I scrambled into the back. The car was even smaller on the inside than it looked from the outside. Frieda sat sideways on to me, her skirt rucked up above her knees. She looked at me shyly.

I felt positively prepubescent. I could feel wave after wave of embarrassing flushes creeping up my neck. Walter swung the car round a corner and Frieda fell against me. Her scent, strong and cloying, went to my head.

'To a bar or to your hotel?' Walter shouted above the roar of the car's engine as he accelerated.

'I had better sign into the hotel first and take my cases to my room,' I shouted back at him. I needed to change too. I had been in the clothes I was wearing since early morning.

'The hotel it is then!'

'This looks like a bit of a dive, as you say in England,' Frieda said, as her brother brought the Horch to a halt outside the Olympisches Gästehaus off Potsdamer Platz.

'My paper booked it,' I said, 'I might find somewhere else later, but it will do for now.'

Frieda was right. From the outside the hotel, or rather guest house, did look a bit of a dive. Part of its facade was stucco and part was brick. It had obviously been damaged in the war and repaired, or rebuilt, on the cheap – a total contrast to what I had seen of Berlin so far. The windows were tall and narrow. They looked as though they hadn't been cleaned for a decade. They probably hadn't.

Walter and Frieda followed me into the hotel's foyer. The inside was no better than the outside. Wall hangings covered what I expect were cracks, the grey tiled floor needed a good scrub and the receptionist looked a hundred years old. I signed the register and was given a key. The woman clicked her fingers and a scruffy looking bellboy appeared.

The boy carried my suitcases up narrow stairs with a threadbare carpet to the first floor – there was no lift. After unlocking the door and placing my cases inside the room, he touched his hat. I had no small change and gave him a mark. He made no attempt to leave, but stood and stared at the coin in his hand.

'Oh, Sidney,' Walter teased, putting his arm round the bellboy's shoulders. 'You have given the young man far too much money. He will now never let you out of his sight.' The lad smiled, said *Danke,* and bowed.

Aware that I shouldn't appear too fluent in front of the boy, I mumbled a half-hearted *Bitte,* without an East German accent.

Frieda, first to enter the room, looked down her nose. 'This room is not good,' she said. 'You must come and stay with Walter and me. He must, mustn't he, Walter?'

'Of course. We have a spare room that you would be welcome to use.'

'Oh,' I said, 'I'm only here to cover the Games. I'll be at the stadium all day and writing my reports for the paper at night, I shall hardly be here.'

'You are very welcome,' Walter said.

I looked up at the ceiling, as if I was giving the Voights' offer some thought, and then said, 'Thank you, it is a very tempting offer, and one that I'll take you up on when I'm not being paid to report on an event as important as the Olympic Games.'

'You could stay on when your assignment is finished,' Walter said, 'and we will paint Berlin red.'

Frieda leaned against me. 'Please... come and stay now,' she said, pouting. God that perfume was strong.

'Frieda, this is my biggest overseas assignment to date. Reporting on the Games will give my career a real boost.

There's another chap from *The Times* staying here. He's a seasoned journalist. I don't want him reporting back that I went AWOL the minute I arrived.'

'Of course you must stay here,' Walter said. 'Now, change your shirt and let us get out on the town.'

Frieda crossed to the window and looked out onto Potsdamer Platz long enough for me to splash water onto my face and change my shirt.

I had no intention of having a late night, or drinking too much. I would hang up my clothes and set up my writing station on the small table beneath the window later.

Talking animatedly, as you do, not listening because there was so much to tell each other – and gossiping like old friends, which we were – the three of us set off for the bright lights of Berlin.

TWENTY-SIX

FIRST NIGHT. OUT ON THE TOWN

'Riesling, Frieda?' Walter said as the barman approached. His sister nodded. 'And beer for you and I, eh, Sidney?'

I started to laugh. 'The first time I tasted beer was at your parents' house. Do you remember?'

Frieda wrinkled her nose. 'Yes. You were sick.'

'*Hundeelend*,' I said, 'as a dog.'

'Your German is still good, Sidney, but you do not sound like a Berliner anymore. You sound like a German farmer speaking the equivalent of pigeon English,' Walter said, as the barman placed a glass of cold beer in front of me. 'Has it been so long that you have forgotten the years you lived here?'

'There wasn't much call for me to speak German with a Berlin accent when I went back to England. When I knew I was coming over this time, I bought a German dictionary, but it didn't give any information on accents.' Frieda laughed. 'All right, you two, give a chap a break. I'll get the accent back now I'm here,' I said, 'I'll be speaking like a Berliner in no time, pronouncing "Ich" as "ik" and changing "au" to "oo."'

Walter burst out laughing and slid a glass of schnapps along the bar towards me.

'No schnapps for me,' I said.

Frieda sidled up to me and, taking Walter's glass of schnapps from the bar she drank it down in one. Still looking at me she picked up my glass and offered it to me.

'Oh, all right then, one can't hurt.' I tipped the glass upside down and choked. I had forgotten how lethal the stuff was.

Walter slapped me on the back. 'Are you all right, my friend? That was wicked of you, Frieda,' he said, and slapped me again.

Shaking my head as if to shake the spirit out of me, I said, 'I must go, I need to eat something.'

'We will come with you. There's a little place nearby. *Wurst und Kartoffeln.* You used to love Berlin sausage and thick-sliced fried potatoes, Sidney.'

'I did. But when we've eaten I will have to go back to the hotel. I need to set up my typewriter in preparation for the start of the Games, and I need to make notes on Berlin. Background stuff, you know?'

'Then come on. What do we wait for?'

With their arms around me, Walter on one side and Frieda on the other the Voights' marched me out of the bar.

The restaurant was a bit Oom-pah-pah for the Voights, I thought. Loud music and raucous laughter. But I soon realised it was a meeting place for patriots. Each time someone entered the restaurant a group of men at a table near the bar stood up and gave the straight arm salute. "Heil Hitler!" The more they drank the louder they became. One of the men heaved himself up onto the table and began to sing the Olympic Anthem, while the others marched round the table. After the first verse the man on the table's friends joined in. By the end of the song everyone, including Walter, was on their feet singing and raising their glasses to Chancellor Hitler.

Later that night, at the hotel, while I waited for the receptionist to finish with an elderly woman asking for directions to somewhere she was visiting early the next day, I heard Walter humming the Olympic Anthem.

He asked me if I had learned the *Olympische Hymne,* that Richard Strauss composed?

I said I hadn't and Walter looked aghast.

'Then Frieda and I will give you a rendition.' He cleared his throat.

'No! Please, my friend, not tonight. I shall get kicked out of the hotel before I've unpacked my cases.'

'Should I whisper the words to you?' Frieda purred, her breath hot and sweet in my ear.

She was so close her hair tickled my nose. She was toying with me. I was enjoying the attention, but I was exhausted. I had drunk too much alcohol. And, although we had specifically gone to the restaurant to eat, no food had materialised. Having been awake for more than twenty hours, I was dropping on my feet. 'Really, both of you, it has been a wonderful–'

Freda said, homecoming. I was going to say night, but for the sake of friendship, I agreed with her. Putting on my serious face, I told them I was meeting up with a fellow journalist for breakfast in – I looked at my wristwatch – four hours. I needed to go to bed.

Walter playfully pushed me away saying we will sing loudly on August the first, and again when Germany wins all the gold medals.

I left the Voights in the lobby of my hotel and staggered upstairs to my room. My suitcases lay where the bellboy had left them. I groaned. Why had I let Walter and Frieda ply me with so much booze? I drank more beer tonight than I had ever done on a bender at Cambridge and that's saying something. Whole weekends were a blur in those heady days.

I forced myself to take my typewriter from its case and set it up on the table by the window, putting two notepads and a selection of pencils and pens next to it. Shirts trousers and jackets I hung on coat hangers and placed in the wardrobe, underwear and socks I left in the case. I took out my tennis shoes and a pair of smart shoes that I had brought to wear with the only decent suit I possessed and dropped them in the bottom of the wardrobe.

That done, I eased off the shoes I'd worn all day, took off my underpants and, sitting on the side of the bed, peeled off my socks and rubbed my aching feet. The shirt I had travelled in and the one I'd been wearing, I dropped in the case. Tomorrow I'd ask reception about laundry. My trousers and jacket, which I'd also had on all day, I took off and folded over the bottom of the iron bedstead. They would need pressing before I wore them again.

Exhausted and woozy from too much strong German beer, I fell backwards onto the bed.

TWENTY-SEVEN

DAY TWO IN BERLIN

I was woken by loud banging. Hardly daring to open both eyes at the same time, I squinted through one and eased myself up on my elbow. I looked around the room. I recognised it, just. I listened for a second. The banging had stopped, thank God. My head was splitting. I lowered it slowly back onto the pillow, rolled over and reached out to pull up the counterpane. I almost leapt out of my skin when the banging started up again. This was a noisy hotel. I groaned. I might give Walter's offer of a bed serious thought. With my head still pounding I buried my face in the pillow.

'Parfitt?'

'Shit!' I sat up with a start. The bloody breakfast meeting. I swung my legs over the side of the bed and grabbed my watch from the bedside table. 'Shit!' I said again. I'd overslept. 'Won't be a second,' I shouted, hauling myself off the bed. As my feet hit the floor waves of pain shot through my body like lightning rods, exploding when they reached my head. With my eyes half shut I stumbled to the door and pulled it open.

'Highsmith?' I said, unable to hide the surprise in my voice when I saw my contact in Berlin outside my bedroom door.

'Good God, Parfitt, you look rough.'

'However I look, I can assure you I feel ten times worse,' I said.

'Mmm... Good idea, tying one on last night. Fits right in with your new persona,' Highsmith said laughing.

I scrunched up my shoulders to help them cope with the weight of my head, and whispered, 'How do you make that out?'

He said I would get a reputation for being a soak. And, even better, I'd get myself noticed.

I thought getting noticed was something I was not supposed to do because of the government thing.

Highsmith said I didn't want to be noticed asking too many questions, but when a chap has had one over the eight and he's a bit out of it, people ignore him and say things that they wouldn't ordinarily say in front of him: things they definitely would not say in front of a foreigner.

I tried to nod that I understood, but it hurt too much.

'So, tell me about last night?' Highsmith said, suddenly.

I told him how I had met an old friend and his sister from my school days here in Berlin and, although I said I needed to prepare for reporting on the Olympics, they wouldn't listen.

'Walter Voight is a strong personality.'

'He is– How did you know I was with Walter Voight?'

'I saw you in the lobby of the hotel with him and his sister late last night. But never mind that. Shake a leg and put some clothes on, old chap. Looking at your tackle is putting me off my breakfast.'

I covered my genitals with cupped hands as best I could, and went to the sink. I watched Rupert Highsmith out of the corner of my eye as he wandered over to the window and looked down at my makeshift desk. He tapped several keys on my typewriter with his middle finger, and then flicked through the empty notepads while I washed and dressed.

To distract the nosy blighter I told him I didn't know

whether I'd be able to eat anything as I felt queasy. He said, with authority, that a cooked breakfast was what I needed. He also said I wouldn't get one in the hotel and suggested we go to the *Frühstücksbar*.

Bleary eyed I followed him to the Breakfast Bar. We had no sooner sat down than a waiter came to our table with a pot of coffee. The strong roasted smell made me heave. My head began to pound again. I asked for a glass of water. The waiter nodded, poured Highsmith's coffee, and then moved deftly through the tables, returning a few minutes later with a pitcher of water and two glasses.

I gulped down a pint of water straight off. I was dehydrated, the reason for my headache.

The waiter returned with a shallow bowl with half a dozen chunks of bread in it. I took one before he had placed it on the table and waved away the dish of pale oily looking butter that he held out to me.

'How well do you know Walter and Frieda Voight?' Highsmith asked, apropos of nothing.

'I was at boarding school with Walter in 1926-27 and I spent a few half-terms and a summer holiday at the Voight family home.'

'And that is when you met Frieda?'

'Yes. Is that a problem?'

'On the contrary, it could be a real help.'

'What do you mean?'

'You don't know do you?'

'What is this, Highsmith, Twenty Questions? For God's sake, man, what don't I know?'

'That Walter Voight was a fully paid up and very enthusiastic member of the Hitler Youth movement.'

I waved the suggestion away with my hand as if I was swatting a dozing fly. 'That's old hat!' I told him. 'It was nothing serious. He was a boy playing at being a man. He wanted to

impress his sister. He wanted to impress me. That business was
a long time ago. He'll have grown out of it now.'

'He was a member until he was eighteen,' Highsmith said,
nonchalantly, 'Frieda was in the BDM – the girls' wing of the
Nazi Party.'

I hadn't considered that possibility. As for Walter, I'd
assumed Nazism had been a flash in the pan thing.

Highsmith laughed. 'Walter Voight has definitely not grown
out of it. He has embraced everything about Nazi ideology;
expansionism, fascism and Nationalism. But that's beside the
point, or rather it is very much to the point where you're
concerned.'

I had no idea what Highsmith was on about and gave him a
quizzical look.

'You, my dear fellow, are going to enjoy every minute you
spend with Herr Voight.'

'If Frieda is with him that won't be difficult.'

'I'm being serious, Parfitt!'

'All right, old man, keep your shirt on. What about my
Olympic itinerary?'

'Leave that to me. The thing is, Parfitt, you understand the
lingo, so you'll do more good getting in with the Voights again
and keeping your ears open.'

'Am I no longer reporting on the Olympics?'

'Of course you are, but Baldwin is keen to appease Hitler.
The man's a ticking time bomb. Baldwin is doing his best to
accede to his demands. As far as the Games are concerned, you
write your reports, I'll read them and if there's anything I think
would provoke Hitler I'll amend it before I wire it to London.'

I didn't think much of that, and told him so. He said that is
how it had to be, because I was answerable to military intelligence, he was answerable to the PM.

I asked him whose name would be on the by-line and he
said, fifty-fifty, give or take. According to Highsmith I didn't

have to be at the games all the time. When he was at the stadium, I was to be drinking in local bars and cafés listening to what the Berliners were saying about Adolph Hitler. When I was at the Games, he would be in the cafés and bars. Because I was fluent in the language it was important that I should spend time being sociable.

'So the next time Walter and Frieda Voight invite you to go out with them, you go. Is that clear?'

'Crystal. They're picking me up tonight. We're going to a cabaret club.'

'Lucky sod! You get to watch totty dancing, while I write up your Games' itinerary.'

TWENTY-EIGHT

As Highsmith was writing up my itinerary, I bought a copy of the *Berliner Zeitung* from the newsagent next to the hotel and found a café. I felt better after I'd eaten, but I daren't risk drinking anything stronger than coffee. I like black coffee, I drink rather too much of it at home, but German coffee is extremely strong and my stomach, although much better, wasn't up to the thick strong stuff Berliners enjoy. I asked the waiter for milk in broken German. And as I'd hoped he asked me if I was English. I told him I was – loudly, as foreigners do – saying I was here for the Olympic Games.

I took my English German dictionary from my pocket, for show, followed by my press card and decided I'd practice my German on the waiter. 'Journalist,' I said, *'Hier – zu – Olympis-chen – Spielen.'*

'Gute. Ja, gute.' The waiter went off laughing at what I thought was my poor attempt to speak his language, which apart from a Berlin accent was grammatically correct. *'Englischer Kaffee,'* he said, wrinkling his nose when he returned with my milk.

I drank my coffee in the busy little café, ordered a second

cup and listened in on the various conversations around me, some funny, some serious, some quiet and secretive, others loud and proud. A man and woman on the table next to me argued about the woman's mother who had come for a weekend some months before and was staying until after the Olympics because she wanted to see *the beloved Chancellor*. The man said his mother-in-law had already cost him a fortune and now he had to buy her a ticket for the Olympic Games just so she could see Hitler.

His wife told him he was wrong. She said he didn't have to buy one ticket, he had to buy two, because she intended to go to the Games with her mother.

Their table was pounced on the minute they vacated it by two young men who looked to be in their early twenties. The more flamboyant looking of the two wore a shirt with a design similar to Scottish paisley-tab in pink and gold. He took a handkerchief from his trousers pocket and blew his nose. His face was blotchy and his eyes red and swollen from crying. The soberly dressed man, in a dark grey suit and white shirt, advised his friend to be more careful approaching men in the future. He said he had got away with it this time, but with so many Nazis in the city, he may not be so lucky next time.

Be careful? Got away with what? I reached for my newspaper with the intention of hiding behind it to hear their conversation better. The suited man saw me looking at them, glared at me, and proceeded to speak in a hushed voice.

The rest of the morning I spent retracing the steps of my childhood. The blocks of concrete apartments where I had lived as a child were as boring now as they had been in the Twenties. In contrast, The Brandenburg Gate, was as impressive as ever. And the newly built government buildings and modern structures in the city of Berlin were nothing less than cosmopolitan. With the city full of foreigners, there to watch the Games, it gave Hitler the perfect opportunity to demonstrate to the world, how efficient Nazi Germany was.

I curtailed my sightseeing when I found a pleasant little café-come-bar in a side street off Potsdamer Platz and had lunch. I ordered a ham sandwich and a small beer. My newspaper was dog-eared. I straightened it out as best I could, read a couple of lines and consulted my dictionary.

The waiter arrived and topped up my coffee. 'Excuse me, sir, there is a student,' he pointed to a young man sitting on his own a couple of tables along. 'He is the son of a friend of mine. He is studying English at university, I'm sure he would be more than happy to help you read your newspaper.'

I looked across and smiled. I had a thousand political opinions when I was a student of his age. He could be just the sort of young chap to give me the information I needed. I thanked the waiter, saying someone to interpret for me would be a great help.

The waiter curled his forefinger in the young man's direction and he left his seat for the one next to me.

When he sat down, I saw he was wearing black pencil round his eyes and rouge on his cheeks.

He asked me if he could be of assistance translating words I didn't understand.

I groaned inwardly. Get out of this, I thought. I told him I spoke some German, enough to get around the city, order from menus in cafés and I knew the German for bier, which made him giggle. 'It's understanding what people are saying when they speak to me that I find difficult. If they speak quickly, or with a dialect, I'm lost.' My turn to laugh, as if I was embarrassed. I was.

'It can be difficult,' he said. 'It is the same with me and English.'

I nodded. 'And when a foreign language is written down, as

it is in newspapers, I am often at a loss to understand whole sentences.'

'It is the structure of the sentence that is difficult for English people,' he explained, 'and the grammar.'

The boy was right. Not that I'd ever had a problem with German grammar. The waiter was attending to a customer at a nearby table. He glanced over and raised the coffee jug, so I asked the boy if he would like coffee.

'*Ja*,' he said, '*danke*,' and tapped my knee.

I flinched and moved my leg. Had inviting him to drink coffee with me given him the wrong impression? Surely not. He was a friend of the waiter, a student at the university. I brushed away my doubts and motioned to the waiter to bring more coffee.

He told me his name was Heinz – which I don't suppose for a second it was – and he said he had no interest at all in politics, the Olympic Games, or Germany's ugly Chancellor.

That was that then, I thought. I'm not going to get any useful information out of *Heinz* to pass on to Highsmith at breakfast tomorrow. I finished my coffee and refused a refill from the waiter who hovered around us with a cynical grin on his face. He knew the type of man he'd introduced me to. Fine, no tip for him. I let a couple of tiresome minutes pass, while the boy batted his eyelashes at me and made lewd comments, and when the waiter arrived to refresh his coffee I put my hand over the cup.

'Do you really think I am stupid?' I dropped a note on the table. 'This will more than cover the food and drink that I have consumed. I bid you farewell,' I said, in my best German.

The boy looked frightened and asked me if I was sure I wouldn't like a more *intimate* service.

I said no and glared at the waiter who had tried to pimp him. I left feeling worried for the boy and the life he was leading and anger for the smirking waiter. I found another bar a couple of streets away. *Die Begrüßungsbar* was more like it. It was a family type of place. I performed the newspaper routine again and in no time men and women nodded and smiled, and asked me if I was an overseas visitor in Berlin for the Olympics.

I told them I was the sports journalist for *The Times* newspaper in England, which sounded impressive and was half true.

Some people told me where they came from in Germany. A couple spoke English. One chap said he worked for Mercedes Benz and had been to England several times on business. He was a Berliner, although he spoke English better than some English people do.

I left the café and strolled through the streets. I shivered. Not from the cold – it was still July – but from seeing fear on the faces of people I passed. There was a disturbing, sinister, feel to Berlin now. People went about their business as they always had. But instead of looking up and smiling, they kept their heads down, afraid to make eye contact with someone. These days they didn't know who that someone might be.

A sudden feeling of horror engulfed me. Hundreds of blood red flags lined Pariser Platz. The Nazi flag flew from every shop doorway and upstairs window. Dense white circles with black swastikas at the centre, like the wings of vampire bats, hung from municipal buildings. They stole the sunlight from the windows of office workers. And they stole my love for Berlin.

The Nazi emblem, once an ancient Indian symbol of spirituality, was for us in the west a symbol of good luck until in the 1930s the Nazis took it as the symbol of their Aryan race identity. I can't remember the last time I cried, but today I cried for this magnificent city that I had once called my home.

I got back to the hotel in time to have a quick wash and change my clothes. My suit had been pressed and the shirt I'd travelled in had been laundered. I washed and dressed with time to spare before I needed to be in the foyer to meet Walter and Frieda.

I looked out of my bedroom window. Dusk was falling. Lights twinkled as they came on one at a time in the city's Mitte district. I looked to my left, to where beyond the rooftops was the Brandenburg Gate and Pariser Platz. My heart grew heavy thinking of the time in 1933 when the Nazis had burned books they had banned because they considered them degenerate. Someone had laid ashes in the same spot today. I wondered whether they had been put there by Nazis to make sure the citizens of Berlin toed the line, or by students in protest of what happened in '33 – and to remind the good people of Berlin if they didn't sit up and take notice, it could happen again.

TWENTY-NINE

KABARET – WHAT A NIGHT

I am writing this entry of my journal twenty-four hours after the event. I was in no fit state to write a shopping list when Walter and Frieda brought me back to the hotel last night.

They picked me up at seven; Walter looking magnificent in a black suit, white shirt with a stiff collar and dicky-bow, and Frieda in a petrol blue silk dress that didn't so much hug, but slid over her slender figure so closely a chap daren't look.

The name of the club we went to was Unterwelt. The band played Hot Jazz, the latest music craze to come out of France – and before France, America.

'Uneducated Berliners,' Walter scoffed, motioning to people dancing. 'They are calling this *jazz* the essence of the era's modernism, a move towards equality and emancipation.'

'You don't look happy about that,' I said.

'A passing phase,' he sneered. 'It will end, as all meaningless pastimes end, when the Chancellor has this club and all the others like it burned down.'

'Ouch. That's a bit harsh, isn't it?' I challenged. Walter ignored me. The look on his face as he watched the dancers having fun was one of disgust. Was Walter showing his true colours at last?

The band played traditional jazz peppered with swing and blues with the occasional 1920s rag-time song thrown in – and the dance floor heaved with bodies dancing a kind of freestyle.

Frieda was swaying to the saxophone and tapping her feet to the beat of the drum so I plucked up the courage and asked her to dance.

Walter immediately stepped between us. I thought he was going to hit me. Instead he grabbed Frieda by the arm and said she was not going to dance to such unsavoury music. The two of them left and I followed.

When we got to the car Frieda shrugged her shoulders in a devil may care way. I pretended I hadn't seen her and opened the passenger door of Walter's car for her to get in. She raised her eyebrows and smiled at me. 'Coward,' she whispered, as she rubbed against me to lower herself onto the seat. I shut the door on her teasing laughter.

I was first to the bar when we got to a club called, Stiefel und Kabarett. Walter wanted a large bier and Frieda asked for wine before leaving to find a table.

Walter came with me to the bar and carried his own beer across the smoke-filled room to where Frieda sat talking to two rather flamboyantly dressed men and a woman.

'Come,' she shouted, 'there is plenty of room.'

The men pushed and shoved each other, giggling, and Walter and I sat down in a space that was hardly big enough for one, let alone two people. The woman stood up, kissed Frieda, and said she must go because she was the next act.

Frieda leaned into me, her lips close to my ear, her breath warm on my neck. 'You'll love Tilly's act. She is very good,' she purred.

I closed my eyes and inhaled. There was that perfume again. 'Oh, good,' I said, lifting my glass to my mouth and taking a drink. My mind wasn't on Tilly or her act at that moment, it was on Frieda, her perfume, and the seductive way she rubbed against me when she whispered in my ear.

Slowly the lights went down until the room was in darkness. There was silence. Then, as the curtains in front of the stage started to open, a spotlight shone on the lovely Tilly singing Marlene Dietrich's, "Ich Bin Die Fesche Lola".

When her set came to an end, Tilly stepped daintily from the stage helped by two male dancers who looked more like all-in wrestlers. Letting go of their hands and shooing them away – all part of the act – she sashayed over to where we were sitting. She was humming a tune that I didn't recognise adding words like *liebe, liebling*, and then, *nehmen Sie mich*. Love and darling are words used in most love songs, but not take me.

'I dedicate my next song to this wonderful Englishman,' she shouted, her arms outstretched towards me while looking around the room. The audience applauded her, she called for a spotlight, and a beam of light picked me out of the gloom and cigarette smoke. She ordered me to stand up, which I did. Unable to look into the light I raised my right arm and waved to what was now *my* audience. Then the spotlight left me and settled on Tilly. I sat down and Tilly began to sing a Marlene Dietrich song called, "In Liebe Fallen".

When she finished singing, Tilly lifted up her numerous skirts to show a pair of bright red satin cami knickers, stockings and garters. She turned round and with the microphone between her legs she wriggled and writhed. The audience went wild. She then swung back to me, took my beer out of my hand, put it on the table and straddled me.

Leaning backwards, she shimmied and arched her back like a limbo dancer until her head was almost touching the floor – and all the while she sang, "Falling In Love Again". I grabbed her hips for fear gravity would get the better of her and she would slip and crack her head on the ground. After the first verse she pulled herself up until she was sitting. With practiced movements, slow and suggestive, she stood up. Her legs still gripping my thighs, she put the microphone on the table next to my drink, took my hands and thrust them at her crotch.

Leaning over me she growled, 'Do you want this, Sidney?'

To my surprise, I felt a bulge beneath her satin knickers that a rugby player would have been proud of. I say to my surprise. I was surprised that this particularly beautiful creature was a man, not that the act was erotic. I'd known about places like this since adolescence. Hard to avoid when you go to an all-boys boarding school.

I pulled my hands from between her legs and in the spirit of the show threw my head back and laughed.

'Hey!' I shielded my eyes, as the stark blue light from the flash bulb of a camera exploded so close to my face it temporarily blinded me. 'Don't waste your bulbs on me. Save them for someone prettier, like this beautiful lady,' I said, as the androgynous Tilly, who looked like Greta Garbo but had the thighs of Herbert Runge, extracted her long legs from mine.

I shot Walter a worried look and flicked my head in the direction of the chap with the camera who was high-tailing it across the dance floor. I didn't want to see my ugly mug plastered all over the *Berliner Morgenpost* or the *Zeitung* in the morning. Nor did I want some bloke following me back to the hotel one day, knocking on my door, and blackmailing me. I'd probably have to pay him a fortune to stop him flogging the photograph to an English paper. There were so many British reporters in Berlin covering the Olympics he would be spoiled for choice.

Walter returned with the film. 'He is what we call a chancer. He takes photographs of people in clubs and bars, and tells them for five Reichmarks he'll develop the photograph for them. Tourists are often eager to take home a memento of their night out in the seedier side of Berlin and as it costs so little they hand the money over. The photographer asks for an address to deliver the photograph and by the time the person gets home, or back to their hotel, they have been burgled. In this man's case, he was happy to take twenty Reichmarks for the film and move to another bar.'

Walter unwound the length of film and let it snake to the floor. I picked it up from among the dog ends and stuffed it into my jacket pocket. The photographer may have taken chances, but I wasn't going to take any.

We laughed and carried on drinking, and in the morning I met Highsmith for breakfast. I told him about Walter's outburst and I agreed that I would learn more about National Socialism and Nazism by spending my evenings with him and Frieda than I would trying to make new friends, which, with the exception of the guy who worked for Mercedes Benz, had only got me into trouble.

THIRTY

THE 11TH OLYMPIC GAMES, AUGUST 1, 1936

Sidney Parfitt, *The Times*.

To get to the startlingly modern Olympic stadium, the 325 acre sports complex five miles west of Berlin, meant me getting up so early there was little point in me going to bed. It also meant I couldn't have my usual meeting with Highsmith over a leisurely breakfast. Instead, I gabbled what I'd learned the night before while eating a piece of dark rye bread.

I set off early to find my seat in the press area and was in good time to see Chancellor Hitler and his top Nazis arrive. Word that Hitler was in sight rippled through 110,000 spectators already seated.

Men, women and children had been herded into the stadium like cattle and ordered to take their seats well in advance of Hitler's arrival. Head held high, giving his trademark straight armed salute and looking ahead, Chancellor Hitler arrived standing up in the front of a large black open-top Mercedes. An entourage of dozens of military cars with faithful Nazi party members followed.

Highsmith was at the Brandenburg Gate and told me later that Hitler had stood, statuesque with his arm out straight from the shoulder, all the way to the stadium. Highsmith lost him after Pariser Platz but there were a couple of reporters stationed en route, and I was at the stadium to report on his arrival.

Hitler arrived to thousands of people screaming and chanting his name. It was incredible to see. Officials opened hundreds of cages and thousands of homing pigeons flew free. Before he mounted a raised seating area built specially for the Chancellor and other dignitaries, a small blonde-haired child – chosen for her Nordic looks no doubt – toddled up to Hitler holding a bouquet of flowers, handed them to him and curtsied.

August 2nd was Highsmith's turn to cover the Olympics. It was my day for frequenting bars and cafés to see what I could learn. After an early lunch in the city, I took a short cut to a quaint coffee house that I'd spotted earlier in the week. As soon as I opened the door I was overwhelmed by the rich, slightly smoky, invigorating aroma of freshly made Berlin-style coffee. The tables were covered in embroidered cloths, there were fresh flowers in the window and at the end of the counter, and a pretty dark haired woman in her middle years greeted me with a welcoming smile as I entered.

I ordered coffee and ogled a glass cabinet where a dozen cakes and pastries were displayed on white doilies, and asked for a slice of strudel.

When the woman brought my coffee and cake, I said, 'I am surprised you are not busier, with so many tourists in Berlin for the Olympics.'

'We are a little off the beaten track here,' she said, pouring my coffee.

I expect she was right. But I still thought it strange that a café as pleasant as this one didn't have *any* customers. 'Do you not have a local clientele?'

The woman suddenly looked terrified. 'Are you from the authorities, sir?'

'Me? No,' I said, wondering what on earth had given her that idea.

'Then why do you ask such questions?' The woman had changed from being friendly and welcoming to guarded and almost hostile.

Not wanting to offend the woman, I took my ID and press pass from the inside pocket of my jacket and showed them to her. I told her I was a journalist and I was here to cover the Olympics for an English newspaper called *The Times*.

She looked at my ID, nodded and apologised, before leaving me to my refreshment.

I sipped my coffee and picked at the edge of the pastry with the fork. I'd lost my appetite, but I ate the delicious sweet for fear of offending the woman further. I looked across the room to where she was standing. She was behind the counter gazing out of the window. I could sense this woman's pain. Something was very wrong. I finished my coffee and wandered over to her.

'I would like another cup of your delicious coffee, madam.'

'Of course!' She turned her back on me and stepped further along the counter to the stove where a pot of fresh coffee was percolating. 'If you go back to your table, I will bring it to you.'

'Thank you.' I did as she said and from a distance watched her wipe tears from her eyes. When she picked up the coffee pot, I picked up my pen and pretended to make notes. 'It is good coffee,' I said when she arrived at my table.

She smiled and nodded. 'Thank you.' Her eyes were still moist. Without realising it I had upset this woman. 'If I have offended you, madam, it was not intentional.'

She shook her head. 'You have not, sir.' She took a deep breath, looked at me but didn't speak.

I started to get up and she stepped back, so I sat down. 'What is it, madam?'

'I should not be speaking to you; to a stranger. These days a misinterpreted word, a word that is misunderstood, or said without thought can get a person... killed.' She looked at me, her eyes dark with fear searched mine, as if she was looking into my soul. 'If you were working for the Nazis you would have arrested me by now, marched me out of here for all my neighbours to see, and I would be on my way to prison.' She dropped into the chair opposite. 'Frankly,' she said, her sad eyes brimming with tears, 'I do not care anymore.' But she did care because she looked over her shoulder at the door.

'Would you like me to lock it, madam?'

She hesitated for some moments before taking a key from her apron pocket. I made my way across the room to the glass panelled door. After locking it, I pulled down the blind. I looked back to where she was sitting. Satisfied that no one could see us from either of the bay windows or the narrow windows at the side of the door, I returned to my seat and gave her back the key.

She clasped her hands around it as if it would reinforce what she wanted to say. 'You are my first customer in months.' She must have noticed the look of surprise on my face. 'I expect you wonder why I keep the café open.'

'It is up to you, madam, it is your business.'

'No. It is not. This café belongs to an old friend of my husband who has disappeared. His wife asked me to run it for him until he returns.' She shook her head. 'I fear he will never do that.

'My husband and I had a restaurant on Potsdamer Platz. It was very popular.' The lines on her forehead smoothed and her face softened. 'My husband was a magnificent chef. The cuisine was International. Our clients enjoyed French dishes, Italian,

some Jewish dishes – in the way the food was prepared – and of
course traditional German fare.'

Her face lit up remembering that time. 'People came from
all over Berlin and from much further away to eat there.' Tears
filled the woman's eyes again, and she looked away. 'Enjoy your
coffee, sir,' she said, pushing herself up from the table.

I put my hand out and touched her arm to stop her from
leaving. She froze. The look of terror on her face made me with-
draw my hand at once. 'I'm sorry I startled you. Please do not be
frightened. I was going to ask why you and your husband left
the restaurant on Potsdamer Platz.'

She gave me a nod and sat down again. 'Brownshirts began
to frequent the restaurant. One or two in the beginning, but
then more. They were loud, rude to other customers, and disre-
spectful about my religion, about Jews. The more brownshirts
that came, the more our regular customers stayed away. In the
end it was just them. Thugs in brown shirts paving the way for
their Nazi masters.'

'And your husband?'

'Beaten and left for dead one night in the alley behind the
restaurant. A Jewish couple found him, or he would have died
in the alley. They took him to hospital, but he died waiting for a
doctor to see him. So, when I was told to leave or go the way of
my husband, I left. I was allowed to take my clothes and some
photographs of my family, but not my jewellery, silver, or the
paintings my husband had collected over the years. They did
not allow me to take anything of value. Friends I knew from the
Synagogue, which had been burned down the year before,
helped me to move my few belongings into the small apartment
above the café. It is furnished. Not in the way my own home
was, but–' She looked up, and then broke down and sobbed.

I left the table and went to the counter, to give her some
time to cry. I took a cup and more milk and returned to her. I
poured her a cup of coffee and topped up my own.

'You must think me ungrateful,' she said. 'At least for the time being I have a roof over my head. What will happen after the Olympic Games?' She clicked her tongue. 'Who knows. Thank God for the foreign visitors. It is only because of them that my windows and doors are not daubed with hate slogans. Until recently, shops owned by Jewish people, "*untermenschen*" subhuman beings, as the Chancellor calls us, were made to paint yellow stars on their doors. And shops owned by what he calls his Aryan people – blonde blue-eyed Germans – had signs in their windows saying, *Achtung Juden* – No Jews here.'

At six o'clock I said goodbye. I hadn't asked her her name. I hadn't told her mine. I said I would be at the Olympic Stadium the next day, but would see her for lunch the day after.

She said she would make me a Viennese dish, Fiaker goulash with Sacher sausages. 'It was a speciality of my late husband, and very popular at the restaurant on Potsdamer.'

I told her I looked forward to sampling the special dish, shook her hand and said goodbye.

She let me out of the café and closed the door. I looked over my shoulder and waved. She smiled and waved back. In the four hours I was in the café that was the only time I had seen her smile.

Walking back to my hotel, I ventured down some narrow alleys and passageways and saw for myself the hatred that was painted on the doors and windows of the Jewish residents who lived there.

THIRTY-ONE

I can't remember a time in my life that I had been more pleased than I was when I was called back to England, the weekend after the Games ended. Walter and Frieda wanted me to stay on, go to the country with them, but I'd had enough, seen enough. There had been too many changes since I was last there. It wasn't the Berlin I'd grown up in, not that I expected it to be. The German capital now boasted the most modern airport, railway station and trains, the widest highways and the most efficient automobiles. Berlin, with its new buildings built with Nazi money, wanted to show the world that it was not only the most magnificent city in Germany, but it was the most magnificent capital in Europe. However, to attain such status, the new regime had breathed hatred and fear into many of its citizens. Places change, evolve, grow, but generally people stay the same. The Berliners of my youth, neighbours, shopkeepers, my parents' colleagues and friends were open and friendly. Not anymore.

I called to say goodbye to the Jewish woman at the café. It was in darkness. I put my hand up to shade my eyes and leaned my forehead on the glass of the bay window. The tables had been stripped of their embroidered tablecloths, and chairs had been turned upside down and stacked on top of them. The stove was still there but the coffee maker had gone, the shelves were empty and there were no cakes on the counter. *Achtung Juden!* was written on the mirror that ran the length of the wall and a yellow star had been painted on the door.

I was sickened by what I had seen. I told Walter about the woman and the Nazi slogans. I criticised Hitler and his Nazi party, but Walter praised him and extolled the party's virtues.

My cases were packed and I was ready to leave when Highsmith turned up with my plane ticket home. Someone was taking my place as an observer, he told me. Someone not from the paper, but from British Intelligence.

I was happy to give up my dream of being a foreign correspondent when the war began. In my naivety I thought by fighting the Germans I might make amends for my folly in Berlin. I had my papers to join up, but it was not to be. Because I was fluent in German I was sent to the south coast and ended up plotting the routes of the Luftwaffe and translating what the pilots reported back to Germany. I enjoyed the job and although I wasn't on the front line, I felt I was doing something worthwhile.

After a couple of years I was told that, because I had an analytical mind and a talent for solving puzzles and crosswords, I was being sent up to Beaumanor in Leicestershire. It was while I was there – and by a total fluke – that I met Frieda Voight again. The landlady of the digs where I was staying made her lodgers sandwiches for lunch. It was part of the rent agreement, as was a cooked meal in the evening. The day I saw Frieda was the only day the landlady hadn't made me lunch.

It was in the summer of 1943. I was in the cafeteria having something to eat and Frieda walked in. I couldn't believe my eyes. She was laughing and chatting with one of my female colleagues. I left my seat and, on the pretence of wanting a hot drink, headed towards the tea and coffee counter. Once I was in the queue I made for the exit, but I wasn't quick enough, Frieda had seen me. She stopped dead in her tracks, as did I. A red rash of embarrassment crept up my neck, as the colour drained from Frieda's face.

She flung her arms around me and whispered, 'I work for the British government, do not say anything.'

I was so shocked I wasn't able to say anything. Anyway, I did as she said. I kept shtum, while she told everyone that we'd met while I was at school with her brother, how Walter and I had become best pals, and how I had spent several weekends at their family home – all of which was true. She omitted to say it had happened in Berlin, thank God. Some of my colleagues knew I had lived in Berlin as a child, but I didn't want to blow her cover, so I changed the subject from our school days to our adult life and said we hadn't seen each other for some years, which was also true.

I learned from one of my colleagues that Freda King, as she was then called, worked for an engineering company making components that she delivered to Beaumanor regularly. That was my cue to ask for a transfer. I was at Bletchley Park for the last couple of years of the war and, apart from a short spell at Scotland Yard, I became a pen-pusher with the Home Office.

I didn't see Frieda again until a few months after I started working for the HO. I had almost forgotten about her. I say almost. No one could completely forget about Frieda Voight. I hadn't been there long when I bumped into her and Walter. It was no coincidence that they were walking down King Charles Street at five thirty, when most of the HO staff were leaving for the day.

Walter, doing the old pals act, armed me into the nearest pub. And Frieda, playing the role of old flame, pretended she still cared for me. I no longer cared for her. I didn't even like her. They were friendly to begin with, then Walter told me he wanted me to use my position in the Home Office to destroy their university and war-work records. Frieda gave me the names that she and Walter had used and the company names and addresses where they had worked.

I told her I wouldn't be able to get hold of her national insurance and tax information, and she laughed at me. She opened her briefcase and when I saw the contents I almost died.

The case was full of photographs and newspaper cuttings of me in Berlin. The first photograph was taken by *the chancer*, as Walter had called him, at Stiefel und Kabarett. It was of me and Tilly the cabaret dancer. It shows Tilly as a boy exposing himself to me – which he didn't do – and me laughing as if I'm enjoying it. I shook my head in disgust and glared at Walter with contempt. He told me I was naïve if I thought he had given me the real film that night.

There's one where I'm sprawled across a bed naked with a man sleeping next to me. That also didn't happen. None of the sordid nonsense happened, even though the photographs say it did. There's another with my head tilted back, laughing. It was taken at the cabaret club. I was laughing; we all were. But instead of the picture showing all of us having fun, I am on my own surrounded by naked women drunk and high on drugs. Again, that never happened. I stopped looking when I saw a head and shoulders shot of me marching with a crowd of Hitler Youth thugs.

I attended some rallies, yes, but I was working undercover for military intelligence in the guise of reporting on the march for *The Times*. It was my job to record the events. But, as you will see, there are several rallies where a photograph of my face has been placed on someone else's body, or where I am wearing a black armband with a swastika on it. Walter said if I destroyed their war records, they would give me the photographs and wouldn't bother me again. So, I put in a request to Director Robinson to follow up a lead I'd been given about a couple of suspected German agents and he gave me permission to see their records.

Within a month, except for a Top Secret file that MI5 had on the Voights, which they knew I didn't have clearance to see let alone destroy, Freda and Walter King didn't exist.

PS I wrote the account of my time in Berlin, and my association with Walter and Frieda Voight, some years ago as an insurance policy. At the time Walter was threatening to blackmail my father about an indiscretion that happened while he was a diplomat in Berlin. I never found out what the indiscretion was, but it must have been bad because my father retired from the corps and left Berlin very suddenly. When Father died the indiscretion died with him, and so did Walter's threat of blackmail. I thought I was free of them because discrediting Father no longer mattered. How wrong I was.

After Walter died, Frieda left me alone. But soon after you saw her in Oxford Street she began blackmailing me again. She said she would tell you about my past if I didn't do as she said. I told her to do her worst because I no longer cared. But when she started threatening my mother and sister, I had no choice but to do as she said.

At first I was no more than a courier delivering letters of introduction and forged documents. (Sorry about your diving licence.) Then she told me to destroy her cold case files. I had no intention of doing that, but I had every intention of finding the files that would send Frieda Voight to hell. I am in no doubt that she and Walter will seek me out when I get there.

I am no longer doing Frieda's bidding, Ena, but I'm staying close to her because I am certain she is not working alone. I'm absolutely positive that someone at Leconfield House is pulling her strings. Someone above suspicion who I believe killed McKenzie Robinson. I expect whoever it is will kill me when I'm no more use to them. Ah! I can hear your key in the lock. To be continued, Sid.

PPS Reading through what I've already written, I think I've covered everything except to tell you how sorry I am. I'm sorry about many things, but none more than letting you down, Ena. One lie led to another lie, and then another – and so it went on until there was no going back. When I was asked to go to Germany and report on the 1936 Olympics in Berlin, I was over the moon. To be an overseas correspondent for The Times *was my dream. Moreover, to work for my country – for military intelligence – I was honoured, proud that such trust had been put in me. Then Walter Voight happened. Bumping into him at the airport was not a coincidence. That he knew the time I was arriving in Berlin when I myself had only known a few days, had to have come from the people who had sent me. I was set up and I fell for it.*

It is too late now for regrets, though I have many: The betrayal of my country is the greatest of them. I don't have an actual account of the work I did for the intelligence service, as my superior – my handler – Rupert Highsmith took it from me at the end of each day, but I kept a record of sorts in a Journal. You may already have read it. If you have, remember that I was young and stupid, swept off my feet by love and false ideals.

Do with this letter, the newspaper cuttings and my journal, what you think best. But, before you expose me as a traitor, which is no less than I deserve, would you go to my house and tell my mother and sister. It would break Mother's heart if she read it in the newspaper.

I need you to know something, Ena. If I could go back to my thirteen-year-old self for one moment, it would be the moment that I replied to Walter Voight when he asked me to spend the weekend with him and his family. At that moment I would say, no!

ENGLAND 1958

THIRTY-TWO

The late morning sky had grown dark; rain clouds blocked out the pale winter sun. Ena had switched on the overhead light, but it still hadn't been bright enough to read small type-print on thin paper. Apart from which there was a lot of it. Ena rubbed her eyes and blinked rapidly to renew the tear film.

Returning the papers to the briefcase and locking it, Ena tightened the screw cap on the small bottle of whisky, which was still three-quarters full, and dropped it into her handbag. She was going to pay for the whole bottle so why leave it.

Where to go from here, she wondered. She could take the case back to Waterloo Station, leave it with the old man in the left luggage department until she needed it again. But then he might become suspicious. He had taken ten shillings from Sid and seen him write one and six on the claims ticket. He had probably seen the rest of the message about solving the case. If he had, he may give the suitcase up if anyone offered him money for it. Ena checked herself. The old man was probably as honest as she was. Even so, bags and cases could be lost or misplaced in station left luggage departments. She decided not to risk it.

Was there anywhere to hide the case at home? She wasn't ready to involve Henry and MI5 in her findings, so she would have to hide it well. But if she took the case home, would she get it from the car to the flat without the green-car-man in the Austin seeing it? Ena doubted she would. And she couldn't leave it in the boot overnight. Green-car-man might decide to search the car. No. It would be safer at the office than at home. But there wasn't anywhere to hide it from Artie. He was bound to want to know what it was. And, while she was certain he wasn't working for anyone but the HO, she didn't want to share what Sid had specifically written to her with him, not yet at least. She needed to do a lot more digging before she shared Sid's outpourings with Artie or anyone for that matter. For a start she needed to find out who was pulling Frieda Voight's strings. Sid was convinced someone at MI5 was controlling Frieda. If Sid was right, Ena owed it to him to find out who the person was and expose them.

Pushing her feet into her shoes, Ena put on her scarf, coat and gloves. Straightening the bedspread where her coat had lain, she picked up her handbag and Sid's case, went downstairs to the outdoor drinks entrance, where she knew she wouldn't be seen by customers in the bar, and paid for the refreshments and the use of the room.

With Sid's briefcase back in the boot of her car, Ena set off for the only place she could be sure the case would be safe.

'Hello, Mrs Green. This is a nice surprise.' Detective Inspector Powell looked down at Sid's briefcase. 'Here on business, are you?'

'In a way, yes,' she said, lifting the case onto a chair. 'I was wondering if you would look after this for me?'

'Take a seat.'

Ena returned the case to the floor and sat down. 'It's a bit of an imposition, but it won't be for long. A couple of days at the most.'

'Why can't you keep it at the office in Mercer Street?'

'It isn't secure. Nor is my flat. They were both broken into recently.'

'Anything taken?'

'No.' Before the DI had time to ask more questions, Ena continued: 'but I'm being followed and there's round-the-clock surveillance on my flat.'

DI Powell sat bolt upright. 'Are you sure?'

'Yes, but that isn't why I'm here. MI5 are aware of it and they're keeping an eye on me. It's likely to be the contents of this case that my tail is after, not me personally. Which is why I don't want to take it to the office or my home.

'The other thing – and this may sound strange to you – I don't want to have to explain what's in the case to my husband, Henry, or to my work colleague, Artie. So, would you look after it for me?'

DI Powell got up from his chair, walked round his desk and perched on the corner. He looked at the case, and then at Ena. 'What's in it?'

'Papers, mostly. An envelope containing a letter addressed to me; a journal recording events during the 1936 Olympics in Berlin, newspaper cuttings and photographs.'

Frowning, the inspector returned to his chair. For several minutes he sat with his elbows on the desk, his hands clasped together as if he was in prayer, and his eyes closed. When he opened his eyes he said, 'No.'

Ena caught her breath. She had been sure Inspector Powell would help her. It took her a couple of seconds to recover from the shock of him saying he wouldn't. She was near to tears and swallowed hard. 'I'm sorry, I shouldn't have asked you.'

'No, you shouldn't. Not without showing me the contents of the case.'

Ena picked up the case. 'I thought you trusted me,' she said, unable to hide the sarcasm in her voice. 'Clearly you don't! I'm sorry to have bothered you. Good bye.' She fled across the room to the door.

'Ena? Stop! Let me explain.'

Emotionally drained, Ena shrugged her shoulders. 'There's no need. I understand.'

'No, I don't think you do. However much I would like to help you by looking after your case, I can't without looking in it. It could contain a hidden device for all I know, a bomb.'

'Do you think I would ask you to look after a bomb? I told you the case contains papers.'

'And I believe you, but if the Chief Super got to hear about it and I didn't know what was inside, I'd be facing early retirement without a pension.'

Ena lifted the case and slammed it down on his desk. 'Open the damn thing then. Go on,' she shouted, taking the key from her pocket and dropping it on top of the case. 'Well if you won't, I will.' She put the key into the small raised brass button lock and turned. It sprang open. She lifted the leather strap, opened the case wide, and pushed it across the inspector's desk. 'Papers!'

'Papers.'

'No bombs, no surveillance equipment, no chemicals– Nothing. The pockets are empty and there isn't a false bottom to the bloody thing either, I've checked.'

DI Powell laughed. 'It's a Gladstone bag, too old to have a false bottom.'

Ena opened her mouth to argue, realised the DI wasn't being serious and said, 'I knew that.' She took out the envelope addressed to her. 'In here there's a letter from Sid Parfitt. It should help me to expose the woman I'm after and close her case file once and for all. But it won't if she, or one of MI5's spooks get their hands on it.

'I want to get this woman, Inspector. I think she killed Sid and I'm almost certain she had something to do with McKenzie Robinson's death. She may not have killed him herself, but I'd gamble she ordered the hit. She once tried to kill me.'

'What?'

'During the war. It's a long story.'

'I have the time.'

'I'm sorry but I don't. I'll tell you one day, over a drink,' she said, with a cheeky grin. She remembered the bottle of Scotch in her handbag, wondered if she should offer the inspector a tot and thought better of it.

'I'll hold you to that.' The DI flicked through the newspapers. 'German!'

'Berlin. The 1936 Olympics. Some Hitler Youth rallies.'

He picked up a photograph, tilted his head to the left and right, turned it sideways, and then upside down. 'Not the kind of thing you should be looking at, Ena.'

Ena glanced over his shoulder and blushed scarlet. 'I wouldn't do if it wasn't important to my investigation.' She laughed nervously. 'Most of the photographs have been doctored, as they say. Like this one.' She held up the photograph of Sid surrounded by naked women. 'The women have been added.' She shook her head. 'They were used to blackmail Sid Parfitt.'

DI Powell took the remaining photographs out and ran the flat of his hand over the base of the bag. Finding nothing he replaced the newspapers and photographs, journal and envelope, and closed it. 'Lock it. I'll put it in the office safe.'

Ena leapt up and threw her arms round the inspector's neck. 'Thank you!' When she had calmed down she offered him the key.

'Keep it. I don't intend to open the case without you being here.'

Ena took her purse from her handbag, placed the key in it, and snapped it shut. 'Thank you again, Inspector,' she said, and followed him to the door. 'I'll be in touch.'

'Don't leave it too long.'

'I won't.'

THIRTY-THREE

Ena left Bow Street police station relieved that Sid's briefcase was in Detective Inspector Powell's safe. She glanced over her shoulder as she walked along James Street where she had left the car. She had been looking over her shoulder since picking up Sid's case from Waterloo Station. Even at The Hope and Anchor she was worried she had been followed. She looked over her shoulder again. She wasn't being followed now.

After picking up the Sunbeam, Ena drove the short distance to Mercer Street and parked. She let herself into the indoor courtyard and then the cold case office. There was no sign of Artie. He had obviously cleared off for the day. Ena didn't blame him. Sid's death had hit him hard. She went over to her desk. Not a single message on the telephone notepad, so she checked the window was securely latched, everything electric had been switched off in the kitchen, and left.

She crossed Mercer Street to the car with a spring in her step, opened the driver's door and slid in behind the steering wheel. 'Home,' she said, turning the key in the ignition.

Looking forward to taking off the clothes she'd been wearing all day and soaking in a long hot bath, she turned into St

Michael's Square. Passing the surveillance car, she parked outside the flat and jumped out. Before she had time to close the Sunbeam's door she heard the powerful engine of the green Austin Cambridge roar into life.

Ena looked in the direction of the sound to see the Austin racing towards her. She dived out of the way, landing on the pavement seconds before the speeding car caught the open driver's door of the Sunbeam. Deafened by the abrading sound of metal being wrenched from metal, as the door of her car was severed from its body and propelled along the street, Ena pressed the palms of her hands against her ears.

Henry ran out of the flat, taking the steps to the pavement two at a time. 'Ena?'

'Over here,' she shouted.

'What the hell happened?' Henry sounded more angry than worried. 'You could have been killed,' he said, hauling her to her feet.

Holding on to Henry's arm, Ena stood on one leg. 'I must have caught my knee on the kerb when I dived out of the way of that maniac.' Looking down, Ena saw blood seeping from a deep graze. 'It's only a scratch,' she said, limping from pain she suspected was nothing compared to the pain she would feel the next day when the bruising came out.

'Come on, let's get you inside.'

'I need my bag. I'll get it from the car and you look for the door. It'll be goodness knows where by now.'

Henry took her arm. 'I'll get your bag and the car door when you are safely inside.'

Ena pulled away from him. 'Get the bag now! Please, Henry, it has work papers in it.'

With a face like thunder, Henry left Ena leaning on the handrail at the beginning of the steps leading to the flat and went to the car. He returned with her bag. 'Now, will you please do as I ask!'

Leaning on Henry, Ena took the steps slowly. Once inside the flat with the door locked, she shrugged off her coat and, with Henry's help, limped into the sitting room. While she took off her laddered stockings, Henry went to the kitchen, filled a bowl with warm water, took a bottle of Dettol and a wrap of cotton wool from the cupboard and returned to the sitting room.

'Let's see.' Putting the bowl at Ena's feet, Henry knelt in front of her. At first the Dettol stung, but it soon began to soothe.

Ena took a pull of cotton wool and dipped it into the warm water. 'Aw!' She opened her hand to reveal a graze from the heel of her hand to the start of her fingers. She leaned forward and submerged her hand in the warm water. Henry pulled off a length of cotton wool and, lifting her hand out of the water, dabbed her palm until there was no grit left in it.

'Thank you, Henry.' Unable to stop the tears, Ena laid her head on his shoulder and sobbed.

'Hey? Come on.' Henry put his arms around her.

'I'm okay. It's shock, I expect.'

'You could have been killed.' Henry moved the bowl of water to the table and sat next to her. 'And not for the first time.'

'No. But I'm safe now.' Ena leaned forward to kiss Henry. He turned his head away.

'You're safe now,' he said, angrily. 'What about next time, and the next?'

'Henry, don't.'

'Don't what, Ena? Don't remind you that you may not have time to jump out of the way of the next car that tries to run you down? Good God, Ena, you may not even see it. It's a dangerous game that you're playing. It's time to stop this obsession with Frieda Voight.'

'How can I? She killed Sid!'

'Exactly. And if you get in her way, she'll kill you.'

'So, what do you suggest I do?'

'Get out of London. Not to Lowarth. It would be dangerous for the family. There must be somewhere you can go that Frieda doesn't know about. Somewhere where you'll be safe.'

There were places Ena could go, but only one where she would be safe and at the same time learn more about Frieda Voight. Helen Crowther's words on the day of McKenzie Robinson's funeral, came into her mind. 'If you want to get out of London for a break, give me a ring.'

'There is,' Ena said, 'Brighton. A friend invited me to go down and see her not long ago.'

'Thank God. Go and pack a bag. The sooner you're out of London the better.'

'What about you?'

'I'll be all right. It's you who's in danger not me.'

Ena ran into the bathroom and grabbed her toiletries, flannel and a clean towel. In the bedroom she dragged a small suitcase out of the wardrobe, wrapped a couple of pairs of shoes in brown paper and dropped them into it. She threw in clean underwear, stockings, skirts, jumpers, and a couple of dresses.

'Are you ready?' Henry shouted.

'Yes.'

She left the bedroom, grabbed her coat from the hook in the hall and put it on. 'I don't want to leave you.'

'I don't see you have a choice. If you'd have left this Frieda Voight obsession alone, when I told you to...' Henry looked angry and hurt. 'I can't take you to the station in the Sunbeam. I'll get a cab. Shut the door after me and don't answer it to anyone. I'll be as quick as I can.'

While Henry was out, Ena telephoned Helen in Brighton and Detective Inspector Powell at Bow Street. Helen answered her telephone almost immediately. Without saying Helen's name, Ena asked her if she could take her up on her offer of a sea view. Helen said yes, let me know what time your train gets in.

DI Powell wasn't in his office. Ena was put through to Sergeant Thompson. 'Sergeant, it's Ena Green. Would you give the inspector a message for me?'

'Of course, Mrs Green, as soon as he arrives in the morning.'

'Tell him I've had to get out of London. Tell him, I'll be in the same neck of the woods as his pal from Hendon.'

The call was interrupted by hammering on the door and Henry shouting, 'It's me!'

'I have to go. Thank you, Sergeant.' Ena put down the telephone and hurried to open the door.

Henry grabbed her suitcase and weekend bag and hustled her out of the flat. He locked the door and walked in front of her down the steps to the waiting taxi.

'Victoria Station, as quickly as you can.'

THIRTY-FOUR

Except that Helen's house was on the seafront, with an unobstructed view of the sea one way and a small jetty where fishing boats were moored the other, the crescent-shaped terrace of fourteen houses could have been an early nineteenth century terrace in West London.

The house was smaller inside than it looked from the outside. The dining room, decorated in fashionable bold greens and deep orange, doubled as a library with built-in bookcases in arched recesses. The room was modern and expensively furnished. Being a PA to the head of MI5 obviously paid well, Ena thought, or perhaps Helen came from money. From the short time she spent with her after McKenzie Robinson's funeral Ena could tell her friend was educated. She spoke well, dressed well – and from the books on her bookcases, she was well read.

Ena browsed the bookcase, settling on a shelf of biographies of nineteenth and twentieth century spies that ranged from the American Confederate spy Isabella Marie Boyd and Mata Hari, to Sidney Reilly, known as the ace of spies, who was recruited by Scotland Yard, and husband and wife team, Julius and Ethel

Rosenberg, American Communists who passed classified information by radio to the KGB.

'I haven't read them all,' Helen said, entering the dining room carrying a tray with teapot, cups and saucers, and two plates of buttered crumpets. She paused briefly by the bookcase. 'Borrow one, two if you like.'

Ena laughed. 'Thank you, but I'll decline. One of these books would take me a month to read.'

'You don't know what you're missing,' Helen said, playfully, over her shoulder. 'Dinner won't be ready for a while, but I thought you looked as if you could do with something to eat now.' Putting the tray down on the coffee table in front of the fire she poured two cups of tea. 'Help yourself.'

'I haven't had crumpets since I lived at home,' Ena said. She took a bite of the small griddle cake. Butter dripped from her chin and Helen passed her a serviette.

By the time they had finished tea the afternoon light had faded. 'Draw the curtains will you, Ena, while I take the tea things to the kitchen.'

Ena got up and went over to the tall sash window. Not quite dark but no longer light, she looked across the road to the pebble beach. The tide was coming in. The sea looked black and cold and unforgiving. Icy fingers ran down her back. Someone's walked over your grave, her mother would have said. Ena dismissed the thought. She didn't believe in such things.

Closing the curtains, Ena stood with her back to them and looked around the dining room, as Helen called it – a combination of studio, library and office. An artist's easel stood in the corner with an unfinished seascape on it. Ena walked around the oval dining table. There was a pile of books in the middle, a table lamp at one end next to a typewriter and notepad.

'Is this where you work?' Ena asked, when Helen returned.

'It was going to be,' she said with sigh. 'I was going to write McKenzie's memoirs.'

'I'm sorry, I didn't mean to remind you.'

'Don't be. I'm over Mac's death. Not over it, but I'm coming to terms with it. I had to be strong for Eve. She didn't like talking about him. She quickly gave away everything that belonged to him – his clothes and shoes – even his golf clubs. I stayed with her for a week after Mac died – and again after the funeral. While I was with her I couldn't grieve. She became upset if I talked about him, so I came home. She's fine about him now. In fact she said the last time I saw her that she would tell me all about McKenzie – the man and the husband – because she wanted me to write his memoirs.'

'And are you going to?'

'I don't know.' Helen went to the drinks cabinet and took a decanter and two sherry schooners from it. 'I know everything there is to know about Mac the director of MI5. I have his papers.'

'Then why don't you?'

'Well, I would *want* to give a true account of Mac's life – his working life and private life – and there are parts of both that would hurt Eve. Sherry?'

'Thank you.' Ena followed Helen to the armchairs at the side of the fire. She didn't know her friend well enough to ask which parts of her boss's life would hurt his wife.

Helen poured the sherry, handed Ena a glass and sat back in her chair. 'I was McKenzie's personal assistant for more than thirty years,' she said, wistfully. 'I would be still if someone hadn't–'

Ena took a sip of her drink. "If someone hadn't" told Ena Helen knew her boss had been murdered. It didn't tell her who she thought had murderer him. Ena was desperate to know who Helen suspected. She looked at her. There were tears in her eyes. Now was not the time to ask.

'For a long time, McKenzie and I thought there was a mole in Leconfield House,' Helen said suddenly. 'We purposely didn't tell anyone. We were getting close to exposing him when you came to see Mac about Frieda Voight.'

Ena held her breath. She felt sure Helen was about to tell her who the mole was. When she didn't, she said, 'Does Mrs Robinson still blame me for her husband's death?'

Helen shook her head. 'No. That Mac died shortly after you came to see him was a coincidence, nothing more.'

Ena exhaled. 'Thank you for telling me.' She wanted to ask Helen if she knew Frieda Voight had visited Director Robinson in hospital. She took another sip of her sherry. There would be time enough, she hoped.

'So, Ena, what brings you to Brighton? Oh,' Helen said, clasping her hand over her mouth. 'Do not answer that question,' she said, laughing. 'Working with McKenzie for such a long time has made me inquisitive. Gentle interrogation, he used to call it. I call it being nosy.'

Ena laughed too. She wasn't ready to tell Helen everything, but she felt she needed to tell her something.

'I don't mind telling you at all. You have a right to know who you are harbouring under your roof. I could be a master criminal.' Ena laughed and took a long breath to give herself time to select from everything that was making her head spin what she could tell Helen without putting her life in danger. If Helen still worked for Five – and there was a mole – she could find herself being stalked by Russians, or worse.

'I'm being followed to and from work. At night a goon in an Austin watches the flat. I went to confront the driver once but he sped off almost knocking me over. This afternoon, as I was getting out of my car, he drove straight at me. I dived out of the way. He was so close he took the door of my car off its hinges.'

'Do you know who has you under surveillance?'

'I can't be sure but I think it's to do with Frieda Voight, who you would know about working at MI5.'

Helen didn't answer, but nodded.

Ena drank the last of her sherry. Nerves always made her mouth dry. The sherry did nothing to alleviate it. 'Frieda was from Berlin, but my colleague Sid,' Ena cleared her throat. 'Sorry, my late colleague, who I believe was killed because of what he knew about Frieda, had proof that she is working for the Russians.'

'And you're under surveillance because the Russians suspect your colleague shared that information with you?'

'I suppose so. But he didn't. He said he wanted to check a file, make sure of something before he told me. He didn't get the chance to tell me anything. He was found dead on the embankment on the south side of Waterloo Bridge in the early hours of the following morning.'

'Do you think he was murdered?'

'I'm sure of it. But I can't prove it.'

The conversation moved into the kitchen. While Helen took a stew pot from the stove Ena washed up the sherry glasses.

'Smells good,' Ena said, watching Helen spoon potatoes, carrots, onion and swede in a rich gravy onto two large plates.

Helen took a crusty loaf from the bread bin and sliced it on a wooden chopping block. 'Do you cook, Ena?'

'When I can. I used to cook every night. These days Henry is rarely home for dinner, so I have something hot at lunchtime with my colleagues.' She corrected herself: 'Colleague.'

'It must nice cooking for someone, eating with them, telling them about your day, sharing problems, discussing and resolving them.'

'It would be, but with Henry working for MI5 and me working for the HO, we can't discuss our work.'

Helen opened a drawer in the kitchen larder cabinet and took out cutlery. She placed a knife, fork and spoon at the side of place mats. 'You don't mind eating in here, do you?'

'Not at all.'

'Tuck in, or it will be cold.'

They ate in relative silence. Ena looked at Helen, she seemed miles away. 'The food's delicious. Thank you, Helen.'

'I'm never sure how much to cook for two. I've been on my own for a long time now.'

When they had finished eating, Helen transferred what was left of the casserole to a large bowl, put it in the refrigerator and dried the dishes after Ena had washed them. They then took cheese and biscuits into the dining room and sat by the fire.

'I'll show you the rest of the house tomorrow, Ena. It's too big for one, really, but I'm reluctant to sell it.'

'How long have you lived here.'

'I was born here.' Helen laughed. 'Those were the days. The house was always full of interesting people. My father was a writer. Biographies mostly. We travelled as a unit of four to wherever in the world my father's next commission was.'

'What an interesting childhood.'

'It was that all right. I met some fascinating people.' Helen laughed again. 'I could tell you stories that would make your hair curl. But seriously, if I had the time, which I haven't, it would be my father's biography I'd write.

'My mother was a teacher before she married my father. She was a strong woman and quite forward thinking. She schooled me at home because she believed in this modern age girls should be educated to the same standard as boys. She was an artist, a painter, but she educated me in science, reading, writing and arithmetic.'

'Is that one of your mother's paintings?' Ena asked, pointing to the seascape she'd admired earlier.

'No, that's one of mine.'

'In that case I think you have a great deal of artistic talent.' Ena got up and went over to the painting. 'Where is this?'

'I'm copying an old black and white photograph that my mother took in Egypt. We lived in Cairo for a while, but...' Helen took a photograph from the mantelshelf and squinted.

'That looks like the port of Alexandria. We were there for some months. It's probably the Mediterranean.'

Ena yawned. 'I'm sorry. How rude of me,' she said, 'it's been a tiring day.'

'And a frightening one. Did you tell anyone you were coming to Brighton?'

'Only Henry. Actually,' Ena said, 'I didn't tell him I was staying with you.'

Helen looked shocked. 'Don't you trust your husband? I assure you he is very trustworthy. McKenzie held him in the highest regard. He called him one of Five's shining stars.'

'Did he?' Ena felt the swell of emotion in her throat. 'We haven't been getting on lately. He doesn't like the work I do. He says it's too dangerous.' Ena bit her bottom lip. 'We had a row before I left.'

'Then go and telephone him. Let him know you've arrived safely. The phone's in the hall. Go on, Ena, put the poor chap's mind at rest.'

THIRTY-FIVE

Ena wanted to talk to Henry, but she didn't feel comfortable speaking on the telephone. It wasn't Helen she was worried about, it was her flat. It had been bugged once and she was worried in case it had been bugged again. Nevertheless, she thanked Helen, and went into the hall. She eyed the telephone with suspicion and quickly unscrewed the mouthpiece. There was no listening device in it. She shook her head at the ridiculousness of imagining every telephone she came across was tapped, picked up the receiver and dialled her and Henry's number.

'Hello?'

'Henry, it's Ena.'

'Thank God. I expected you to ring when you got to Brighton; let me know you'd arrived safely. I've been worried sick.'

'Sorry. I meant to phone from the station, but my friend was on the platform waiting for me when I arrived. And by the time we'd eaten and we had caught up with each other's news it was gone ten. Truth is, we hadn't seen each other for such a long time we've only just finished chatting.'

'As long as you're all right.'

'Of course I'm all right. What about you?'

'Fine. I found the car door. I couldn't leave it in the road so I lugged it back here. As luck would have it, the lights were still on at Stockwell Garage when I came back from Victoria. I rang them and they came out and tied a tarpaulin over the car. They said they'll pick the car and the door up tomorrow. If it can be repaired they'll give me a quote.'

'If it can't, a new door will be expensive, Henry.'

'I don't care about the expense, as long as you're all right. You could have been killed.'

'I know,' Ena whispered. 'I should go. I don't want to be on my friend's phone too long.'

'What's the number, I'll ring you back?'

'I can't remember and it isn't on the telephone. I'll call you tomorrow.'

'At least give me the address of where you're staying.'

'No, Henry. With all that has been going on recently, I don't trust that our telephone isn't tapped. I'll give you the address and telephone number tomorrow. I'll ring the office and we can talk on a secure line. I'd better get back to my friend. Good night.'

'Night, darling. Sleep well.'

Guilt swept over her as she replaced the receiver. It wouldn't have hurt to give Henry Helen's telephone number. It wasn't Henry she didn't trust, it was the situation – and whoever the mole was at Leconfield House.

Ena met Helen as she was coming out of the kitchen. 'I'll show you your room, Ena,' she said, leading the way across the hall to a short passage near the front door. 'And, as promised, it has a sea view.' Helen opened the bedroom door and switched on the light. 'And this,' she said, turning on her heels and opening a door on the left, 'is the bathroom.' She pointed to two large bath towels hanging from hooks on the wall just inside the door. 'I'm on the first floor. This space is all yours.'

Feeling tearful, Ena took a deep breath. She hadn't felt safe since seeing Sid's body on the pathologist's table in the mortuary at St Thomas's. 'I think being watched, followed, almost run down, has finally got to me,' she said.

Helen patted her shoulder as a mother might do. 'Get a good night's sleep. You're safe here.'

Ena tossed and turned, annoyed with herself because she was dog tired and yet, try as hard as she may, she could not sleep. She got up and went to the window. She drew back the curtains. The moon was almost full. It looked as if it was tilting slightly to the right. Dark craters brought it to life in the shape of an old man's face. Two eyes, deeply set, and beneath them a broad nose ran down the centre of the orb. A jagged dark line across the bottom of the face looked like a mouth, lips smudged with dull charcoal coloured lipstick.

She reached for the bedspread, pulled it from the bed and wrapped it around her shoulders. Tiptoeing out of the bedroom, she made her way across the hall to the kitchen and out through the back door. On the narrow wooden veranda she pulled the quilt tightly round her and flopped into a big old rocking chair. Tucking her feet under her, she leaned back on half a dozen soft cushions and looked up at the sky. The moon dimmed as clouds drifted lazily in front of it, shining brightly again as soon as they had passed. She breathed the tang of salt air and listened to the comforting sound of the sea rolling in and breaking without urgency against the low wall where several boats swayed and bumped each other.

She would have liked to have stayed on the veranda looking up at the moon and stars all night, but it was too cold. Shivering she returned to the guest bedroom and crawled into bed.

. . .

Running faster along narrow passages Ena was getting nowhere. Every time she saw a light someone switched it off. Frightened, she turned the corner and there they were.

Who is Collins? the faceless ones howled. Ena ran again until she had left them behind. She was hot and slowed her pace. Needing to catch her breath she stopped and leaned forward, put her hands on her knees and inhaled deeply several times. She could hear them running, their feet pounding the cobblestones. They were behind her, then they were in front of her. She ran this way and that. The faceless ones chased her onto Waterloo Bridge and stood in a row. Like a police cordon they barred her way. She couldn't go forward, she couldn't go back. She looked over the bridge at the cold black water of the River Thames. It was her only escape.

She ran down the steps of the landing jetty and, clutching a mooring rope, crouched between two wooden boats. They bumped and swayed with the swell of the incoming tide. The terrifying faceless ones – tall and angular – came out of the sides of the boats and marched towards her. To get away from them she let go of the mooring rope and slipped soundlessly into the Thames.

She closed her eyes and let the icy black water wash over her. No one was chasing her now, nor were the boats bumping her. She felt safe at last. Lulled by the current she drifted into sleep. Then, in a net, she was hauled out of the water. In a catch of fish, she was landed. And like the fishing boats she was anchored, tied to the embankment.

She pulled, pulled again, hard this time, but couldn't free herself. Her body rocked and swayed, and collided with other dead bodies. She screamed for help. But her cries only alerted the green-car-man.

Help me, she called, but the green-car-man only laughed at

her. Again she was running for her life. The faster she ran the faster the green-car-man ran. It seemed he was around every corner, in front of her and behind her, waiting for her. There was no escaping him.

Eventually, she stopped and confronted him. *Why are you chasing me?*

He didn't answer. He towered over her in a black overcoat with a high collar, and a trilby tilted low over his eyes. Ena stretched up and lifted the brim of the hat. But as hard as she tried, she could see nothing between hat and collar but a black aperture.

Ena woke in a sweat. She turned over and for several seconds didn't know where she was. Light crept into the unfamiliar room above the curtains, creating eerie patterns on the ceiling. She heard seagulls crying, reminding her that she was in Brighton at the home of her friend Helen Crowther.

Relieved that it was morning, Ena did what she always did when she'd had a bad dream; she jumped out of bed and threw open the curtains.

Spikes of rain dashed the window and the flags on the seafront whipped and flapped, a warning to fishermen that it was not safe to be out on the sea. Nor on the beach, Ena thought. The sea was choppy. High waves thrashed against the lattice piles of the pier.

There was a knock at the door. Ena spun round. Her heart rate doubled, but calmed when she heard Helen's voice. She hurried across the room and opened the door.

'Not a day for strolling along the font,' Helen said, setting a tray with tea and toast on the bed. 'Did you sleep well?'

'Yes,' Ena said, which wasn't the truth, but she didn't want to worry Helen.

'Ena?'

'What?' she jumped. 'Sorry, I was miles away.'

'You didn't have a good night, did you?'

Ena shook her head. 'A man, green like the car that tried to run me down, was chasing me. And there were others. Faceless men like the anonymous men in the cold cases I investigate.'

'Do you want to talk about it?'

'No. I'm fine. I often have strange dreams. Mostly where I'm being chased. It's always the same dream, it's just different men doing the chasing. Happens when I'm worried or stressed.'

'Well,' Helen said, crossing to the window and looking out, 'perhaps we should go out today after all. How about a trip to the fishmonger, buy something for tonight's dinner, and have a cup of coffee in one of the new coffee shops on The Lanes?'

'Sounds perfect,' Ena said, putting all thoughts of being caught in a fishing net in the Thames out of her mind. 'We'll stay in town and have lunch. My treat.'

'It's a deal,' Helen said. 'I'll get dinner, you get lunch.' At the bedroom door Helen turned and said, 'I'm going to enjoy having you here, Ena.'

'I'm going to enjoy being here,' Ena said. She went to the bathroom and ran the bath. Her hand and knee stung when she lowered herself into the hot water. The cuts soon became acclimatised and felt only a little sore.

Refreshed, Ena dressed, brushed her hair, and took her breakfast tray down to the kitchen.

Helen was finishing a cup of tea, but left it and took the tray out of Ena's hands.

'I'll wash these.' Ena took the tray back and headed over to the sink.

'Unless you want more tea we'll go when you've washed up.'

'Yes. Let's blow the cobwebs away.'

Before they left, Helen gave Ena a headscarf. 'You'll need this,' she said, 'tie it tight. What size shoes do you take?'

'Six, usually.'

Helen took a pair of thick soled leather walking shoes from the cupboard. 'Try these for size. They're not glamorous but you won't get twenty yards in your high heels,' she said, dropping the brogues at Ena's feet.

Helen put on flat boots and tied a scarf around her head, knotting it tightly under her chin. Ena did the same.

'Ready?' Ena nodded, and her friend opened the front door.

The wind gusted in. The nets at the windows on either side of the door billowed and a painting hanging on the wall swayed on its cord.

THIRTY-SIX

Walking along the front arm in arm, the sound of waves crashing onto the shingle and the wind buffeting them along, the two women huddled closer. At the pier, Helen stopped and pulled on Ena's arm. 'Coffee?' She mimed lifting an imaginary cup to her lips. Ena nodded and shimmied her shoulders to indicate she was cold.

She followed Helen into the Palace Café. Hanging on to the last vestiges of summer, three walls sported summer posters. The first, a pretty blonde girl on a beach wearing a black and red bathing costume advertised Vimto for health. A poster of two ice creams sitting in deckchairs in the blazing sun was coming away from the wall and the third, a selection of ice cream sundaes had begun to fade.

When they'd finished their coffee, they left the café and made their way to the Lanes. Ena marvelled at the antique shops, fabric and gift shops. A penny arcade caught her eye and she dragged Helen inside to play the slot machines. She put a penny in the first and waited. It pinged and whizzed and lights flashed on and off, leaving two apples on the screen. While she waited for her reward, Ena read the small hand-written card stuck to the corner of the machine's glass front. "Rich pickings when three apples light up." She put another penny in. This time only one apple was left on the screen.

From somewhere further along the arcade they heard coins clacketing into a metal tray and the laughing policeman burst into hysterics.

'Had enough?' Helen asked.

Ena pulled a disappointed face. 'Yes, I'm hungry. Let's get something to eat?'

They found a café on the front with a sea view. Ena peered through the floor to ceiling window. Thick in sea salt, it was like looking through frosted glass. Inside the pleasant café was warm and the fish and chips were delicious. After their second cup of tea, Ena paid the bill and the two friends set off for the High Street where Helen bought meat and vegetables for their evening meal before they caught a bus home.

Closing the bedroom curtains, Ena saw a taxi pull up on the far side of the road. A man got out with a bunch of flowers in one hand and a bottle in the other. Ena watched him pay the driver, and then run across the road to Helen's front door. A second later she heard the bell.

The door to her room opened into the small front hall. She put her ear against it.

Helen said, 'Hello. What a lovely surprise.'

The man said something Ena didn't catch followed by, 'I called on the off chance, but if it isn't convenient...'

'No, it's fine,' Helen said. 'Come in, let me take your coat.'

Ena went back to the window and finished drawing the curtains. She switched on the bedside lamp and sat on the bed. She hadn't reckoned on Helen having visitors, but then why wouldn't she? Checking her hair in the mirror, Ena teased a curl that had fallen onto her brow back into place. After straightening her skirt she put on her shoes and left her bedroom.

Opening the door to the dining room, she saw Helen talking to the man by the fire. Her friend was looking up into the man's face and he was smiling down at her. They were enjoying an intimate conversation, Ena thought, and turned to leave.

'Ena?' Helen called.

'I'm sorry. I didn't know you had a guest,' she said, feeling like the proverbial gooseberry.

'Come and meet Shaun. Shaun and I worked together at Leconfield House until he was head-hunted by MI6.'

'Don't believe a word of what Helen says, Ena. I was sidelined. Five didn't know what to do with me, so they handed me over to Six like a lamb to the slaughter.'

Helen slapped him playfully on the shoulder. Then, taking him by the arm, walked him across the room to Ena. 'Shaun O'Shaughnessy, this is my friend, Ena Green.'

'Pleased to meet you, Ena.'

'And I you, Shaun.'

Shaun looked into Ena's eyes for rather too long, and he smiled too confidently for Ena's liking. He was good looking with fair, almost blond hair, strong features and piercing green eyes. A charmer her mother would have called him; one for the ladies. Not this lady, Ena thought. She offered him her hand. Instead of shaking it, he kissed it.

Ena laughed. 'You wouldn't be Irish by any chance, would you, Mr O'Shaughnessy?'

'I would. Shaun O'Shaughnessy at your service,' he said, with a sweeping bow. 'But how did you know? Was it my natural good looks, or my emerald green eyes?'

Ena laughed. 'It was your accent.'

'Tell the truth, Ena, it was the Blarney,' Helen said, handing Ena a glass of wine. 'Make yourself at home, Shaun, I'm going to check on the dinner.'

'I'll help,' Ena said, putting her glass on the table.

'No, darling. You stay here and keep Shaun amused. Ha!' Helen said, 'I expect it will be the other way around. There is no stopping O'Shaughnessy when he gets going. Ta, ta,' she said, and holding her glass aloft, left the dining room.

Shaun dropped into the chair nearest to the fire, crossed his legs and pointed to the chair opposite. 'Well, Ena, tell me about yourself,' he said, raising his glass to her.

She laughed. 'Is that what they call a "chat up" line, or is it the way MI6 interrogate women these days?'

'I'm sure I wouldn't know. Come now, spill the beans. What are you doing hiding yourself away down here in this quiet little suburb of Brighton, when you could be *rocking and rolling* the night away at the Palace Ballroom?'

'I'm not hiding, I have temporarily left the hustle and bustle of city life behind for a few days of peace and quiet.'

'There? Didn't I say you are no fun at all?' Shaun closed his eyes, leaned sideways and swung his long legs over the arm of the chair.

Ena laughed again. Having got over the initial shock of seeing a stranger in the house, she was enjoying herself. Although he was a bit full of himself, she was warming to Shaun O'Shaughnessy and was enjoying his company.

Shaun's glass was empty. Ena left her seat and replenished his drink. She topped up her own. 'Is Shaun O'Shaughnessy your real name?'

'Of course,' he said, indignantly, opening his eyes, 'why do you ask?'

'It sounds like the name an actor would choose.'

'When they join Equity, do you mean?'

'It is, isn't it? Go on, admit it. O'Shaughnessy isn't your real name.'

'Don't you like it?'

'I don't have to like it, it isn't my name.'

'Mm,' Shaun sat upright. He took his glass by the stem and squinted at her through the top of the bowl. 'No,' he said, 'it wouldn't suit you.'

Ena laughed at his performance. 'No, it wouldn't.'

'Then I shall keep it,' he said.

A knock at the door interrupted their conversation. Ena was nearest and opened it.

'What are you two laughing about?' Helen, balancing dishes of hot food and serving spoons on a large silver tray, crossed to the table. 'Ena, dear, would you take mats and cutlery from the drawer in the dresser and lay three places?' she asked, setting the steaming food down in the middle of the table. 'Won't be a tick.'

By the time Ena had laid the table, Helen was back with plates and another bottle of red wine. 'Shaun, make yourself useful and open this.'

'Yes, ma'am.' Shaun saluted, downed his wine and stood the glass in the hearth. Helen handed him a bone-handled corkscrew. 'What have we here?' He lifted the bottle and examined the label. 'Chateau le plonk, 1958 – and a very good year it is too,' he said, plunging the metal spike of the corkscrew into the top of the bottle. He embedded the cork up to its handle, gripped the bottle with one hand and heaved the corkscrew out with the other. The cork made a dull pop as it parted company with the bottle and Shaun put it up to his nose and sniffed.

'For goodness' sake, Shaun, just pour the damn stuff.' Helen said, 'it doesn't have a bouquet.'

Shaun giggled as Helen dished up. 'Smells good. Beef bourgeoning?' he teased, sampling the beef and vegetables in a thick herb gravy.

'Beef stew, darling, with half a bottle of red wine in it. And before you ask, no it wasn't Chateau le plonk, it was something even cheaper.'

'Whatever you put in it, Helen, it's delicious,' Ena said, helping herself to more gravy.

When they had finished the main course, Helen piled the dirty dishes on the tray and took them to the kitchen, returning shortly afterwards with coffee pot, cups and saucers, and a selection of cheeses.

Nibbling on chunks of cheese and drinking wine, the three companions talked and laughed. Ena observed how easy the conversation flowed between Helen and Shaun. Listening to them reminded her how easy it had once been between her and Henry. They never threw dinner parties, which their friends often did, but there was always food in the cupboard and refrigerator that she could whip into a meal if anyone called, which they did often when she and Henry were first married. When did their friends stop calling? When did she and Henry become too busy to call on them?

Suddenly aware that the conversation had stopped, Ena looked up. Shaun, with his head tilted on one side, was grinning. Helen was looking at her with anticipation. 'I'm sorry,' Ena said, 'I was miles away. What were you saying?'

'That the three of us should go to the Dome tomorrow night. Chris Barber's Jazz Band is on. How about it?'

'I'd love to go,' Ena said.

'Then I shall book a table for three.'

THIRTY-SEVEN

From the outside the Dome, like the Brighton Pavilion, was a mixture of Regency grandeur with exotic Indian and Chinese influences. Inside it was 1930s Art Deco with wall-to-wall walnut panelling. Ena and Helen went to the ladies' cloakroom to leave their coats and powder their noses, while Shaun headed off to the bar. When they arrived in the ballroom, Shaun was sitting at a table tapping his feet to 'Bugle Boy March'.

'May I have this dance?' he said, as soon as Ena was seated.

She looked at Helen. 'Do you mind?'

'Good Lord, no. Go on,' Helen said, 'enjoy yourself.'

Out on the dance floor Shaun took hold of Ena's hands and flicking his feet out, rocked back and forth and then stepped sideways. Ena copied him and in no time she was spinning round and going under Shaun's arm. Shaun next danced with Helen and Ena sat the dance out.

The three friends – for Shaun had proved himself to be a friend – talked and joked, laughed and drank wine. Ena wished she led a more normal life, met up with friends, and went to jazz clubs; there were enough in London. She was having fun for the first time in years. She wanted this life. Not the life of spies and shadows.

'Penny for them?' Shaun whispered in Ena's ear.

'Not worth it,' she said, getting up. 'Come on, let's dance.'

They danced the Lindy Hop to 'Mama Don't Allow' and rock and rolled to 'Rockin' in Rhythm'. When it was time to leave, Ena was exhausted.

'Hello again,' Shaun said, swanning past Ena when she opened the front door the following night. 'Helen, darling,' he called, waving a bottle of red wine and crossing the hall to meet Helen coming out of the kitchen.

Helen turned and laughed. 'I don't see you for donkey's years and then I see you three nights on the trot.'

'Trot? Don't speak to me about dancing,' he grimaced, 'my feet haven't recovered from last night yet.'

Helen laughed again. 'Un-cork the wine, I'll get the glasses.'

Shaun followed Helen into the dining room and took the corkscrew from the sideboard where it had been left the night before. 'How are you feeling this evening, Ena?' he asked, taking the cork out of the bottle.

'Good, thank you.'

'Good? Who wants to be good?' he said, putting the wine bottle on the table and taking Ena by the hand.

'If you'll excuse me.' She extracted her hand from his. 'I'll see if Helen needs any help in the kitchen.'

Shaun raised an eyebrow and looked disappointed, which annoyed Ena. He was very forward. They had only known each for other a couple of days – and he knew she was married. Unless Helen had told him she and Henry hadn't been getting on. But no, Helen wouldn't break a confidence.

'Shaun is getting fresh,' Ena said, stirring the carrot and onion soup.

Helen laughed and flapped her hand. 'Getting fresh with you? Shaun?'

And why not, Ena thought. She was put out by her friend's rejection of the possibility.

'Yes! He held my hand as if he was trying to woo me.'

'He was flattering you, darling. Shaun is as queer as a row of pink tents on a Brighton campsite on St Valentine's night.'

Ena had wondered, but she didn't make assumptions. Some of the old biddies in Lowarth had assumed Henry was a homosexual because he wasn't married with children by the time he was twenty-five, as most men they knew were. There was nothing *queer* about him, then or now. As she stirred the soup Ena wondered how Henry was managing without her. She hoped he was lonely, missing her, and the next time she telephoned he would beg her to come home. A sad smile played on her lips. Truth was, although she'd had fun in Brighton, she was missing him.

'Are you trying to burn the soup, Ena?' Helen took the spoon out of her hand and turned off the gas. 'Thick enough, don't you think?'

Ena bit her bottom lip. 'Sorry, I was thinking about Henry.'

'Missing him?'

'No. Well, yes, a little.'

Helen poured the soup into a tureen. 'Take this in, I'll bring the bread.'

While they ate, they talked about all manner of things – from the Dome to the Minchin Club – owned and frequented by gangsters.

'The Minchin Club sounds familiar,' Ena said.

'You may have read about it in the *News of The World*. The Minchin Club is quite possibly the most famous – or infamous – club outside south London.'

'Because of gangsters?'

'And movie stars, producers, West End actors. They all come down from London to the Minchin,' Shaun boasted.

The conversation moved on to London's nightlife, work, and then the possibility of there being a mole at Leconfield House.

Shaun gasped and clasped his hands over his mouth. 'Maybe the mole is your hubby.'

Helen laughed, but Ena didn't think the joke was funny. 'Not high enough up the food chain,' she said, without thinking. She waited for one of them to ask her why she thought the mole was high ranking. They didn't so she quickly changed the subject. 'How long did you work at Leconfield house, Shaun?'

'Too long. I was a minion, a shuffler of papers. The most interesting thing I did at Five was rubber-stamp documents. Classified this, highly classified that. No, Five wasn't for me. It was so *boring*.' He gave a theatrical shudder.

'But never mind about me. I was an office drudge. You, on the other hand, have an interesting job. You work for the Home Office, don't you?'

'I wouldn't call it interesting, exactly. It's admin work.' Ena laughed. She wasn't going to tell her fellow dinner guest anything she was sure he didn't already know. 'The kind of documents that you rubber-stamped my colleague and I put in folders and file in alphabetical order.'

'I was sorry to hear about your other colleague, the one that jumped – or was pushed – off Waterloo Bridge.'

Ena shot Helen a questioning look. Helen lifted her shoulders as if to say, I didn't tell him.

Ena felt her heart rate speed up. She suddenly felt very hot. 'Who told you about Sid?'

'Oh heck. Is it a secret? The spooks at MI6 are such gossips.'

'No, it isn't a secret that Sid committed suicide.'

Exaggerating the expression, Shaun pressed his lips together and rolled his eyes at the ceiling. A childish reaction, Ena thought.

'What is it, Shaun?' Helen pointed a finger at him. 'Come on, out with it. What do you know that we don't?'

'My lips are sealed. I've said too much already.'

'What are they saying at Six?'

'No. I'm saying no more. I've upset Ena.'

'Tittle-tattle doesn't upset me,' Ena said, 'though I'd have thought your lot at Six would have had more respect for someone in the same profession.'

'I agree with Ena,' Helen said, getting up. 'I am going to fetch another bottle of wine from the kitchen. By the time I get back, I want you two to have kissed and made up. We're on the same side, after all.'

As soon as Helen had left the room, Shaun extended his hand to Ena. She didn't take it. 'Look,' he began, 'I was told that a bloke named Collin, or Collins, shoved your pal off Waterloo Bridge.'

Collins? How the hell has he heard about Collins? Ena's heart thumped against her ribcage and her stomach lurched, but she managed to stay outwardly calm. 'I have to say, I haven't heard that name on the HO's gossip grapevine. But you never know.' Ena put her forefinger to her lips and frowned. 'Collin?' she mused. 'If Sid was *queer*,' she said, in an attempt to embarrass Shaun, 'Collin might have been his lover.' She saw Shaun stiffen. She had touched a nerve. '*If* Sid was queer,' she said again, 'but he wasn't.'

Ena hated the word, queer. It was offensive and it implied a person wasn't right somehow. But this bloody man brought out the worst in her.

'Ena, I'm sorry. I must have been misinformed.'

'Yes, you must.' Damn the man. Who told him about Collins? Only four people knew about the piece of paper in Sid's mouth with Collins written on it: Director Bentley, Detective Inspector Powell, Artie and herself. She would gamble her life that it wasn't Dick Bentley or DI Powell who had talked out of place. It could only have been Artie. Ena felt tears of anger building up at the back of her eyes and blinked.

She didn't want to protest too much, or O'Shaughnessy would guess she knew about Collins, but she wasn't going to let him off without giving him a piece of her mind. 'Sid Parfitt was not only my colleague, he was my friend. That he committed suicide is bad enough for his friends and family, but to hear gossip that implies some homosexual thug killed Sid is unkind and unnecessary. I shall wait for the police report. I suggest you do the same.' She turned to see Helen coming in with the promised bottle of wine. She refused a refill saying she'd had enough alcohol.

Helen said she had too and left the room again to make coffee. When she was out of earshot, Shaun asked Ena not to tell her that he had made a stupid assumption about Sid Parfitt's death. Ena thought about saying she wouldn't tell Helen if he told her who had given him the name Collins, but decided against it. She didn't want him to think the name meant anything to her and kept quiet.

'I won't say anything. Helen has been very good to me. I don't wish to upset her.'

Shaun offered Ena his hand again. This time, although she wanted to stab it with the corkscrew, she took it. 'Friends?'

'Friends,' she lied.

'Thank goodness you two have made up,' Helen said, returning with a tray of coffee. Brrrr! it's cold in the kitchen.' She poured coffee for the three of them and, although the conversation had lost its earlier feel of camaraderie, Ena smiled in the right places and contributed often enough to appear as if she was enjoying herself.

At midnight, Shaun said it was time he left. Ena wanted to agree with him, but said nothing. Helen offered to telephone for a cab, but he said he would walk, it would do him good. When Helen went to fetch his coat Shaun apologised to Ena again, and again he asked her not to tell Helen what he'd said about her friend Sid. Ena, for the second time, said she wouldn't say anything. And when Helen returned with his coat, she allowed Shaun to give her a peck on the cheek, by way of saying goodnight.

It was one o'clock by the time Ena and Helen had cleared the dining room table and washed up.

'Good night, Helen. Thank you for the lovely meal,' Ena said, hugging her friend when they had put out the lights and were in the hall about to go their separate ways – Helen upstairs to her bedroom and Ena to the spare room on the ground floor next to the front door.

'Good night, Ena. I'm glad you and Shaun made up before he left. He's not a bad chap.'

'Of course he isn't. It was the wine. I'm not used to drinking so much. Night, night.'

Ena watched Helen go upstairs and when she was out of sight, went into her room. From the gap under the door, she saw the hall light go out.

Suddenly frightened, Ena went to lock the bedroom door. There was no key. She leaned against it. Her legs were shaking. Artie must have told the obnoxious Shaun O'Shaughnessy, if that was his name, about Collins. She'd lay money on it. Thank God she hadn't told Artie that Collins was Sid's dictionary. It was bad enough that he, and now O'Shaughnessy, assumed it was a man who had killed Sid.

Ena crept out of the bedroom and into the hall. She turned the front doorknob. It was locked. She told herself she was stupid to think O'Shaughnessy had anything to do with the people who were after her and went to bed. By the morning she had tossed and turned most of the night unable to sleep, so she got up and packed her bags.

After breakfast she telephoned Henry. It felt like an eternity before he answered.

'Hello?'

'It's Ena. I'm coming home.' There was silence. 'Are you there, Henry?'

'Yes, I'm here. I can't tell you how pleased I am to hear you say those words. I've missed you so much.'

'I've missed you too. I can't wait to see you. What time will you be home from work?'

'Six at the latest.'

'That'll be seven then?'

Henry laughed. 'Oh blast! I'd forgotten. There's a meeting at six, but it should be finished by seven. I'll be home at eight.'

'Dinner at eight o'clock, then. I love you, Henry.'

'I love you too. I have never loved anyone but you, Ena.'

She put the phone down and went into the kitchen. 'I'm going home, Helen.'

Helen looked surprised. 'Are you leaving because of Shaun?'

'No,' Ena assured her friend, 'I'm going because I miss Henry. I know we have a lot of stuff to sort out – and we will – but being away from him these last few days has made me realise how much I love him. I've enjoyed my time with you, and hope I'll be welcome to come down again in the future.'

'You will,' Helen said, 'and you can bring Henry next time.'

Ena laughed. 'Are you sure?'

'Yes.' Helen laughed too. 'And I promise not to invite Shaun.'

Ena put her arms around her friend and thanked her. 'And when you're next at Leconfield House, come and have dinner with us.'

. . .

The train was in when Ena and Helen arrived at the station. The two friends hugged again, and said they would see each other soon.

'Helen? I promised Shaun I wouldn't say anything to you, but he told me he knew a chap called Collins was involved in Sid Parfitt's death. The thing is, that piece of information hasn't been released to anyone, not even to MI5 and MI6.'

'I'm sorry, Ena. I damn well knew he'd said something to upset you.'

'I'm not as upset as I am worried. I'm worried that because I stayed with you, you could now be in danger. I mean, who is Shaun O'Shaughnessy? You haven't seen him for years and he turns up out of the blue when I'm staying with you. Please be careful.'

'I will,' Helen said thoughtfully, as she walked with Ena to the train. 'And you're right, Shaun turning up was a bit of a coincidence.'

When she had boarded the train, Ena closed the door and pulled down the window. 'I don't believe in coincidences,' she called, as the train began its journey.

'Nor do I,' Helen shouted before she was consumed by steam and smoke.

THIRTY-EIGHT

'Henry?' Ena ran into the hall, unlocked the door and flung it open. 'Frieda!'

'Hello, Ena.'

The nerves on the top of Ena's stomach tightened and her heart began to thud.

'Where are your manners? Aren't you going to ask me in?'

Ena stepped to the side of the door to allow Frieda to enter. She scanned the street. There was nothing out of the ordinary to the left or right. Closing the door slowly she focussed on the shadows in the shop doorway opposite, and then scrutinised the narrow unlit alleyway further down the road. There was no one. Frieda hadn't brought anyone with her, nor had she been followed. 'Can I take your coat?'

'No. I won't be staying.'

Ena led the way into the sitting room. The two women stood and stared at each other for some time. It was Ena who spoke first. 'How did you know where I lived?'

'I saw you in Selfridges in the summer. If I'd seen you, chances were you'd seen me. I knew if you had you'd go straight to MI5 and tell Henry. So I took a cab to Curzon Street and got there before you. I watched you from the coffee house opposite the café where you and Henry had lunch. It wasn't difficult to find out where you worked. I followed you home from Mercer Street several times. You take the same route too often, Ena. You should know better.'

Frieda was right, she should have known better but she wasn't going to admit it. 'Why wouldn't I take the same route home? I work in the administrative office of a non-sensitive government department. The work I do is of no interest to anyone.'

'If you say so.'

'I do say so!' Ena was annoyed with herself for being care-less. One of the basic rules, if you worked in any department of the Home Office, was vary your journey to and from work daily. Trying to keep her voice calm, she said, 'What do you want, Frieda?'

'To tell you to stop looking for me. Stop meddling in things you know nothing about. If you don't stop, the people I work for will stop you.' Frieda suddenly looked terrified. She reached forward, gripped the edge of the table and lowered herself onto a chair. She took a pack of cigarettes and a lighter from her handbag. 'They are bad people, Ena. They would think nothing of killing you.'

'Good God, Frieda, who are these people?'

Frieda took a cigarette from the packet and lit it. She offered the pack to Ena. Ena shook her head. Placing the cigarettes and lighter on the table, Frieda said, 'I shouldn't tell you. It's too dangerous. If they knew I'd come here tonight they would–' She took a drag of her cigarette and inhaled deeply. Exhaling a stream of thick smoke she cast her eyes down as if she was ashamed of what she was about to say.

'What is it, Frieda?'

'I work for the Russians.'

Ena had suspected as much. She dropped onto the seat of the dining chair opposite her old friend.

Frieda lifted her head and looked searchingly into Ena's face. With a shuddering breath, she said, 'When I was caught in forty-four MI5 gave me an ultimatum. Or, as Five put it, a chance to avoid the hangman's noose.' Frieda gave a short cynical laugh. 'They were right of course. As an enemy agent, if convicted, I'd have been given the death penalty.'

'Was Henry your handler?'

'No. Henry was *supposedly* on the run with my brother Walter,' Frieda said, her voice cold and brittle. 'Henry wasn't on the run with Walter, he was using him to find out if he was part of a spy ring. More importantly, he wanted to know who we had reported to in the war.' A cynical smile played on Frieda's lips.

'Go on.'

'Walter didn't know. All correspondence with Germany came in and went out through me. When your husband worked that out, he gave Walter up to the authorities and they put him in jail. Shortly afterwards, McKenzie Robinson came to see me. "Hang, or work for us. The choice is yours." Some choice! Eventually I said I'd work for the British as a double-agent if they took the death penalty off the table for Walter – and Robinson agreed. So I sold my soul to the British government and became their puppet. My job was to feed the Russians false information, which I was happy to do. The arrangement worked well for several years, and then the Russians found out.'

'How?'

'I don't know. I was very careful. I took no risks. Someone must have told them.'

'What? You mean, someone at MI5 informed on you to the Russians?'

'I don't know for sure, but I've had cause to wonder more than once if there's a mole at MI5; someone who works at Leconfield House, who passes information to the Russians. It's the only thing that makes sense.' Frieda raised and dropped her shoulders. 'So, then the Russians gave me an ultimatum – work for them or they would have Walter killed.'

'But Walter was in prison.'

Frieda laughed. 'The Russians have a long reach. There is nowhere to hide from them, not even if you're locked up in a British prison.'

'I'm sorry,' Ena said.

'Are you?'

'Yes. Couldn't Henry have helped you?'

'What, lock me up in a safe house? Hide me away in some damp old building in a backwater somewhere never to be seen again?'

'Better than being on the run, or dead, I'd have thought.'

'Would it?' Frieda said, her voice thick with cynicism.

'What about McKenzie Robinson. Why didn't you go back to him?'

Frieda looked into the mid-distance, as if she was unsure how much to tell Ena.

'Frieda?'

'Because the first time the Russians questioned me about my loyalties was after a meeting I'd had with McKenzie Robinson. I didn't trust him not to sell me out to the Soviets.'

Suddenly it all fell into place. 'Frieda, did you kill Mac Robinson?'

'No, I didn't.'

'But you went to see him when he was in hospital.'

'Yes, to tell him there was a mole in his department. And, I was scared. I was out of options and I asked him if he would help me to get out of the country.'

'And what did Mac say?'

'He said he would help me as soon as he came out of hospital. But he didn't come out, did he?' Frieda shrugged. 'It doesn't matter now, anyway. Robinson's dead and I no longer care what happens to me. What do I have to live for? My brother is dead, my country has been defeated, *and I am the enemy*. Ena, I am a–'

'Spy,' Ena said.

Frieda shook her head vehemently. 'A traitor.' Her voice was hardly audible. 'I'm paid in roubles by the enemy of my homeland. Paid by a government who not much more than a decade ago ordered hundreds of thousands of my countrymen to be killed.'

Ena got up and went to the sideboard. She took a bottle of brandy and two glasses from the cupboard. After pouring a double measure into each glass she passed one to Frieda.

'Thank you.' Frieda picked up her glass, took a substantial drink and closed her eyes. 'That's good.' She took another drink, a sip this time, and savoured it for a second before swallowing. She looked into the copper-coloured liquid. 'I'm tired, Ena. So very, very tired.'

Ena's natural instinct was to get up and go to her; her gut feeling was to stay in her seat.

'They would have killed me if I hadn't worked for them. I wanted to live, but now...' Tears rolled down Frieda's face. Ena wanted to say to the woman she had worked with in the war, who she had socialised with in the local pubs and dances – and who she had called her friend – that everything would be all right. But she knew as Frieda did that it would never be all right again. Frieda was a spy and according to Henry, a killer.

Ena refreshed their glasses. She needed to stay alert and poured more brandy into Frieda's glass than she did her own. She wanted to know what the Russians were up to – and hoped that because Frieda seemed happy to talk she would tell her.

Aware that Frieda was watching her, Ena took a sip of her drink. Frieda looked curiously at Ena's glass and a smile, more akin to a smirk, crossed her lips. Had she noticed Ena had given herself less brandy? Fearing she had, Ena took the bottle and topped up her glass. She didn't drink. Frieda said she had come to warn Ena that the Russians would kill her if she didn't drop the investigation. Frieda had tried to kill her once before; Ena couldn't be sure she wouldn't try to kill her again, now.

'I'm sorry,' Frieda said. Ena's heart began to beat faster. It felt heavy and sounded so loud in her chest that she felt sure Frieda would hear it. Frieda drained her drink and put down her glass. With her elbows on the table, her hands clasped together, Frieda leaned forward and looked into Ena's eyes.

Ena shifted uneasily in her seat.

'I've been ordered to kill you, Ena.'

THIRTY-NINE

The adrenaline that until now had kept Ena alert drained from her body. She felt weak with fear, her stomach lurched and she swallowed to stop herself from being sick. 'So,' she said, doing her utmost to keep her voice calm, 'that's the real reason you came here tonight is it, to kill me?'

'I came to warn you, to tell you to stop looking for me, stop asking about me. Forget about me and the Russians. The Russians think because I blame MI5 for Walter's death that I work exclusively for them now. They are satisfied that the information I pass to British Intelligence about the hydrogen bomb is only what they tell me to pass and nothing more.'

'But it isn't?'

'Of course it isn't. I am an engineer, I know how much hydrogen fuel they have, how much uranium and how many bombs they have stockpiled. There has been a race between the United States of America and the Soviet Union to see who can build the biggest, the most powerful atomic bombs since 1946.'

Stunned, Ena sat and listened to what Frieda had to say.

'After Stalin's death in 1953 one of the four top brass who took over from him has been assassinated and two have resigned. Jumped or pushed, who knows – who cares – but their demise left Nikita Khrushchev as the Soviet Union's sole leader. Khrushchev now has what he has wanted all along: a new policy for dealing with the west and a free pass to kick the Americans out of Europe. If he has his way, there'll be another war. If there is, Western Europe – including the British Isles – will be obliterated. The arms race is on. The Americans have developed missiles that can be dropped from aeroplanes. God knows what the Russians have, but you can be sure it's something many times bigger than the one dropped on Hiroshima. The next war will be nuclear – and quite possibly the end of civilisation as we know it in the west.'

'I still don't understand why the Russians think I'm a threat.'

'Your meddling has got them worried. They're beginning to wonder whether my job, passing on false information to British intelligence, is worth the risk they're taking.' Frieda picked up her cigarettes and lighter, took a cigarette from the pack and lit it. 'Sorry, would you like one?' She put the packet back on the table, placed the small lighter on top of it and moved both nearer to Ena.

Ena took a cigarette and lit it. She rarely smoked and found the cigarette too strong. 'So,' she said, wishing she hadn't bothered, 'what happens now?'

'Forget about me. I am dead as far as you're concerned. Or I should be. You went to my funeral, remember?'

'I remember.' Ena took a drag of her cigarette and said, 'Who was buried in your place?'

'What? No one! My coffin was empty. There might have been a bag or two of sand in it, so it felt as if there was a body inside, but I assure you the only person buried on that day was my brother Walter.'

'Thank God for that.'

Frieda glared at Ena, her expression at first was anger, and then pain. 'I love my brother. I tell him every day.'

'I'm sorry. I didn't mean thank God your brother was dead. I meant I'm glad MI5 didn't bury some poor person in your place.'

'Most of the spooks at MI5 would bury their grandmothers if it served their purpose,' Frieda spat, 'so would the Russians.' The two women finished their cigarettes in silence. When she had stubbed hers out, Frieda said, 'Talking of Russians, if you don't stop asking questions they really will kill you, and then they will kill me – and we'll both end up beneath the slabs of a Russian diplomat's townhouse in Holland Park and British Intelligence will be out in the cold as far as the Atomic Bomb programme is concerned.'

Ena didn't believe for a second the Russian government were interested in her. Frieda was trying to put the wind up her. No matter. Talking was buying her time. Henry said he would be home at eight. She glanced at the clock, it was ten past. She needed to keep Frieda talking. 'I don't know anything about the atomic bomb or any other kind of bomb, and I don't want to know.'

'No?' Frieda lit another cigarette. 'Sidney didn't tell you, then?'

'If you mean my late work colleague, Sidney Parfitt – who I had a lot of respect for – why would he know anything about bombs and Russians?'

Frieda burst into laughter. 'Ena, you are such a bad liar.'

'And you are such a good liar, Frieda. You always were.' Silence fell for the second time. It was Ena who broke it. 'Did you have anything to do with Sid's death?'

'Suicide,' Frieda said.

'Murder!' Ena corrected.

'The official line was *suicide*.'

'But we both know it wasn't suicide,' Ena said. Frieda shrugged. 'You didn't answer my question.'

'No, I did not have anything to do with Sidney's death. What makes you think I did?'

'A woman telephoned his mother on the night he was killed. She said she was me. At least that's what Sid's mother told the police the following day when they went to tell her Sid's body had been found. His mother said I had telephoned Sid at ten o'clock and asked him to meet me at the office.'

'And you didn't?'

'No! Why would I ask you if you'd telephoned him if I had?'

'I did not telephone anyone, Ena. But then I am not the only woman on the *Bloc*, if you'll excuse the pun. I'm afraid you will have to look elsewhere,' Frieda said smirking.

'What's that supposed to mean?'

Frieda ignored her, stubbed out her cigarette, picked up her handbag and made for the door.

'Where are you going?'

'To Walter and to hell, I shouldn't wonder.'

Ena jumped up. 'I'm coming with you.'

Frieda laughed. 'You are so easy to tease, Ena. I am going to the bathroom, if that's all right with you?'

The blush of embarrassment coloured Ena's cheeks and she sat down. 'Of course, it is. First on the right.'

Frieda pulled open the sitting room door and let it swing shut behind her.

Ena waited for ten minutes and when Frieda hadn't returned, went into the hall. Frieda's coat had gone. She grabbed her own coat and put it on. 'Damn you, Frieda, where have you gone?' Ena deliberated for no longer than a second. 'Walter!'

FORTY

Ena caught a glimpse of Frieda on the Northern Line going south, and again exiting the train at Brixton underground station. She followed her, though she knew where she was going. In the churchyard of St Leonard's, Ena saw Frieda fall to her knees on her brother Walter's grave. She picked a flower from the metal vase beneath his headstone and began pulling off its petals. Ena hid behind a large conifer tree, too far away to hear what Frieda was saying as she talked animatedly, flicked petals in the air and laughed. Suddenly she rocked back on her heels and got to her feet. It had started to rain. Waving her arms in the air Frieda looked up and cursed the heavens. Then, repeating his name over and over, she blew Walter a kiss.

From behind the conifer, Ena caught the words, *you* and *soon*. She looked out from her hiding place again. Frieda had gone. Ena scanned the area. A shaft of light coming from the arched porch of the church caught her attention. Frieda had opened the door and was about to disappear into the building. Ena waited a few seconds before following her into the nave. She looked from the font at the back of the church to the altar beneath the east window. Frieda was nowhere to be seen.

Ena walked down the aisle scanning the pews, the choir stalls, and the Lady Chapel. Frieda must have known Ena had followed her and slipped out of the side door when Ena came in.

Opening the door to leave, Ena heard a door on the other side of the church close. Opening one door had created a draft, causing another door to shut. Ena ran across the back of the church. There was a door set back in an alcove with Bell Tower written on it. Ena opened it and climbed the steep narrow stone stairway to the roof.

'Frieda, don't!'

'How did you know I was here?' Frieda said, leaning over the parapet of the bell tower.

'When I asked you where you were going and you said, to Walter and hell, I guessed you'd come to his grave. But never mind about that. Come away from the edge, will you?'

Frieda leaned over the parapet again. 'I can see mine and Walter's grave from up here. Look, the moon is shining on it.' She stood up and turned to Ena. 'A slip, a step in the wrong direction,' she taunted. 'It would be so easy.'

'Stop it, Frieda!'

'Why? I'd be better off dead. I'm in so deep with the Russians, MI5, the Americans, and God knows who else.' Frieda reached out to Ena. 'Don't you see. Dead is the only way I'll ever be free of them.' She slid down the wall until she was sitting on the wet leads. With her legs stretched out in front of her, she buried her head in her hands. 'I want to be with Walter,' she cried.

Ena went over and sat down beside her. She edged closer and laid her hand on Frieda's arm.

'Walter and I were a team. We were no good on our own. We needed each other and we loved each other.'

'I know how fond you were on your brother–'

'But you don't. You can't know. No one does.' Frieda looked

at Ena with contempt. 'I wasn't *fond* of Walter, I was in love with him. And he was in love with me.'

Ena's hand slipped from Frieda's arm and she slumped against the cold stone of the parapet in shock. 'But you were brother and sister...'

'No. We weren't. Walter wasn't my real brother. There were no blood ties. We were both adopted. When Walter wanted to join Hitler Youth, he needed to prove he was racially pure. A true Aryan. Father, or the man we called father, was away on business and Mother was out hob-nobbing, raising money for one or other of Hitler's causes, so Walter searched the house. Hidden behind a pile of Father's private papers in a drawer at the back of his bureau, he found two birth certificates. One, a boy, born on the same day as Walter, the other a girl, born on my birthday.'

'What did Walter do? Did he confront your father?'

Frieda took a long breath. 'He wouldn't have dared. No, he put them back where he found them and waited until Father came home at the weekend. As we knew he would, Father produced Walter's false birth certificate immediately and told him he was proud of him. A year later, Father gave me my birth certificate so I could join BDM.' Frieda laughed. 'The irony was, neither of our real birth certificates proved we were German, let alone Aryan.'

Frieda leaned her head back and rested it on the embrasure of the parapet. 'Walter was the only man for me, and I was the only woman for him. There was never anyone else for either of us. What we felt for each other was real love,' she said, her voice hoarse with emotion.

Out of the corner of her eye, Ena saw a movement in the doorway to the bell tower. Someone was listening to her and Frieda's conversation. Her heart began to race. She glanced at Frieda. Her eyes were bright and piercing, as they penetrated the darkness of the bell chamber.

'Is that you, Henry?' Scrambling to her feet on the slippery leads, Frieda took a small pistol from her pocket and pointed it into the darkness beyond the door. 'Ena and I are having a chat. Why don't you join us?'

'No, Henry,' Ena shouted, getting to her feet, 'Frieda has a gun trained on the door. Get out of there. Go down and wait for me in the church.'

With his hands above his head, Henry appeared out of the darkness and stepped over the sill of the narrow door. He slowly walked across the leads. 'I'm not leaving you up here, Ena,' he said, before turning to Frieda.

'Well, I'm here. What shall we talk about?' He took several steps backwards until he was so close to Ena he was shielding her completely. 'Shoot me, if you're going to, Frieda,' Henry shouted, opening his arms wide. He turned away for a second and looked over the parapet. Beneath it, the church clock; below that, a sheer drop to the ground.

Henry swung round to face Frieda and something bumped against Ena's wrist. There was something heavy in his pocket. Whatever it was, her husband was trying to draw her attention to it. She touched his shoulder and he backed closer to her.

'Come on, Frieda, shoot me or put the damn gun away,' Henry said. 'Let's go down. It's bloody dangerous up here.'

It had rained on and off all day, now it was raining heavily. A sudden gust of wind blew sheeting rain across the leads, soaking Frieda. She shouted something that was lost in the wind, lifted the hand with the gun in it and wiped the sleeve of her coat across her face.

'Give it up, Frieda!' Henry shouted. 'Give me the gun. We need to get out of this damn rain.'

'To hell with you, Henry Green!' Frieda shouted and aimed the gun at him with an unsteady arm.

Behind Henry, Ena slid her hand into his overcoat pocket. Her fingers, numb and wet, quickly made contact with the cold steel of his gun. Her heart was pounding as she lifted the weapon from his pocket and slipped it into her own. That done, she tapped Henry on the shoulder again. He stepped to the side. Ena took the gun from her pocket and pointed it at Frieda in one smooth movement. She had a clear shot. But she didn't take it.

'Do as Henry says, Frieda. Please,' Ena shouted.

'No!' Frieda put the back of her hand up to her forehead and pushed stiff stands of dripping wet bleached hair from her face. 'Why are you making Ena do this, Henry?' she screamed.

'Henry isn't making me do it, Frieda. It is you who is making me *do it*; making me hold a gun on you. You're threatening to shoot my husband. I can't let you do that.'

'I don't want to hurt you, Ena.'

Ena took a step closer to Frieda. 'I don't want to hurt you, either. So, please, let the three of us go down and talk about what to do for the best; the best for you.'

Frieda looked to the heavens and began to shake her head wildly. She rocked back and forth on her heels screaming, 'No, no, no!'

'Frieda? Listen to me,' Henry shouted. 'I want to help you.'

Frieda froze and looked at Henry, her eyes black with hatred. 'You? You want to help me?'

'Yes. I'll get you to a safe house.'

'A safe house?' she repeated.

'Yes. And from there I'll arrange for you to go home.'

Shaking from the bitterly cold wind and soaked to the skin with rain, Frieda looked up at the sky and screamed, 'For me there is no going home.' She thrashed from side to side, howling like an animal caught in a trap. Henry leapt forward and made a grab for her gun, but Frieda was too quick for him. She kicked out and caught the back of his hand. Henry halted for a second. It was long enough. Frieda raised her gun.

'Frieda?' Ena shouted. Frieda turned and Ena lifted Henry's gun. 'Don't do it!'

For a second Frieda closed her eyes. Leaning against the wall of the church spire, the symbol of pious medieval man reaching for the heavens, Frieda cried, 'Why are you making Ena do this, Henry?'

Ena was shaking, not from the wind and icy rain but from fear. She took a breath to calm herself. It didn't work. 'Henry isn't making me do anything, Frieda, you are. I told you, if I have to shoot you to save my husband, I will. I will shoot you in a heartbeat, make no mistake.'

'All right!' Frieda wiped the rain from her eyes. 'Don't shoot me, Ena... Killing me, taking my life, will eat away at you like a cancer. Every time I close my eyes, I see the faces of the people I have killed. They haunt me now, and they will haunt me till I die. Do *you* want that?'

Remembering the two years of nightmares when she thought she had killed a man, Ena began to tremble. 'No, Frieda, I don't.'

'Then, I won't let you shoot me.' Smiling at Ena, Frieda put her gun down on the wet leads.

Ena smiled back at her old friend and laid Henry's gun next to it. A second later Frieda stepped back and disappeared.

'No!' Ena ran to the edge of the parapet screaming Frieda's name.

Henry caught her by the arm and pulled her to safety. 'It's too late, Ena. She's gone.' Holding Ena, his arms around her in a vicelike grip, Henry rocked her until she stopped sobbing.

FORTY-ONE

Ena fell to her knees. Blinded by the rain and wind, she reached up to Henry. He took off his coat and wrapped it around her shoulders. It was sodden and heavy. 'Come on, love, let's get you out of this rain.' Two policemen appeared in the doorway of the bell tower. Henry beckoned to one of them to help him. Together they lifted Ena to her feet.

With his arms around her, Henry walked Ena into the belfry, across the wooden floor to the arched doorway and out to the stone staircase. He nodded to the police officer to descend the steep steps in front of Ena, while he stayed behind her to make sure she didn't go back to the roof.

They were met at the bottom of the flight of steps by a uniformed policeman who directed them to a row of pews where two middle-aged men in civvies sat talking.

As Ena and Henry approached, the men got to their feet. One man left, the other turned and greeted them. 'Mr and Mrs Green?' the man remaining said, 'Detective Inspector Burke, Brixton CID.'

'Detective Inspector, my wife has had a terrible shock and she's soaked to the skin, I would like to take her home.'

'I appreciate that, sir, but a woman has just fallen to her death.'

Ena let out a heart-rending sob. 'I want to see her,' she cried, her teeth chattering from being cold for so long. 'I want to tell her I'm sorry.'

'You can't see her, Ena.' Henry held her tightly. He looked at Burke. 'Couldn't this wait until tomorrow, Inspector?'

'Mr Green, it is imperative that I find out who this woman is. The sooner I ask your wife a couple of questions, the sooner you can take her home.' Henry nodded half-heartedly and the inspector turned his attention to Ena, 'Mrs Green did you know the woman who– The woman?'

'Yes,' Ena whispered.

'Could you tell me the woman's name?'

'Frieda. Her name is Frieda Voight.'

'And how did you know, Frieda Voight?'

Henry started to interrupt.

Without looking at him, DI Burke showed Henry the palm of his hand. 'Mrs Green?'

'We worked together in the war. She was my friend.' Tears fell from Ena's eyes and her legs buckled beneath her. Henry caught her and she leaned on him.

'I am sorry to have to ask you this, but did Miss Voight fall, or did she jump from the church roof?'

Henry again opened his mouth. This time it was to save Ena from having to say the words.

Again the inspector put up his hand.

'Mrs Green?'

'She jumped,' Ena whispered, 'because she didn't–'

'Enough!' Henry shouted. 'You've had your *couple* of questions, Inspector. If you wish to speak to my wife further, you can do it tomorrow at our home.' Henry thrust his hand into the inside pocket of his jacket and took out a small white card. It was sopping wet and the address unreadable. 'Our address is number seven, St Michaels Square, Stockwell. Now if you'll excuse us, my wife is soaked to the skin and shivering with cold. If I don't get her home soon she'll catch pneumonia.'

'Take Mr and Mrs Green out through the vestry, Constable. Give Mr Green's address to my sergeant and tell him to drive them home.' He turned to Henry. 'Until tomorrow, Mr Green. Mrs Green.'

The constable led the way down the aisle to the vestry door. They walked in on a conversation between several policemen speculating on whether the dead woman had jumped, fallen, or been pushed. As each one became aware of Ena and Henry they fell silent.

'Is DI Burke's driver here?'

'Yes.' A sergeant stepped from among a cluster of blue uniforms.

'The DI said to take Mr and Mrs Green home, Sarge.'

The sergeant gave a tired smile. 'Follow me.'

As they left the church, Ena said again that she wanted to see Frieda, and again Henry said she couldn't.

Beyond the church gates was a row of police cars. 'Over here, madam, sir.' The sergeant unlocked the doors of an unmarked car and Henry helped Ena into the back.

The drive from Brixton to Stockwell didn't take long. As soon as they were home, Henry hung up their coats, went into the bathroom and turned on the hot water in the bath. He then helped Ena out of her wet clothes and wrapped his old dressing gown around her.

While Ena bathed Henry threw off his wet clothes, put on dry ones, and lit a fire in the sitting room. In the armchair at the side of the fire, he made mental notes of what they could and could not tell Detective Inspector Burke the following day. The real reason, the historical reason, why Frieda jumped off the roof of St Leonard's Church must remain secret.

Everything to do with Frieda Voight was classified. No one could know about her past or Ena and Henry's part in it. A thought came into Henry's mind that he wished hadn't. If the investigation into Sid Parfitt's death led to Frieda, both his and Ena's covers would be blown and the already fragile security service he worked for would again be under the microscope.

Henry wondered how much Ena knew about his involvement with Frieda. He hadn't told her Frieda was a double agent working for the British and Russian governments, nor that she was suspected of killing several British government personnel. Henry sucked in a sharp breath. 'Oh my God,' he said aloud. Ena didn't know he'd been Frieda's handler. He was in for an ear-blasting when she finds out. But then, Ena couldn't tell Burke about her job, or that she was investigating Frieda after exposing her and her brother as enemy agents in the war. For the time being he decided to keep quiet.

Henry got up, went over to the table and grabbed the bottle of brandy and a glass. Sitting down again he poured a double, took a swig, and as the smooth liquid slipped down his throat he wondered how he was going to satisfy Inspector Burke about Frieda's death and, at the same time, keep his and Ena's jobs secret. He leaned back in the chair deep in thought.

'Henry?' Ena came into the room. She was wearing her pyjamas and her own dressing gown. Her face was shiny and clean, her hair combed but still damp from washing. She sat at his feet in front of the fire, laid her head on his knee and yawned.

'You ought to be in bed, Ena.'

'I don't want to go to bed, I want to stay here in the warm with you.'

'In that case.' Henry gently lifted Ena's head from his knee and eased himself out of the chair. He moved the coffee table

out of the way and pulled the settee forward. 'Lie on here.'
Already half asleep, Ena held on to the arms of the chair and
hauled herself up. She flopped onto the settee, brought her
knees up to her chin, and was asleep in seconds.

Henry went to the bedroom and returned with a pillow that
he slipped under Ena's head, and a blanket that he laid over her.
Switching off the overhead light he returned to the armchair. By
the light of the fire he watched Ena sleep.

After a night of shallow and fitful sleep, Ena was aware that
someone was stroking her hair. She jerked her head and
shrugged her shoulders, but they didn't stop.

'Ena?' Henry whispered, 'the police are here. They want to
speak to you.'

Ena stirred when she heard the familiar voice say, 'Do you
have to talk to my wife this morning. Couldn't you come back
this afternoon?'

Ena opened her eyes. 'Inspector?' She pushed herself up
into a sitting position.

'Sorry to wake you, Mrs Green, but I need to speak to you
and your husband about Miss Voight.'

'It's all right. What do you want to know?'

'You said last night that Miss Voight was a friend of yours?'

'Had been a friend, Inspector,' Henry cut in.

Inspector Burke shot Henry a look of exasperation. '*Had*
been a friend of yours. When was the last time you saw her,
before last night?'

'Except for once in Oxford Street in August when I saw her
coming out of Selfridges, I hadn't seen or spoken to her since the
autumn of 1944.'

'When you worked together?'

Ena nodded.

'And where did you both work?'

'In an engineering factory in the Midlands.' The Inspector tilted his head and raised his eyes as if to say tell me more. Ena wasn't going to tell him about the work they did for Bletchley Park and Beaumanor. 'Silcott Engineering, in Lowarth, Leicestershire. We did work for the RAF and the Navy.'

'Do you know where Miss Voight lived and worked after the war?'

'No. As I said, I hadn't seen her since forty-four.'

'How did you and this friend that you hadn't seen for fourteen years come to be on the roof of St Leonard's church?'

The most obvious question. The one the inspector was bound to ask and the one Ena most dreaded. The Home Office training was, stick as close to the truth as possible without giving anything away. She took a breath. 'Well, I didn't know it at the time, but the day I saw Frieda in Oxford Street she had seen me.' Ena frowned and made a show of thinking. 'She didn't tell me how she knew where I lived – and I didn't think to ask – but she knew I'd married Henry.' Ena saw Henry flinch out of the corner of her eye. 'So I expect she looked up H Green in the telephone directory and found our address.'

'Did she telephone?'

'No.'

'She just turned up on your doorstep on the off chance that you were in?'

'Yes. I suppose she did. It was eight o'clock at night, Inspector. Most people are home from work by then.'

'Of course they are.' The inspector took a pack of cigarettes from his pocket and offered it to Henry and Ena. Henry took one, Ena shook her head. He's making a meal of lighting the damn cigarettes, Ena thought as the DI struck one match after another that wouldn't ignite. Eventually Henry fetched the table lighter from the sideboard and their cigarettes were soon lit. He's trying to catch me off balance, Ena thought. He's stalling, playing for time.

'Would you like to know why she came here?'

Henry took a drag of his cigarette and choked.

'Yes, Mrs Green, I was just about to ask you.'

'Well, as I would like to get washed and dressed, which I can't do while you are here, I'll tell you. Frieda's brother, Walter, is buried in St Leonard's churchyard and Frieda, who had been suffering from severe depression, told me last night that she wanted to be with him. She was here about an hour before she asked if she could use the bathroom. When she didn't come back after five minutes, I went into the hall and saw that her coat had gone.'

Like lightning Ena's brain calculated the possible questions the DI would need to ask her from the information she had given him. 'Frieda had told me where her brother was buried, so I put two and two together. I scribbled Henry a note, put on my coat and headed to Brixton after her. I saw her at her brother's grave, and then she disappeared into the church. I didn't see her inside, but I noticed the door to the bell tower was open and I guessed where she'd gone.'

'And you went up after her?'

'Of course. She had already said she wanted to be with her brother, so when I realised she had gone up the roof, I was frightened she wanted to be with him literally and would jump...' Ena looked from Henry to Inspector Burke. 'And she did, didn't she? She went up there specifically to kill herself so she could be with Walter.'

'Thank you, Mrs Green.'

Ena got up from the settee. 'If you've finished questioning me, Inspector, I should like to get dressed.'

'I have, Mrs Green, for now, but–'

'Don't leave town.'

The DI didn't see the humour in Ena's interruption, thanked her for helping him with his enquiries and said, 'I may need to speak to you at a later date.'

At the sitting room door, Ena looked back at Henry. She smiled briefly. When she got into the bedroom she fell onto the bed and sobbed.

Sometime later Ena heard the muffled voices of Henry and the inspector in the hall. After a few hushed words the front door opened and closed, and then there was silence.

FORTY-TWO

'I lied to the inspector. I told him I had left a note telling you that Frieda and I had gone to St Leonard's church, but there was no note.' Henry didn't comment. 'So, how did you know where to find us?'

'It isn't important. Nothing is except you are safe,' Henry said, pulling Ena to him. 'I don't know what I'd have done if–'

'Tell me, Henry! How did you know?' Ena backed away and put up her hand. 'Oh my God!' Suddenly everything that had happened since she'd seen Frieda Voight outside Selfridges in the summer began to make sense. 'It was you! It was your bloody lot at Five who bugged the flat.' She made fists of both her hands and beat them against Henry's chest. 'You bastard! Are they listening now?' She looked up at the light in the ceiling. 'Well?' she shouted. 'Can you hear me? Over and bloody out!'

'Ena, stop! I had to know what you were doing. It was the only way I could keep you safe.'

Ena brought her focus back to her husband. 'Sid told me he'd got rid of them all. Oh, no,' she said, 'are you telling me Sid knew MI5 had planted the bugs?'

'He might have recognised they were ours.'

Ena dropped onto the armchair. 'Why?'

'Why what?'

'Why did you, Five, have our flat bugged?'

Henry knelt down in front of her and took her hands in his. 'Don't, Henry!' she said, pushing him away.

'Sorry, I–'

'Just tell me why you felt it necessary to bug our home.'

'For your safety.' Henry rocked back on his heels and stood up. 'As soon as you told me you'd seen Frieda, I requested a tail.'

'I know. And he was rubbish at his job. He might as well have been dressed as a clown the number of times I spotted him. And the cars that followed me?'

Henry nodded.

'You went to a lot of trouble.'

'You were in a lot of trouble.'

'Enough trouble for Five to have me run over? The spook driving the green Austin almost killed me.'

'He wasn't one of ours.'

'What?' Ena felt suddenly sick. 'Then whose was he?'

Henry didn't answer her.

'You don't know, do you?'

'No. But now Frieda's gone and the case is closed, no one has any reason to hurt you. The case *is* closed, isn't it?'

Ena wasn't going to argue with Henry. She wasn't going to lie to him either. 'Why the listening devices here?' she asked, changing the subject. 'I can understand why you bugged the office. You needed to know where we were in the investigation, but our home?'

'Five's man who was following you had spotted Frieda in Mercer Street. Sometime later the guy in the surveillance car saw her outside the flat. I was worried that, because she knew where you lived, she might follow you home one night and... And she did.'

'Go on.'

'After Sid was killed we stepped up your security. We knew it was Frieda who had killed him. And we knew she'd killed Mac Robinson or had him killed.'

'Calling herself by my name and using my driving licence.'

'Don't you see? You were getting too close to the truth about her. You already knew too much. I asked you time after time to drop the case, begged you to stop looking for her, but you wouldn't. One of the ways I thought I could keep you safe was by knowing what you were doing and who you were talking to, which is why I had your office and our flat bugged.'

'Did you have to break the window?'

'It wasn't me who did it. I was–'

'In Berlin.'

Henry ran his hands through his hair and exhaled loudly. 'I was Frieda's handler.'

'She told me. I also know about her work in nuclear research. She used my engineering qualifications and ID to help get the job.'

'She wasn't a physicist, was she?'

'You know she wasn't. She would have used someone else's qualifications.'

'Good Lord, did she confess everything to you?'

'Frieda didn't tell me, Sid did.'

'Did you know he was mixed up in this business?'

'Yes, Sid went to the same boarding school in Germany as Walter Voight. Frieda had something on him from the time he lived in Berlin and later when he covered the 1936 Olympics.' Ena wasn't sure how much Henry knew, but she was sure as a diplomat in Berlin Sid's father – and his mother and sister – would have been known to MI6.

'Which is how he first met Frieda. We're not sure how involved Sid was. We know he wasn't spying at the time Frieda was passing information to the Soviets. Most of it was old news.

I think she enjoyed playing the Russians off against the Americans – and at the same time feeding us false information. She played a dangerous game, Ena, one that she knew she couldn't win.'

'And in the end, she didn't care about any of it. All she wanted was to be with her beloved Walter.'

'Frieda and Walter were not brother and sister.'

'I know. They were both adopted. She told me when we were on the roof of the church.' Ena shuddered at the memory. Not because Frieda and Walter loved each other, were *in love* with each other, but because Frieda had become so tangled up in a web of lies and deceit that she felt there was no way out. 'Poor Frieda.'

'The trouble she was in was of her own making,' Henry said. 'And, as tragic as it was, death was the only way out for her.'

'You said you'd help her. Get her to a safe house, and then home to Berlin.'

'I would have tried, but she had caused so much trouble playing one government off against the other that I knew, and she knew, Five had washed their hands of her. She was out in the cold, which is why she killed herself.'

'That may be why she wanted to die, but it wasn't why she killed herself. Frieda fell to her death because she didn't want me to shoot her. She knew if I did, it would haunt me for the rest of my life. The image of her falling off the roof is bad enough, but, as she said, to take another human being's life is something that is with you twenty-four hours a day forever. Frieda killed herself so I wouldn't have to; so I wouldn't have her death on my conscience.'

Ena reached out to her husband. 'Hold me, Henry,' she cried, 'hold me.'

FORTY-THREE

Ena stood in the doorway lost for words. The office was empty, gutted. There was not a file, a cabinet, or stick of furniture left in it. She took a sharp breath and found her voice. 'Artie?'

Artie poked his head round the toilet door. 'Ena?' He flew across the room, arms outstretched and wrapped them around her. 'They've moved us.'

'Who has?'

'The Home Office.'

'On whose authority?'

'Dick Bentley's. Three heavy-set goons marched in here yesterday as if they owned the place and stripped it. Took everything. The only place left to sit down is the lav.'

'Did they have the correct documentation?'

'Yes. Removal of classified materials. Authorised and signed by Director Bentley.'

'My typewriter isn't classified materials. I'll ring Dick and ask him what's going on.'

'You can't. They've taken the telephones.'

'The telephones aren't *classified* materials either.'

'Nor is the kettle, cups and saucers, tea and coffee, but they took them all the same.'

Ena walked around the room. A nail was left in the wall, but the calendar that hung on it was gone. 'What's Dick Bentley playing at?' Whatever it was it couldn't have happened at a worse time. She needed to read the Voight files again. She also needed to speak to Artie about Shaun O'Shaughnessy, find out how Artie knew him and, more importantly, if he had told O'Shaughnessy about the piece of paper that the pathologist found in Sid's mouth with the name Collins on it.

She circled the room again, ending up where her desk should have been. She glanced at Artie. Maybe it wasn't the worst time after all. She knew Artie well enough to know he'd be too wound up for the conversation she wanted to have with him about O'Shaughnessy at the moment. He would need to get the missing files and the pending office move off his mind first. And she would let him. Because they weren't able to make a hot drink, she would suggest they went out to a café for coffee. Then, as there was nothing they could do back at the office, she would offer to buy him lunch and while they ate introduce the subject of, *Mr* Collins.

She checked the store room and the lavatory. 'You're right, Artie. The only thing they didn't take is the toilet seat.'

Artie followed Ena huffing and puffing. Then, as Ena knew he would, he said, 'We can't even make a hot drink.'

'No,' she tutted, 'and I could really do with one.' She over-acted a shiver. 'It's cold. So, as we can't do anything here, let's go to the Lyons Corner House on the Strand and have a cup of coffee?'

Artie grabbed his coat from the hook on the back of the door, put it on and, as he always did, he wound his college scarf around his neck. 'I'll lock up,' he said, and then threw his arms in the air. 'They took my bloody keys,' he screamed.

'I expect they thought with nothing left to steal it didn't

matter.' It did to Ena. 'I have mine,' she said, taking her set of keys from her handbag. She looked up at Artie and followed his gaze. He was looking across the empty room, his eyes misty with tears.

'That's it, isn't it, Ena?' he said, when she had locked the street door. 'That's the end of the Cold Case Office.'

'Not if I have anything to do with it, Artie.' She put her arm in his and they strolled through Covent Garden to the Strand. 'I'll go and see Dick Bentley, find out what's going on.'

Ena gave Artie a pound note and he went to the counter for their coffees. Lyons Corner House was always busy. It was popular with young and old, office workers and shoppers alike. Ena looked around. Lots of woman with shopping bags. Most from shops on Oxford Street and Regent Street. Early Christmas shoppers, stopping off for a reviving cuppa on their way to or from Charing Cross Station, Ena thought.

'No sugar,' Artie said, placing a large cup of coffee on the table in front of Ena. 'Two in mine. You'd think I was sweet enough,' he giggled, 'and, an iced bun.' He handed Ena her change and took a bite from the end of the sticky cake.

Ena sipped her coffee and told Artie a watered down version of why she went to stay with friends in Brighton. He looked horrified that she had almost been run over.

'I knew you were away, Henry came into the office and told me, but he didn't say why you had gone.'

'I was scared. What with Sid being killed, I thought I was next.'

Artie gasped. 'And then it could have been me. Do you think there was something incriminating in the files we've been working on? Oh, my God. I bet that's why the intelligence service took them today. Thank God they did,' he said. 'The bull-neck goons have probably saved our lives by taking those files. If we haven't got them we can't find out anything can we?'

'No,' Ena said. 'Anyway, the Voight case is closed.'

'Why? Did Frieda Voight kill McKenzie Robinson? Did she kill Sid? We can't be sure either of their deaths were down to her. We think they were. But what we think and what we can prove are two very different things.' Artie forced the last of his iced bun into his mouth.

'Frieda killed herself last night.'

'No!' Artie almost choked. 'How?'

Ena felt sick and the nerves on the top of her stomach tightened. 'She jumped from the roof of the church where her brother is buried.'

'I thought he died in prison. How did he get to be buried in the grounds of a church?'

'An agreement military intelligence made with her when she agreed to work for our government. She was handled by MI5 – and since they are convinced Frieda killed Mac Robinson and Sid, they have shut our investigation down.'

Artie swiped his cup from its saucer as if he was angry with it. 'That's why they sent the clowns in to remove the files,' he said, getting to his feet. 'Fancy another coffee?'

'Yes, and something to eat. We'll have elevenses.'

Artie beamed his usual smile when anyone mentioned food. Especially if they were buying his. 'Here,' she gave him another pound. 'Get what you want and I'll have one of those bread rolls with egg and salad dressing.'

'I was thinking when I was at the counter,' Artie said, returning to the table with a tray of assorted sandwiches and two cups of coffee, 'at least we're safe now Voight has gone.'

This was the chance Ena had been waiting for. 'I hope you're right, but I'm not so sure.'

'What do you mean? Is there another threat?'

'I don't know, Artie. I was hoping you could tell me.'

A curious look crossed his face. He frowned and lifted his shoulders.

'I need to ask you about a friend of yours?'

Artie couldn't speak. His mouth was full of food. He made circles with his right hand as if to say, 'Go on'.

'Shaun O'Shaughnessy.'

For the second time Artie almost choked. He chewed quickly, swallowed, and said, 'He is no friend of mine. What has he been saying?'

'He asked me who Collins was?'

Artie looked to the heavens. A rush of embarrassment emblazoned his cheeks and beads of perspiration appeared on his brow.

'Did you tell him Sid had given us the name Collins?'

Artie shoved his plate of food into the middle of the table, placed his elbows where the plate had been and put his head in his hands.

'Well? Did you?'

'I might have said something. Truth is, I don't know.'

'Tell me what you do know.'

'I met O'Shaughnessy on my way home the night I heard Sid had been killed. I was in a bit of a state and called into the Salisbury for a drink. I only intended to stay for one, but I started talking to this chap. Or rather he came over to the bar and started talking to me. He bought me a drink and told me his name was Shaun O'Shaughnessy. He made small talk, said no one ever believed that was his real name, that he was an actor and had been booked for the end of the pier revue in Brighton next summer. He entertained me with anecdotes of the famous actors he'd worked with. He was a real wag, and at first his stories took my mind off Sid dying. I laughed, but then I felt guilty. I thanked him for the drink and said I was going because I'd lost a friend that day and felt sad.

'He said a problem shared and all that – and insisted I had another drink. I'd only had two, but they must have gone straight to my head, because I felt dizzy. I couldn't see straight.

Anyway I told him my friend Sid had died in the early hours of that day and he gasped.

'He said his friend Sid had died that day too. He said it was too much of a coincidence to think two men named Sid had died on the same day and he asked me if my friend's surname was Parfitt.'

'And you said it was.'

'Well, yes. I didn't see anything wrong in it. He already knew Sid's surname.' Artie looked around and, although no one was close enough to overhear what he was saying, he put his hand up to the side of his mouth and whispered, 'He said Sid had been murdered. Well, I knew that, but it wasn't common knowledge. As far as the public was concerned a man had jumped off Waterloo Bridge, not been pushed off it. Anyway, because I was upset he bought me another drink and said he was sorry for telling me in such an offhand way.

'We raised our glasses to Sid, and he said, "I'll find out who killed our old friend, Artie, that's a promise. And when I do I'll sling *him* off Waterloo Bridge." He said we must put our heads together, pool our information.

'He said Sid had gone to meet a woman on the night he was killed. He said it could have been a woman called Frieda Voight. He said Sid had told him about Frieda. Or, he said, it could have been the married women Sid was seeing. Apparently Sid told him the woman's husband had found out about Sid and was gunning for him.'

From what Sid had written in his letter, Ena found it hard to believe Sid would meet Frieda on his own anywhere, let alone on a bridge in the early hours of the morning. And as for seeing a married woman, that was not Sid's style. 'How did the name Collins come up in the conversation?' Ena asked.

'O'Shaughnessy said Sid had told him the name of the bloke whose wife he was seeing. He couldn't remember but said it was on the tip of his tongue.'

'So you asked him if it was Collins?'

Artie whispered, 'Yes. He said we should find out who this Collins chap is and go round and sort him out on behalf of Sid. He asked me if I knew him. I didn't, so I couldn't tell him anything else. You don't know who Collins is, do you Ena?'

'No,' Ena lied. Thank God she hadn't worked out the reference to Collins before Artie left the office that day. She shuddered. The various and anonymous ways in which someone could be killed and their bodies never found, were endless. It didn't do to dwell on the subject.

'How did you leave it with O'Shaughnessy?'

Artie looked downcast. 'He said we should keep in touch and let each other know if we find out anything that would help us to get this chap Collins, Sid's killer.' He looked up, caught Ena's eye and looked away. 'The truth is, I can't remember. I was so drunk when I left the Salisbury I fell into the back of a taxi. The bloody thing started to spin so I shut my eyes. The next thing I remember the taxi driver was shaking me and shouting at me to wake up. That was outside my flat. I stumbled out, fished in my jacket pocket for money to pay the fare, but the taxi driver said O'Shaughnessy had already paid it. Well, he said, a woman had given O'Shaughnessy the money which he then gave to the taxi driver.'

'A woman? Did you see the woman who paid for your taxi?'

Artie slowly shook his head. 'I don't remember anything, really, except what the taxi driver told me.'

'Have you heard from O'Shaughnessy since?'

'No.'

'Did you give him the office telephone number?'

Tears welled up in Artie's eye. When he nodded the action sent them spilling onto his cheeks. 'I'm so sorry, Ena.'

She reached out and put her hand on his arm. 'Got a hankie?'

He shook his head.

Ena took a handkerchief from her handbag. 'Here. Dry your eyes.' When Artie had recovered, she said. 'Fancy a drink? Something stronger than coffee?'

Artie grimaced. 'Not at the Salisbury?'

'Yes, at the Salisbury. You might remember something about the woman with O'Shaughnessy. She might have been in the Salisbury while you were in there. Come on, something might jog your memory.'

FORTY-FOUR

Dragging his heels, Artie ambled along at Ena's side. From the Strand they cut through Bedford Street and turned left onto New Row where, at St Martin's Lane, they crossed to the Salisbury. With wall to ceiling mahogany panelling, large etched mirrors behind the mahogany bar – and plush seating in dimly lit corners where men and women wanting to be discrete could sit in relative privacy – the Salisbury was the epitome of opulence.

'I'm going to have a Scotch and water. What do you want, Artie?' Ena asked, as they entered the luxurious old Victorian pub.

'Same for me. Make mine a large,' he said, in a huff because he didn't want to be there.

Ena ordered their drinks; a single Teachers for herself and a double for Artie. When she had paid for them, she added a splash of water to her Scotch. 'Water?' she asked, the water-jug still in her hand. Artie shrugged, so Ena added the same quantity of water as there was whisky and gave it to him. 'Where were you standing?'

Glass in hand, he promenaded to the end of the bar and stood next to a bust of Oscar Wilde. Ena followed.

'Now what?'

'Now, tell me *again* what happened when you first saw O'Shaughnessy.' Ena tapped Artie on the shoulder. 'You can't do that if you're leaning on the bar with your back to the door.' She was losing her patience. 'Come on, Artie. You must have been facing into the room to see him come in from the street.'

Artie swung round, his right hand raised with his glass in it, his left elbow on the bar. And in an exaggerated gesture of campery, put his glass up to his lips. He didn't take a drink. 'Oh, my God!'

'What is it?'

'A woman,' he said, without taking his eyes off the door. He took a swig of Scotch and continued speaking as if he was narrating a film. 'O'Shaughnessy entered, looked around, saw me and smiled. He lifted his right hand and waved. I think it was his right. Yes, it was, because a woman came in behind him and tapped him on his left arm.'

'What did she look like?'

'I didn't see her face. She stood sideways onto him. She said something–' Artie stopped and looked at Ena. 'It could have been something as simple as "Excuse me" because O'Shaughnessy nodded and made a beeline for me.'

'And the woman?'

'She sat at the first table inside the door. I wasn't paying attention to her, but I think she had her back to the room. Anyway, O'Shaughnessy swaggered over and you know the rest.'

Artie knocked his drink back in one. He put his empty glass down on the bar with a thump, which caught the barman's attention.

'Same again?'

'Singles, please,' Ena said, her glass still half full. She needed a clear head, not one foggy with alcohol. She didn't want Artie drunk either. She wanted him to recall what happened outside the pub, when O'Shaughnessy put him in the taxi.

'Tell me again, what happened when you left that night,' Ena said, when the barman had poured the drinks and was out of earshot serving someone else.

'I told you, O'Shaughnessy put me in a taxi.'

'Before that. When you were leaving, you must have passed the woman who came in at the same time as O'Shaughnessy.'

'If I did I didn't see her.'

'Okay. So, you went outside?'

'And O'Shaughnessy threw me into the back of a cab. He was a rough bugger, come to think of it.' Artie shuddered, flicked his head back and finished his whiskey. 'Aren't you going to drink that?' he said, eyes widening at the sight of Ena's untouched second Scotch.

She shook her head. 'But first,' she said, her hand on top of Artie's as he seized the glass, 'I need to know what the woman with O'Shaughnessy looked like.'

With an exaggerated pained expression, Artie turned and slouched on the bar.

Ena finally ran out of patience. 'Do you know how deeply you're in the shit, Artie?' He didn't reply. 'I need something, anything, that will help me to dig you out of it. Come on!'

'The HO will give me the chop anyway, so what does it matter?' He held his empty glass up and shook it at the barman.

Ena grabbed his arm, yanked it down, and gave the barman a disparaging look. 'It matters to me, and it should matter to you.' Ena saw tears in Artie's eyes. She didn't care. She had been too easy on him. 'Don't you want to know who murdered Sid?'

Ena watched the moist sadness in Artie's eyes turn to flashing anger. She thought he would explode in a fit of rage.

Instead he turned his back on her and quietly sobbed. Ena put her hand up to his shoulder. He shrugged it off. 'I do care, Ena, I do.' Turning to face her, he cuffed the tears from his face.

'I know you do. And I know you're sorry that you got involved with O'Shaughnessy.'

'You'll never know how sorry.' Artie wiped the palm of his hand across his face.

'But, now you have a chance to turn the tables on him. I know he was involved in Sid's murder, but I can't prove it.' Just thinking about O'Shaughnessy left a bad taste in Ena's mouth. 'He's a nasty piece of work. I wouldn't be surprised if he enjoys hurting people.'

Artie took a sharp breath and put his fist up to his mouth.

'He followed you here and he got you drunk to get information out of you.'

'And I gave it to him.'

'That wasn't what I meant. Artie, O'Shaughnessy played you.'

Artie looked as if he was going to cry again. Ena couldn't have that, she needed him to listen to her not wallow in self-pity. 'It's good you told him about Collins.' Artie's head shot up. 'If you hadn't given him something you too could have ended up–'

Ena left the unspoken word hanging in the air and changed direction. 'You broke the Official Secrets Act when you talked to O'Shaughnessy about the work we do, but, as I said, you have the chance to make amends.'

Artie closed his eyes, squeezed them tight, and then shook his head. 'I'm sorry. I don't remember seeing the woman again after she came into the pub.'

It was no good pushing Artie any further, he was spent. Ena handed him her untouched whisky. 'Drink it. It's time to go.'

Artie downed it in one. 'I'm going to stay for another.'

'No you are not!' Ena looked at her watch. 'For the next

four hours at least you are being paid by the HO. And, as your boss, I am ordering you to go home and make yourself something to eat. Do you have any food in?' Artie looked up at the ceiling. 'Silly question. Here,' Ena took her purse from her handbag and took another pound note from it. 'I can't keep doing this, Artie,' she said, slapping the note into the palm of his hand. '*You* are going to clean up your act, or *you* will find yourself out of a job. Stop on the way home and buy some food, cook it, eat it, and then take a bath and have a shave. And stay in. Have an early night. I don't want you to leave your flat until tomorrow morning. Got it?'

'Got it,' he whispered. 'Thank you. How shall I ever repay you?'

'By doing as I ask. I'll see you in the morning. We're due at King Charles Street at nine. Now,' she said, 'let's get you a cab.'

Ena hailed a black cab and asked the driver to take her friend to Clapham. She gave him an extra five shillings and asked if he would drop Artie off at the Co-operative Store on the way, wait for him, and then drive him home. He said he would and the taxi pulled away from the kerb with a miserable looking Artie slumped in the back seat.

'Wait!' Artie shouted, hanging out of the window. The taxi screeched to a standstill. 'I do remember something,' he said excitedly when Ena caught up with the cab. 'The woman who came into the Salisbury behind O'Shaughnessy was standing in the doorway when the swine shoved me into the taxi. I did see her.'

Ena opened her mouth to ask what the woman looked like, but Artie put up his hand.

'She was older than O'Shaughnessy, and shorter by four or five inches.' He looked back at the door of the Salisbury and squinted. 'And she had short fair hair with grey in it.'

FORTY-FIVE

Ena lifted the telephone handset from its cradle, fed three pennies into the coin slot at the top of the box, and dialled the number for Bow Street police station. As soon as the call was answered she pressed button A.

'I need to speak to Detective Inspector Powell.'

'Who shall I say–'

'Ena Green.'

The telephone went from background chatter to silence. She was about to put the receiver back on its cradle when she heard the voice of Inspector Powell. 'I was wondering when you were going to call.'

'Sorry I haven't been in touch, but things have been a bit hectic.'

'So I hear. How are you?'

'Shook up, as you can imagine, but at least I'm alive. I was wondering if I could see you today?'

'Of course. I'll come over to Mercer Street.'

'No. The office is closed... I'd rather not discuss it on the telephone. Could I come into the station?'

'Yes. What time shall I expect you?'

'Now. I'm in the telephone box across the street.'

Ena heard the inspector laugh.

'I'll get someone to make a pot of tea.'

WPC Jarvis, the policewoman who had been with the inspector the day Ena was questioned about Sid's death, was waiting for her in the entrance foyer of Bow Street police station.

Constable Jarvis gave Ena a welcoming smile. 'The telephone rang as the DI was leaving his office. It was a call he had to take, or he would have come to meet you himself.'

Ena followed the WPC to the inspector's office. She knocked the door and waited until the inspector called, 'Come in.'

WPC Jarvis opened the door, stood back to let Ena enter and closed the door behind her.

'How are you really feeling, Ena?' Inspector Powell asked, getting up and pulling out the chair under his desk for Ena to sit on. Returning to his own seat, he said, 'Well?'

'As I said, I'm shook up but I'll be fine.' The truth was, Ena felt sick with worry, exhausted trying to make sense of what had happened the night before with Frieda, and frightened of what might have happened to Artie. Thank goodness she had sent him home in a cab. But then, if O'Shaughnessy already had her young colleague in his sights, he would probably know where he lived. Ena hoped he didn't. She must talk to Artie, make him see the danger in picking up strangers in pubs.

But first, she needed to speak to Helen Crowther. Ena was even more convinced now that O'Shaughnessy turning up when he did on the pretext of renewing his acquaintance with Helen was because Ena was there and to find out what she knew about Collins.

O'Shaughnessy had bought Artie drinks to get to know him, and bought Helen flowers to get to know her. Ena caught her breath. She was the common denominator between Sid, Mac Robinson, Artie and Helen. It was too late for Sid and Mac, but she could keep Artie and Helen safe by shutting down the Voight case.

'Ena?'

Bringing her focus back to the inspector she made fists of her hands to stop them trembling.

DI Powell leaned on the desk and smiled sympathetically. 'Are you sure you're all right?'

'No, actually I'm not. I'm drowning in worry, sickened by Frieda's suicide last night, and scared that whoever murdered Sid and McKenzie Robinson will come after me again – and next time it won't be to warn me off – or he'll get to my colleague, my husband, or my friend in Brighton.'

'You could drop the case, leave us to find Mr Parfitt's killer.'

'What about Mac Robinson? If it was Frieda Voight who murdered him, his wife should be told. It would give her closure.'

'My colleague in Brighton and his team are working round the clock to find his killer.'

There was a knock at the door and WPC Jarvis brought in a tray of tea and biscuits and set them down on the inspector's desk. 'Is there anything else, sir?'

'No thank you, Jarvis.' When the constable left, the inspector picked up his cup. Ena followed his lead and, refusing a biscuit, drank her tea.

DI Powell gave Ena a wry smile. 'It would be flattering to think a lovely young woman had come to the station just to have tea with me. Alas,' he said, getting up from his chair and going over to the safe, 'I suspect it's the briefcase you've come to see, not me?'

Ena laughed despite feeling upset. 'How did you guess?'

'*Guess?* Detective Inspector's do not *guess*, they deduce.'

Ena liked the inspector and laughed again. 'Of course they

do, sir. The truth is, I didn't want to mention the briefcase on the telephone. You never know who's listening to your calls.'

'I think my telephone is safe,' he said, taking the case to the table next to the window overlooking Covent Garden. He moved several papers and put the case down. 'It's all yours.'

Ena took the key from her purse and unlocked it.

'If there's anything I can do...?'

'No, but thanks...' Ena said, taking out Sid's journal.

'Then I'll get on with some paperwork.'

Ena read the title of each entry, skipping any mention of the 1936 Olympics and giving extra attention to passages where Walter and Frieda's names were written. She saw nothing new. She turned to the last half dozen pages and read them again. There was nothing there that she hadn't read before.

She yawned. Her back ached from sitting hunched over the table. She stretched to rid her spine of tension and yawned again.

'Are you tired, Ena?'

'Yes, but I'm not as tired as I am cold. I yawn uncontrollably when I'm really cold. It's irritating, I know. It drives Henry mad.'

'But it isn't cold in here. Perhaps you're coming down with something.'

'I hope not,' she said, still reading.

'When did you last eat?'

'Err,' she lifted her head and looked out of the window, as if the answer lay on the other side of the pane of glass. She hadn't touched the egg roll in Lyons Corner House. 'I had a slice of toast this morning.'

'Which was also the last time I ate. So, as it is three thirty, how about I take you for something to eat?'

'Inspector Powell, I am a married woman!' Ena joked, swinging round in her chair to look at him. 'It's very kind of you. I am hungry. My rumbling stomach is stopping me from

concentrating. I had to read the last page of Sid's journal twice.'
She returned the journal and the letter to the case, locked it,
and put it under the table out of sight. The inspector took her
coat from the chair by his desk and held it up for her to slip her
arms in.

'Wait!'

'What is it?'

'There was nothing in the journal that I hadn't read before,
because what I'm looking for isn't in the journal.' On her knees
Ena scrambled under the desk, dragged the case out and hauled
it onto the table. 'It's in Sid's letter,' she said, unlocking the case
and taking out the brown envelope containing the letter. 'Sid
said something that... Damn it! What's wrong with my bloody
brain?'

The inspector picked up his telephone. 'Sergeant? Get one
of the lads to go to the café in the market and get four rounds of
sandwiches. Anything will do: meat, cheese – and tell him to
put a spurt on. Stick an IOU in petty cash, will you? Oh, and
get Jarvis to bring a jug of coffee and two mugs up to my office
as soon as she can.'

When the inspector put down the telephone, Ena lifted her
head from the case and frowned. 'Something Sid wrote is
niggling me.' She shut her eyes. She could see the typewritten
page, but whatever it was that he was trying to tell her was just
beyond her memory's reach. She turned to the last few pages of
the letter and began to read. And there it was:

'... I attended some rallies, yes, but I didn't march. I was
working for *The Times*. It was my job to record the events, and
then Highsmith wired them to the newspaper. But, as you'll see,
there are several rallies where my face has been placed on
someone else's body. That was it, the sentence that had lodged
in her memory. *Ena, please look at the photographs with the
Hitler Youth articles. Look closely at them and you'll see it isn't
me.* Walter said if I destroyed their war records, they wouldn't

bother me again. So, I put a request in to McKenzie Robinson to follow up a lead I'd been given about a couple of suspected German agents and he gave me permission to see their records...'

Ena glanced at the remainder of the letter stopping when she got to the bottom of the page. Sid said again that she shouldn't be shocked by the photographs, that they were clever forgeries, but it wasn't a photograph of Sid that she wanted to see.

It hadn't registered with her at the time, but she had seen someone, a couple. It was them Ena was interested in.

"There's something else, Ena. I don't think Walter or Frieda worked alone. It isn't the uncle we talked about. It is someone at Leconfield House. Someone above suspicion. Ah! I hear your key in the door. To be cont. Sid."

Ena put the letter to one side and took out the newspaper cuttings. She laid them out on the table and examined them one at a time.

'Inspector, do you have a magnifying glass?'

DI Powell rummaged in the top right drawer of his desk, then the left, found a magnifier with a handle and took it to her.

'Look at this photograph. That's Sid in thirty-six.'

DI Powell put the glass up to his eye and then lowered it slowly until it was just above the newspaper cutting. 'He looks very young.'

'He was very young,' Ena said.

At that moment there was a knock at the door and Constable Jarvis entered balancing coffee, milk and mugs on a tray. The inspector handed Ena the magnifying glass and took the tray from the constable. A second later the sandwiches arrived.

'Ena, food. Come and eat something. That is an order!'

Ena reluctantly left the table and sat down at the inspector's desk. She took a sip of coffee. It was hot and strong. 'Mmmm... Just what I need.'

DI Powell ripped open several paper bags to reveal four rounds of sandwiches that had been cut in halves. Ena took one that was nearest to her. It was cheese and tomato. She devoured it in minutes and washed it down with coffee.

When they had finished eating, Ena leaned back against the circular backrest of the chair. She closed her eyes. Words raced round in her head: *request to McKenzie Robinson... someone at Leconfield House... someone above suspicion...*

She jumped up. 'I am going to examine the newspaper cuttings.'

'Can I help?'

'Yes, but should you be? Helping me, I mean? Aren't you supposed to be out there catching criminals?'

'I've told you before, I'm the boss. If anything important comes in I shall leave you to it. Until then, I'm in here catching criminals.'

'Good!' Ena pointed to two photographs of her late work colleague when he was in his early twenties. 'This is Sid.' DI Powell took a pair of spectacles from his breast pocket. 'Do you want the magnifying glass?' He shook his head. 'Okay.' Ena separated the cuttings into two piles. 'You look for Sid in this lot, and I'll look through these. When we get to the end we'll swap and look again, in case either of us have missed him.'

Ena had scrutinised the first pile of newspaper cuttings and armed with another cup of coffee began looking through the second pile. 'Oh my God!'

'What is it?'

Shock took her voice. 'I'm not sure,' she said at last, tears filling her eyes.

'Is it Sid?'

'No.'

DI Powell leaned over and peered at the photograph that

was upsetting Ena. He held the magnifying glass directly above the face of a woman in her late-twenties. The woman was looking up at a much younger man. They were both laughing. She was small with a tipped up nose, wide mouth, full lips, and short fair hair. On closer inspection, the young man was a teenager. His hair was cut in the cropped style of Hitler Youth and looked lighter than the woman's. Ena took the magnifying glass from the inspector and held it over the woman's face. Picturing her hair with grey in it, add two stone and twenty-two years, and there was no mistaking her.

FORTY-SIX

'Who is she?' the inspector asked.

'*She,*' Ena said, a bitter edge to her voice, 'is the woman I have just spent four days with in Brighton. Her name is Helen Crowther, personal assistant to the late Director of MI5, McKenzie Robinson.'

'And the boy?'

'Shaun O'Shaughnessy, if that's his real name. He is a nasty piece of work who manipulated Artie and got him drunk to get information out of him. And who I suspect, killed Sid and threw him off Waterloo Bridge. Oh no!'

'What is it?'

'Frieda was telling the truth. When I asked her if she had killed McKenzie Robinson she said she hadn't. She said she went to the hospital to warn him and to tell him there was a mole at Leconfield House.' Ena wiped her tears. 'I didn't believe her.' She buried her head in her hands and wept.

'I know what you need,' Inspector Powell said, going to his desk and taking a bottle of brandy from the top drawer. He tipped what was left of their coffee back into the jug and poured each of them a drink.

Ena took her brandy with shaking hands. 'Thank you.'

'Medicinal purposes,' the DI said, smiling thinly.

'What are you going to do?' he asked, when Ena had stopped crying.

'I don't know. Perhaps nothing – yet.' She looked briefly at the table of incriminating evidence. 'I ought to hand it over to MI5, but I don't know who I can trust.'

'You can trust your husband.'

'Yes.'

'And you can trust me.'

Ena said yes again. 'But, I'm not going to do anything until I have spoken to Sid's mother. I must tell her first. I owe Sid that much. She needs to know that what she will be reading in the newspapers about her son is not true. There's always the possibility that Five won't go public with the story. They may well bury it because Helen Crowther is one of their own.'

DI Powell downed his brandy. 'Come on,' he said, 'put that lot back in the case, I'm taking you home.'

Ena returned the damning evidence against Sid, Helen Crowther and Shaun O'Shaughnessy to the case and locked it.

'Ready?'

'Almost.' She handed Inspector Powell the large brown envelope. 'Keep this for me, will you?' He raised his eyebrows. 'There is no need for the Home Office or MI5 to see falsified photographs of Sid in compromising positions. The pictures Sid talks about in the letter to me I've put in the case. They will be enough to show that Sid was being blackmailed by Frieda Voight. These,' she extended her hand holding the envelope to the inspector, 'serve no purpose. They won't help Sid's case, nor will they help in the case against Crowther and O'Shaughnessy.'

. . .

Henry was at home when Ena and Inspector Powell arrived. Ena told him briefly about the letter Sid had written to her. She didn't mention Helen Crowther but said, 'I know who the mole is at Leconfield House. The evidence is in this briefcase. I don't think I should show it to you, do you?'

'No, darling. I'll be under suspicion, the entire department will be. The less I know the better.' Henry turned to Inspector Powell. 'I suppose you've seen the contents of the briefcase?'

'Yes. And,' he said, turning to Ena, 'I can't ignore what's in it. Sid Parfitt's murder is still my case. I shall be telephoning Director Bentley at the Home Office tomorrow... afternoon.'

Ena saw Inspector Powell to the door. 'And the envelope you're keeping for me?'

'What envelope?'

Ena put her arms around the inspector and whispered, 'Thank you.'

Artie was waiting in the reception area of the Home Office when Ena arrived. Washed and shaved with his hair clean and neatly combed, he looked the smartest she'd ever seen him look.

'You'll miss the old office in Mercer Street,' Artie said.

'We will, but we'll be safer here.'

'We?'

'Of course, *we*. A lot has happened since I put you in that taxi yesterday. There's no time to explain now, but if you hadn't met that toerag O'Shaughnessy, none of it would have come to light. So,' Ena looked at Artie sternly, 'let me do the talking when we're with Dick Bentley. You–'

'Follow your lead.'

'Exactly. Ena Green and Artie Mallory to see Director Bentley,' Ena announced to the receptionist.

'He's expecting you, Mrs Green.'

Ena led the way to Dick Bentley's office.

She knocked on the director's door. 'And remember,' Ena said to Artie, 'don't speak unless the director or I speak to you. If either of us ask you a question, answer, but don't volunteer anything. Oh, and don't look surprised when I mention O'Shaughnessy.'

Artie took a sharp breath. 'You're going to tell him?'

'No, of course not.' Ena straightened his tie. 'Relax. Don't look so worried.'

The director's door opened and his secretary came out. She held the door open for Ena and Artie to go in. 'Come in, Ena.' Director Bentley reached over his desk and shook Ena's hand. 'And Mr Mallory?' he said, his arm outstretched. Artie took his hand and gave it a shake. 'Good to see you. Take a seat. Now, what happened on that church roof?'

Ena told the director everything, including Frieda insisting that she hadn't killed Sid or McKenzie Robinson. 'I believe she was telling the truth,' Ena said. She opened Sid's briefcase and took out his journal, part of the letter and the three photographs Sid referred to in the letter, along with the damning newspaper cutting where Helen Crowther was on a Hitler Youth march with Shaun O'Shaughnessy. She gave the newspaper cutting to the director first.

'Is this what I think it is?'

'Yes, sir. It's a Hitler Youth rally.'

'Good God!' Director Bentley held the newspaper closer. 'And is this *who* I think it is?'

'Yes, Director.'

'Who's the fellow she's with?'

'His name is Shaun O'Shaughnessy.'

Out of the corner of her eye, Ena saw Artie flinch.

'Do you know him?'

'Yes. I met O'Shaughnessy in Brighton with Helen Crowther.'

'And did you know about this at the time?'

'No. Crowther befriended me after McKenzie Robinson's funeral. I think I told you that Eve Robinson blamed me for her husband's death.' The director nodded. 'Crowther was sympathetic and said she would speak to Mrs Robinson on my behalf. She gave me her number and said if I ever need to talk, I could ring her. She said I'd be welcome to visit her in Brighton. So, the evening that I was almost run down, I got in touch with her and she invited me to stay with her for a few days. I thought it was a good idea, give things time to cool down here.' Ena took an envelope addressed to Director Bentley from her handbag and passed it across the desk to him. 'It's all in here, sir.'

The director put it in the top drawer of his desk. 'I shall read it later.' He picked up Sid's journal, photographs and some of the pages Sid had written to Ena. 'These I presume are for me too?'

'Yes, sir. Together they explain why Sid Parfitt was forced to work for the Voights, and why he was killed.'

'Your husband's at Leconfield House, isn't he.'

The director was not asking Ena a question, he was making a statement. 'Yes. And because Helen Crowther was his boss's personal assistant, I haven't told him anything about her, or what is in this briefcase.'

'Your husband was Frieda Voight's handler?'

That *was* a question. 'Yes, sir. Frieda told me when we were on the roof of St Leonard's church.'

'And is that why she was going to shoot him?'

The director had been well informed. 'She told me she was going to shoot Henry because he had lied to her. She said Henry had promised to get her brother out of prison and back to Berlin if she worked for MI5.'

'The things we have to do to keep our country safe, Ena. Not always morally right, but always necessary. Leave this with me. I'll read it thoroughly over Christmas. A meeting has been convened for January first. What to do about Helen Crowther will be decided then. For now,' he looked from Ena to Artie, 'it goes without saying that what we have discussed today stays within these walls.'

'Yes, sir.' Ena looked at Artie. He nodded.

'Well, we had better find our new office.'

'That won't be necessary. You'll be breaking up for Christmas in two days. Go and do your Christmas shopping, better still, go home and rest. By God, you deserve a rest after all you've been through, Ena.'

Ena laughed. 'We have been busy, haven't we, Artie?'

The director didn't give Artie time to reply. 'I was thinking that, as your new office is piled high with boxes, Mr Mallory here might like to unpack them. Get your new work space ready for your return after Christmas. New Year, new office, new cold case.'

Ena looked at Artie and pulled a sorry frown.

'I'll get straight to it, sir,' Artie said, beaming a grateful smile at Ena.

'Well, if you're sure,' she said, 'I do need to do some shopping. Henry and I are going home to Lowarth for Christmas. Oh.' A worrying thought crossed Ena's mind. 'Henry will be able to go away at Christmas?'

'Of course. Your husband has given a full account of his work with the Voights. As for the Crowther case, nothing will happen about that until the new year.'

'Thank you, then I'll go.' Ena said, shaking Director Bentley's hand.

Reaching up and hugging Artie, she whispered, 'Behave yourself.'

At the door, Ena turned back and looked at both men. 'Happy Christmas.'

A LETTER FROM THE AUTHOR

Dear reader,

Thank you for reading *Confessions*. I hope you enjoyed meeting Ena again as she solved murders and exposed spies as a cold case investigator for the Home Office. Ena has come a long way since *Redemption*, since she worked in an engineering factory in WW2 with Frieda, became involved with Bletchley Park and exposed Frieda and her brother Walter as spies. If you enjoyed *Confessions*, and I hope you did, perhaps you would like to join other readers to hear about my new releases and bonus content and sign up for my newsletter.

www.stormpublishing.co/madalyn-morgan

Also, if you could spare a few moments to leave a review, I would really appreciate it. Even a short review, if it is positive, can make all the difference in encouraging other readers to discover my books for the first time. Thank you very much!

It wasn't one thing that inspired me to write *Confessions*, but many. Plot points and ideas came to me while I slept. I would get up in the middle of the night and write them down. By the end of Ena Dudley's story, *Redemption*, she had met Henry Green, liked him and felt there was a deeper feeling between them than friendship.

So, I thought, why not have Henry as Ena's love interest? But, it was now 1958, and the end of *Redemption* was at the end of WW2, thirteen years earlier. So, as both of them were single, I scribbled in my notebook – Ena and Henry, married. Ena and Henry's love is not the hot passionate love that her sister Claire experienced in *Betrayal*, nor the deep love that Bess had for James in *Foxden Acres*. In Henry, Ena had found someone she could love. There was an age difference of quite a few years – and I put a question mark in brackets by the words 'age difference'. I didn't know until I began writing *Confessions* if their love would grow. I quite fancy the unmarried detective, DI Powell, and wondered if Ena would fancy him too. But I don't think my readers would have liked it.

Having been at Bletchley Park, I couldn't have Ena going back to working in the engineering factory. So, because she was almost killed by her colleague Freda King, real name Frieda Voight, who Ena had exposed along with her brother Walter as a German spy, it was obvious that Ena was intelligent, had initiative, had a strong character and could hold her nerve.

At the end of *Redemption*, Walter escaped, but Frieda was sent to prison. What if Frieda had been killed in prison? She was a double agent, which was a dangerous game. Ena might have gone to her funeral. In that case, if she saw Frieda in London in 1958, it would give me scope to invent some great storylines. One storyline I thought of would kill two birds with one stone. If Henry had been Frieda's handler, and she threatened to kill him, it would make Ena and Henry's love stronger.

I then looked at the history I had written for Ena's work colleague, Sid Parfitt. Because his father had been a diplomat in Berlin, Sid would have been educated in Berlin. He could have met Walter and Frieda Voight at school. Sid had also been a journalist. That is when the idea came to me to send Sid to Berlin as a journalist, working for *The Times* newspaper covering the eleventh Olympic Games – Hitler's Olympics – in August 1936. That was the beginning of months of research, which I loved. After that, *Confessions* wrote itself.

Thank you for being part of my writing journey. I hope you'll stay in touch, as I have many more stories and ideas to share with you!

Best wishes and happy reading,

Madalyn x

www.madalynmorgan.wordpress.com

 facebook.com/madalynmorgan1
 twitter.com/ActScribblerDJ
 instagram.com/madalynmorgan1
 pinterest.com/madalynmorgan

ACKNOWLEDGMENTS

I would like to thank Rebecca Emin, Maureen Vincent-Northam, Cathy Helms, Rob Woodward, author Debbie Viggiano and Derek Eastwood for his advice on cars in England 1958 and Berlin 1936.

Printed in Great Britain
by Amazon

56758360R00179